ANOTHER ELVIS
LOVE CHILD

Born in Bolton in 1965, Janette Jenkins studied acting before completing a degree in Literature and Philosophy and then doing an MA in Creative Writing at the University of East Anglia. Her first novel, *Colombus Day*, was published in 1999. She has a young daughter and lives in the north of England.

ALSO BY JANETTE JENKINS

Colombus Day

Janette Jenkins

ANOTHER ELVIS
LOVE CHILD

V

VINTAGE

Published by Vintage 2003

2 4 6 8 10 9 7 5 3 1

Copyright © Janette Jenkins 2002

Janette Jenkins has asserted her right under the Copyright, Designs and Patents Act, 1988 to be identified as the author of this work

First published in Great Britain in 2002 by
Chatto & Windus

Vintage
Random House, 20 Vauxhall Bridge Road,
London SW1V 2SA

Random House Australia (Pty) Limited
20 Alfred Street, Milsons Point, Sydney
New South Wales 2061, Australia

Random House New Zealand Limited
18 Poland Road, Glenfield,
Auckland 10, New Zealand

Random House (Pty) Limited
Endulini, 5A Jubilee Road, Parktown 2193,
South Africa

The Random House Group Limited Reg. No. 954009
www.randomhouse.co.uk

A CIP catalogue record for this book
is available from the British Library

ISBN 0 09 943098 3

The Random House Group Limited supports The Forest Stewardship Council (FSC®), the leading international forest certification organisation. Our books carrying the FSC label are printed on FSC® certified paper. FSC is the only forest certification scheme endorsed by the leading environmental organisations, including Greenpeace. Our paper procurement policy can be found at www.randomhouse.co.uk/environment

MIX
Paper from
responsible sources
FSC® C018072

Printed and bound in Great Britain by Clays Ltd, St Ives PLC

In memory of my friends,
Gary Faulkner and Martin Brouwers

THE CARTER MUSEUM OF GARDENING
AND NATURAL SCIENCE,
LYNFORD PARK, DORSET

Wednesday 11 August 1999

'JACK?' SOMEONE ASKS. 'WHAT TIME IS IT? HOW LONG
have we got?' I look at my watch. *'I don't know. It's gone eleven.
I'll go and ask Danny. He's got the TV in his office. He said he'd
let us know.'*

Danny works next to me, in our small but growing Commu-
nity/PR department. His office is little more than a cupboard, full
of guides, postcards and rolls of purple entrance tickets. He sits
in a corner with his knees hunched up, drinking instant coffee. A
wasp blows in. The three tiny windows have been wedged, with
last year's free diaries and a Ground Force mug.

'Listen to this,' he nods. And so I'm watching a girl (Sally,
Land's End) shivering in a vest, and talking earnestly into the
camera. She smiles. Rubs her forehead. Frowns. On the screen, the

news is full of cloud and empty Cornwall, but here the sky is bright, and there's plenty of blue left in it.

'They're just saying the same things over and over again,' Danny tells me. 'And none of them sound like they're experts. Look at her. The blonde. Does she look like an astronomer to you?'

'Try turning over. You're watching Channel 5.'

I leave him, channel hopping and cursing under his breath. My office next door is bigger. I have a sign on the door that reads: J. Trench. Head of Department. Polished brass. It looks official, but it's a hands-on job, and inside it's cluttered with my work boots, socks and pairs of old ripped jeans. Books and papers sit in piles across the desk. Soil samples. Letters, mostly handwritten, from people with gardening queries. Photos and sketches of (maybe) rare plants found in between the dandelions. Of tools found right at the back of their sheds. In attics. Cellars. 'Is it antique?' they ask. 'What is it?' 'What does it actually do?' Then, 'Would you like to buy it for your museum?' 'I'll donate this rake/hoe/unknown ancient artefact, for a small sum, or a free family pass and a meal in your restaurant.' But the object is usually worthless and the plants turn out to be herbs.

Across the walls, there are pin boards full of postcards, Post-its and pictures of my wife with our round-faced golden daughter. Jo and Lily, laughing in the garden. Lily smiling, chewing her dimpled fists, propped against the sandpit. Leaning against the wall, I watch the sunshine making lines across the table. It's warm. Stuffy. Brushing down my shirt, I stroll into the main museum, blowing down my collar. My boots make a creaking sound.

On the second floor, the rooms are almost empty. A boy races round with a smashed-up paper plane and a white-haired old couple find an empty padded bench and start an early picnic. The woman looks shy, but as soon as the food comes out, the hard-boiled eggs and coffee, she forgets. The birds sound real. The water-feature soothes, and the dazzling white lights make her slip off her shiny grey cardigan.

Danny appears. 'Well, you should see it now. Amazing. It looks *pretty bad down south. My sister will be disappointed, mind you, she only went to get her boyfriend in a tent for the night.'*

We walk towards a window. Across the courtyard, with its café and old-fashioned sweet shop, rows of necks are craned. We put on our red tinted glasses and stare hard at the sun and the thin arc of black that's already settled across it. Some girls from a summer school have pinhole projectors, they giggle and squirm; the moon just isn't fast enough, so they go back to their whispers and strips of bootlace liquorice.

'It isn't a bad view, is it?' Danny sniffs. 'They said we'd see nothing, but we can. Still, I'm going back to the telly for a bit. I'm getting bloody neckache.'

I lean out further. I can smell the flowers from the Victorian cottage garden. Roses. Freesia. Night-scented stocks. A girl calls out, 'Miss! She's looking at the sun. She'll go blind! Tell her, miss! Tell her!'

Then, later, there's the darkness, and everyone falls silent. It's cold. Prickly. It only lasts for a minute or so, but the birds are totally confused, and now you can see them, looping through the treetops in tight black circles.

Behind me, the couple have finished with their picnic. They haven't left the sunshine. The man wipes eggshell from his hands and the woman's blinking hard, as if she's suddenly just remembering where she is.

As the brightness reappears, people start to move again. They're looking at tour guides, wall maps. They rifle through their purses. A van pulls on to the gravel. There's the rip of the handbrake. Music. The radio carries on. 'Sexbomb'. The man from Cearns and Brown swaggers to the café with a flapping sheet of paper. He stops at one of the benches and looks at an abandoned projector. He stares through the pinhole, half wiggling his hips. Someone laughs. 'He thinks he's Tom Jones! Look at him! Look!' He gives them another few moves. His shoulders start. His white shirt ripples. 'He's good,' someone shouts. 'He can do it!' The music stops. The man looks up, and I quickly move my head inside, burning.

The sun is huge.

It is 100 times greater in diameter than the earth. It is also extremely hot. In its centre the temperature is around 15 million degrees Celsius.

1979

WHEN THE DOOR HAD SLAMMED CLOSED FOR THE SEVEN-teenth time, I came downstairs to watch him again. With his face pulled down and his shirt half open, he was doing Tom Jones to himself on the opposite wall. Through the bevelled mirror, his reflection swayed in and out of the frame. His arm. Profile. Arm again. His hips and tiny stomach circled, leaving his belt behind.

The room felt warm. Smoky. Behind him, the old tiled fireplace was lined with empty bottles and plates of bread and lipstick. Hitching my pyjamas I slunk round to the back of the sofa and made myself small. Through the spindle legs I could see the balls of his feet sliding. He was wearing old socks that looked wet underneath. From the kitchen door, my mum appeared.

'Joey. Have you seen the time?'

Suddenly my dad stopped moving as Tom carried on with a crackled kind of 'Delilah'.

'That's dust,' he hissed. 'Evie, the bloody record's ruined.'

'It'll be fine.'

'It will?'

'Yes.'

'Fine?'

She nodded.

'You mean fine, like the Drifters was fine?'

'That was an accident.' She tugged at the back of her hair.

'So why did you sneak it back in? Why didn't you just own up and say that you'd scratched it? Ruined it? What were you doing playing it, anyway? You don't even like the bloody Drifters.'

'I don't know.' Softly, she leant against the wall, her eyes slowly closing, then jerking wide open. Her voice was going. She kept looking at the door.

I rolled backwards, following the words from the record as they slid and spun together. I could picture that dust ball. Fat and clinging. Dangerous. I wanted to run up there. To blow the needle clean.

'It's late,' she said. 'It's over.'

'I know the time. I can see the clock. There it goes. Tick, tick, tock.'

'I'm going up.'

'So, what about the mess?'

'It can wait.'

'It can what?'

'Well . . . You know. I'll do it tomorrow. Early. Really early. I promise.'

'Shit.'

He turned and stopped the record. He blew it. He wiped it over his shirt and held it up and to the light.

'Looks all right,' he said. 'But there's bound to be some damage.'

Mum looked relieved. From the corner of my eye I watched as she edged her way past the rug. With her head down, she looked smaller than ever. Her new dress had wrinkled. Her party shoes with the suede high heels had been left side by side, by the sink.

'And don't put that blue thing on.'

'What?'

'You know. In bed. It's enormous. And there's too many buttons,' he said. 'Fiddly.'

Turning his back, he clumsily changed the record. I wanted to move, but somehow I felt trapped inside the carpet. The red and gold squiggles ran in and out of my eyes. Now it was Elvis. 'Suspicious Minds'.

'Are you joining in then, or what?'

I looked up and he was kneeling on the sofa, his head swaying, hanging over the back of the cushions.

'I don't know,' I swallowed. 'I'm tired. I, well, I want to go to sleep.'

'Well, you won't get to sleep with this on.' He turned the volume higher. 'We might as well make the most of it, with those Murphys back in Ireland for the week.'

Lifting the arm of the record player, he let the needle hover. I moved slowly. My legs felt wobbly, like they were going to buckle under me. But I wasn't exactly scared, because he was always like this after any kind of party. It was as if he couldn't stop. When people started to leave he'd go into a frenzy. Singing. Dancing. Then he'd shout down the street, telling them to stay. He'd stand by car doors with his arms outstretched. He'd say that all the local taxis had been booked for the next three hours.

'It's that time of night you see. Busy, busy, busy.'

I was tired. Aching. My throat hurt. I'd lasted until midnight at the party, before hiding upstairs, wrapping myself in blankets just to turn the noise into a muffled kind of thud.

I'd seen the first few leave. Rita Jackson felt sick. A neighbour's girl had been scooped into her father's giant overcoat and left to sleep on the back seat of his ancient black Wolseley.

'I haven't locked up,' he'd said. 'In case she needs the toilet.'

The last to leave was a man called Terry. He'd been dancing wildly, with his shirt off, sweeping the air in his tight black trousers and authentic lizard-skin boots. He had a crew cut. A fierce-looking dragon tattooed across his back.

'I'm into kung fu,' he said. 'Bruce Lee. *Enter the Dragon.* I've seen all the films.'

But this Terry was skinny, and his wife kept crying into her gin and bitter lemon.

'Men,' she whimpered. 'They don't know when to stop.'

Holding on to the back of the sofa, I looked up at my dad. His knees were buckled, Elvis-style. His face looked pink and his shirt was circled with sweat.

'Come on, come on. You know the start of this one.'

I licked my lips and closed my eyes tight as he yanked me by the sleeve.

'Here. Now.'

He dragged me. Like always, the rug was our stage.

'Think. We could be anywhere,' he panted. 'The Lyceum. The Palais. The bloody London Palladium.'

'All right.'

'So where, Jack? Where?'

'What about on the telly?'

'The telly? Not enough scale. We need stalls. A balcony. A bloody third tier for the teenies to hang over the cheap seats.'

'The Palladium then?'

'Right.'

'But that's on the telly.'

Cracking the side of my shoulder, he hissed and narrowed his eyes. He slipped down the needle. Elvis. The King. He moved into the starting position, tipping back his head. Then, pouting, he gave me the nod.

My shoulder was burning, numb, but I started off, shuffling a bit. Then I moved in half circles, Showaddywaddy-style. The first few lines I managed, but then my voice sounded way out, so I mimed, watching my toes as they moved around the tassels.

'You're bloody crap, you are,' he said, when it finally went into fade. 'You're supposed to look up at the audience. Give them a bit of something. Not just the top of your scruffy-looking head.'

'I'm tired.'

'Tired?' he pushed me. Tiny. Jolting. 'Go on then, soft lad. Shift.'

'What?'

'I said, shift. Shift yourself off to bed. You're not much bloody use as a backing singer. No concentration.' He tapped the side of his head.

'Goodnight then—'

'Oh, and while we're at it, don't you think that Elvis ever got tired. The Tremeloes? Bill Haley and his Comets?'

I turned. Almost safe and out of the room. 'Well, yes,' I said, remembering the books and documentaries. Elvis with his head between his knees. 'But they were getting paid. The buzz would have kept them awake.'

Biting my bottom lip, I dug in my nails, waiting for it. But then suddenly, he smiled.

'You wait till next Saturday,' he said.

'Saturday? So I can come?'

'Definitely. Only get there later than me.'

'Why?'

'Because on a Saturday, nothing starts buzzing until after they've called out the bingo.'

59 Palma Street, Bolton, Lancs.

THERE WERE ONLY THE THREE OF US BUT IT STILL FELT squashed. My dad, Joseph Trench wig salesman/stylist and semiprofessional singer. My mum, Evelyn-Maria, part-time receptionist for a firm of solicitors specialising in 'family matters'. And me. Jack Aaron Trench, aged eleven.

There weren't too many Trenches about. The family had moved from Exeter in the late 1800s to work the Bolton cotton mills. Most died young. In a shoe box we kept some painted sympathy cards and thick cardboardy photographs. The cards were full of dust, black ribbons and faded pointy writing.

'Look at the date,' Dad would say, whenever he got them out. '1905. Look at this, Evie. They're practically relics. Don't chuck them out whatever you do. They might be worth a bob or two. We could sell them off to Sotheby's.' Then he'd dance around a bit, rubbing his hands with glee.

Most of the photographs were ripped around the edges. A fat man with a pipe. A baby. Two ugly girls holding hands. They were wearing long white dresses and big black clogs.

'Who are these girls?' my mum often asked my grandma.

First it was Ada and Mary. Then it was Kitty and Beryl. Later it was 'family', and 'she has a look of our Myrtle'.

More recent photographs showed mill workers embarking on an outing. Men in caps. Smart jackets. Starchy shirts and ties. The women at the front smiled stiffly, holding handbags over one arm, and all white-gloved, like the queen.

My grandma was in a couple of these. Young and slim. She'd be wearing a hat. Narrow pointed shoes. She'd have a spray of something wilting pinned to her left lapel.

'Corsage,' she'd say. 'We all had them then.'

'Where were you going?'

'I don't know. Somewhere.'

But she used to say, 'Morecambe.' 'Southport.' 'The Lights.' The mill was called 'Dove'.

'All those steps,' she'd say. 'And the noise.'

At Dove she spun cotton, then went somewhere else,

hemming nurses' aprons. She cleaned offices. She iced fancy cakes at the back of Hattie's tea shop.

'All day long. Cakes that looked like dominoes.'

Her husband, Arthur, was asthmatic. 'And in a way I was glad,' she'd say. 'Because he didn't go to war.' Instead he worked as an aircraft mechanic, and he came home every night, smelling of oil and Swarfega. His nails would be black, and the creases in his hands looked like spiders' webs, even on a Sunday.

'But at least he was where I could see him.'

They had two sons. My dad, the favourite, and Frank, the baby who went behind her back and married a French Canadian on his twenty-first birthday, then emigrated to Lachine, Montreal.

'It was only supposed to be temporary,' she told us. 'But you know what these foreigners are like, once they stick their claws in.'

'Foreigners.' She'd say the word with relish, looking at my mum. 'Just my bad luck. Two daughters-in-law with strange-sounding surnames and fancy ideas. How did it happen? Do they all step off the boat and sniff their way up to the Trenches?'

But no. How could they? My mum was born Evelyn-Maria Keldiles at her home in Farnworth, Lancashire. Her sister, Claudine, was already at primary school, winning ribbons and *The Best Little Book of the Bible*.

My Bretonese grandparents came from Le Faou, Finistère, as newly weds in 1937. At first, my grandpa drove lorries through the night and my gran crocheted cardigans in their rooms at Marsden's Boarding House. Her small metal hook would keep on making the holes, while she'd stare at the sticks of borrowed furniture, drinking the thick smoky coffee they'd brought with them in the trunk. In a night, she could make three baby coats to sell to Mrs Johnson on the market. 'They might be too fancy for here,' she'd say. 'But we might as well give them a go.'

And later, in the strange damp room, she'd lie in bed alone, listening to the shipping forecast. The man with the serious-sounding voice would say Finistère too fast, but she still felt thrilled, because he'd proved that it was real. Out there. And she supposed it was just where they'd left it.

'Oh, how I missed it,' she said. 'And I still do, even now. But then. Then everything was different. I don't know about England. We could have been anywhere. China. Timbuktu. Anywhere.'

'But you like it here now?'

'Well,' she'd say. 'Thirty-eight years and I supposed we're getting used.'

But by the time they were used, they'd saved enough to go home. They'd managed to sell their little garden terrace, their shaky red Citroën, with the lease on the lock-up garage. For years they'd done without holidays, making do with weekends and drives down to the coast. My grandpa was proud they could do without unnecessary luxury items. Like washing machines and a colour TV.

'Work keeps us sprightly,' he'd say. 'Look at us. Do we look over sixty? Look at your grandmother. Not a day over forty,' he'd beam, while she'd pat her hair, coyly, blushing into the carpet.

MUM WAS UP EARLY. I COULD HEAR HER RUNNING WATER and moving things. Stopping and starting the Hoover.

'Jack,' she said. 'God, did I wake you?' She was easing all the ornaments back into place. The over-bright Polaroids in their mock-gold frames. Tutting, she held up her favourite glass fruit bowl. It had been used more than once as an ashtray. 'Pigs.'

'It's too early to be cleaning.'

'I couldn't sleep anyway,' she said, fishing out the apples.

'It isn't eight o'clock.'

'I know.'

'I could help, I suppose.'

'You? You just sit right there, and don't make any noise.'

Spraying everything in sight with All-in-One furniture polish, she started finding things. One squashed court shoe. A tie. A small blue handbag.

'Not much in it,' she sniffed. 'I think it must be Maureen's. There isn't even a purse.'

'Are we having any more?'

'Any more what?'

'You know. Parties. Before the Murphys get back.'

'Not if I can help it.'

Her hands started picking at the cushions, arranging them into diamonds. She scraped at some food that had hardened on the coffee table. Her dressing gown gaped, showing scarred white knees and a glimpse of something netty.

'Oh, I'll soon have it done,' she said, lighting her third cigarette of the morning.

She sat on the edge of the armchair, rubbing her forehead, staring at the bright orange glow of her fag end. Her feet bounced and circled. She couldn't keep them still.

Mum was small. Tiny. Shorter and thinner than most of the girls in my school class. For years, with her hair pulled tight into a high bouncing pony tail, she was often mistaken for a tired-looking minor. Bus conductors would automatically ring out the half fare. Boys would do a double take. The woman at the Odeon refused to sell her tickets for *The Wild Bunch*.

'Still, petite has plenty of benefits,' she'd told me, choosing half-price dresses in a shop called Junior Miss. 'And look at these shoes,' she'd beamed. 'You would never believe it, would you?'

'What?'

'Well, look,' she said, 'they were really made for kiddies.'

She waved a foot, proudly. They had oval-shaped buckles and mock leather stitching. Most of the girls in my school wore these kind of shoes. Mum's feet did look tiny, but she didn't look young. What could those boys have been thinking of? She had dust-coloured creases round her eyes, a way of hunching over, so instead of looking youthful, she looked shrunken down, and older.

'ARE'N'T YOU TIRED?' SHE ASKED. 'YOU SHOULD BE.'

'Not really.'

'You look it.'

'So do you.'

'Well, I've not had a wash,' she said. 'And that always makes such a difference.'

Smoothing down her dressing gown, she went over to inspect the record that my dad had left on the turntable, lifting it carefully, with the ungreasy edge of her hand.

'Open the sleeve,' she said. 'Quick, before I drop it.'

'He doesn't look after them. He just leaves them. Plonks them down.'

'Well, I wouldn't like it scratched,' she said. 'I've always liked "Something".'

I WENT TO GET DRESSED. THROUGH MY THIN BEDROOM wall I could hear Dad snoring. The rain thudded down. Grey sheets. Cold again. Freezing. I threw my clothes on. My Bolton Wanderers T-shirt and green school jumper. My faded denim jeans with the label picked out from the pocket. Now there were only stitch marks I hoped everyone would think that they were Wranglers instead of the Happy Jean brand my mum always bought me from the market.

'They're the same thing anyway,' she'd say. 'Denim's denim, and they're only your casual trousers.'

'But—'

'But nothing. Wranglers are a rip-off. Mr Patel says they're all made in the same factory anyway.'

'PUT SOMETHING QUIET ON,' DAD SAID. 'I'VE GOT A thumping headache. Look at me. Can't you bloody tell?'

Mum padded round him, silently pouring tea and moving his messy plates away. She'd put up her hair and dressed extra smart for Sunday. A blue and white skirt. Flower patterns. An apron so it kept nice.

'I'll turn the record off,' I told him. He had the paper spread out. Girls in swim suits. Blondes. An actress with her hand across her face was carrying a couple of poodles. It was his favourite half-page showbiz column.

'Not off,' he said. 'Listen to me. I didn't say off. I said something else. Something quieter. Like Frank. Or Deano. That's it. That's perfect. Put Dean Martin on.'

He swayed his shoulders to 'Volare'. He was wearing the satin-look dressing gown that mum had bought for him at Christmas.

'All the big stars have them,' she'd said, with all her fingers crossed.

'I know. I know. You think I don't know?' But the present was a hit. He'd worn it all day. 'Like that fucking Noël Coward.'

'Here's another one.'

'Another what?' Mum stopped what she was doing and beamed at him. Her voice was all soft, and interested.

'Another Elvis love child.'

'Oh?'

She went and sat next to him. She wobbled. It took at least three cushions and a few *Woman's Own*s for her to reach the edge of the table.

'Aged twenty-five,' she read. 'From Reno, Nevada. Well, he looks like him.'

'Billy Jackson's dad is the spit of Prince Philip, but it doesn't make him royalty.'

'True.'

The room was stifling. The kitchen and upstairs were freezing. I tried sitting in between the two, but I got a stiff neck and stomachache. Their voices droned on about nothing. The party.

The window cleaner's bill. Someone from work who'd just moved down to London.

'Lives in the same bloody street as Danny La Rue. Would you credit it? Well, apparently, he looks like a woman, even in trousers.'

I stared down at the book I was reading, concentrating on the words, the hiss of the gas fire, the shush of the rain outside. *The Amazing Sky At Night*. The Pole Star. Ursa Major. Cassiopeia. Everything floating in silence. And I'd seen it on the *Alien* poster. Outer space is dark and silent. There is no air to carry sound, so no one will hear you scream.

For a while, Mum and Dad just sat there, drinking tea, staring into the *People* and lighting more fags. Then Dean Martin started crooning 'That's Amore' and my dad went and turned it up three, to 'Hi'.

'You can't beat this one for the ladies,' he said, swaying with his chipped Best Dad In The World mug. 'I'm adding this one to my repertoire. They all love the French stuff. Just like your grandpa, eh?' He practised fluttering his eyes at me, sticking out his hips as his belt slipped off. His thing was just dangling. He hadn't got a clue.

'*That's amore.*'

'That's Italian,' I said.

He stopped. 'What?'

'It's a funny Italian record. It's even got pizza in it.'

'Funny? Italian? Pizza my arse. What are you talking about? "That's Amore." Amore's bloody French. Ask your mother. She should know. Evie!'

'What?'

'Tell him. Tell him that it's French.'

'Yes, it's French,' she said. 'For love.'

'Thank you,' Dad breathed. '*Finally*. But now I've gone and missed the bloody thing, so I'll have to put it on, all over again.'

By two o'clock, I felt drugged. The curtains fluttered. There was a haze above the ornaments. My dad was snoring in his *Viva Las Vegas* T-shirt and shiny yellow running shorts. His chin was speckled with Bisto.

'I've splashed cold water on my face,' my mum came out of the kitchen. 'I need to waken up a bit. Have you seen the weather? It's black outside. Pouring.'

'What about Grandma?'

'Your dad'll take us. We'll be all right in the car.'

'No way.'

He told us he was running out of petrol and flicked 30p for the bus fare.

'So, you're not coming?' I asked, prising the hood from the inside of my anorak.

'Not this fucking Sunday, I'm not.'

The rain was hard and freezing. We sheltered in the doorway of Smiley Pets, Mum rushing out every few seconds to see if the bus was in sight. Through the window there was a thin violet light from all the silent aquariums. Dog leads. Get 'Em All! (easy use) flea powder.

The number twelve bus came ten minutes late. It threw dirty water on mum's best coat. Inside it was full of pink-haired girls, laughing, while a snarling giant Rottweiler had the back seat to itself.

Grandma Trench was a widow. She had diabetes, emphysema and puffed-out, shapeless ankles. She lived in a room at SS Peter and Paul's: A Home For Elderly Ladies. Everything was provided. Paid for by the council. But she'd had to sell her house, give them her pension book and cash in all her life assurance.

'Rip-off merchants,' Dad said. 'They must have seen you coming a mile off.'

'Well, I think it's worth it,' she'd tell him. 'That house was full of rising damp. No wonder my chest was always bad. At least it's warm in here. And I don't need money. What's the point of buying new things for yourself at my age?'

Grandma stayed in bed all day. She'd sit with a magnifying glass, reading *People's Friend*. She'd watch all the programmes on her giant television. *Coronation Street*. Documentaries. *Wildlife on One*. But her favourite channel was ITV because she'd read somewhere that they'd just booked Des O'Connor.

'And he's such a clean-living boy. A true entertainer.'

'Des O'Connor? You like Des O'Connor?'

'Oh yes,' she'd say. 'But he just isn't on enough. And with all that talent, well, he should be.'

WE ARRIVED WET THROUGH. DRIPPING. SISTER ELIZABETH let us in. A woman called Maude had her nose pressed hard against the window, peering through the raindrops.

'She's waiting for George,' Sister said.

'George?'

'Her husband.'

'Is he coming?'

'No,' she told us. 'He doesn't like leaving the dog.'

My grandma eyed us up and down.

'What are you doing?' she asked. 'You're dripping. Both of you. You'll bring all sorts in here, coming like that.'

'Like what?' I hung my anorak next to the heater. It was already starting to steam.

'Margie next door got the typhoid from a visitor.'

'The what?' We bit our wet lips.

'The typh— well, it was something like that. And now she's immune to all her medications. Joey not with you?' She strained looking over our shoulders.

'He's working.' Mum sat down, shivering. Her dirt-splashed coat dripped down the back of the chair.

'Again? Well, that's good. That's what you want. He's such a hard-working boy. Even at school. He was always late home. Always in the library, looking things up.'

Mum didn't look surprised. She pulled a ball of tissue from the soggy end of her sleeve. Grandma ignored me.

'Jack still the same?' she asked.

Mum smiled, sniffing. 'Oh, he's fine,' she said. 'He likes his books. Don't you? He wants to be a scientist. Imagine.'

'A scientist? What kind of a job is that? You can't beat chiropody if you want a steady wage. People will always need their feet looking at.'

We sat and watched grandma watching television. Soon Mum was staring at the screen with her. There was brass-band music and some boys on old-fashioned push-bikes freewheeled down a slope.

'Daft buggers,' said Grandma. 'They'll end up under a bus like that boy from Southall Street. Wayne. Duane. Shane. Something. What a mess. And that poor driver. He was never the same after that. Lost his job. Then his wife ran off with that butcher.'

I looked at other things. The crank on the hospital bed. Her Ex-Lax instructions. A nearly dead pot plant. Mum's shoes were leaving footprints. They'd changed from blue to black.

'Teatime,' Grandma said, suddenly sitting up, straightening her nightie. 'Lovely.' She almost looked excited as an orderly called Janet winked and swung out the bed tray. She was wearing white clogs and her heels were covered in plasters.

'It's a dog end of a day,' she said. 'The kitchen's full of wet things and broken umbrellas. Here we are Mrs Trench, this should keep you going.'

She put down the plate and a fan-shaped serviette. It was red and covered with holly. 'From Christmas, of course,' said Janet.

'We've hundreds to get through, though most people seem to like them. They're cheerier than the white.'

'Well,' Grandma said when she'd gone. 'They try their best here. It's plain. None of that fancy foreign muck.'

The food was mashed and the fork had a bend in it, like the ones that babies use when they're learning to feed themselves. While she ate I flicked through her magazines. You could win an Austin Allegro, or a holiday in Spain. I'd choose the car – then I'd sell it. On page nineteen, knitwear. *Be A Dream In Navy Blue!* The problem page wasn't a bit like Mum's *Woman's Own*. No sex stuff here. Dear Nurse Susan was all about arthritis, gallstones and painful varicose veins.

Scooping her dessert (runny egg custard), Grandma's eyes moved up and down the screen. She stopped, her spoon swayed midair. She pulled down her forehead and frowned.

'Is that a man or a woman?' she asked.

'Who?'

'That one there. That one reading the news.'

'That's Angela Rippon.'

'A woman? Really? Well, I thought it was,' she said. 'It's the earrings that give her away.'

Mum looked twitchy. She started wandering around. Picking things up, then putting them down. She squared all the magazines, then she stared through the window, describing what she saw.

'And four black dustbins,' said Grandma. 'I know.'

We all drank tea, watching Margaret Thatcher as she strode across a car park. Soon my mum started clock watching. Fiddling with her wristwatch. She stared at the pink Our Lady of Lourdes alarm clock, blessed by the Pope and ten minutes slow.

My legs felt itchy, squashed beside the cabinet full of photographs, baby powder, half-empty bottles of lemon barley water.

'You're lucky to have him at home, you know.'

Mum looked up; her watch strap was loose, it slipped towards her knuckles.

'My Joey could be anywhere now. A real full-time professional. He's as good as Des O'Connor. And Butlin's are crying out for acts. Family acts. Redcoats. Acts that can really sing instead of just shouting and strutting about. I've told him.'

'Told him what?'

'He should get on *New Faces*. Get himself an agent.'

'Oh, he likes his job too much,' said Mum, staring at her shoes. They were squelching. They'd left blue marks on her tights.

'Have you seen how much they get, just for making a record?'

'Well, I—'

'I know what it is. Are you worried he might leave you? You hear about these big stars and all their shenanigans. But my Joey's not like that. He never has been. Fame and fortune wouldn't change him. And let's face it, Evie, he could have had anyone. That girl he used to go out with, that Linda, well, she modelled clothes for Littlewood's. She lives in Cheshire now.'

Mum raised her eyebrows. A crack of sunlight trickled down her shoulder. From the next room we could hear a muted radio. Chatter. Then YMCA.

'You'd hate it if he went away,' I told her. Mum was straightening her coat now, patting down the sides. 'Look at uncle Frank.'

'Frank? Frank's nothing but a mechanic. He could do that here. Frank didn't need to go abroad to mend cars,' she said.

'Dad's just a club singer, Grandma. He isn't Mick Jagger.'

'And thank goodness for that. They have clubs in London you know. Big glitzy places. He won't be discovered up here.'

'Well . . . ' Mum said, but she wasn't really listening anymore. She was looking at the weatherman sticking on his rain clouds.

'That voice. It's a real gift from God,' said Grandma. 'We shouldn't be holding him back.'

WHEN WE WERE LEAVING, WE BENT IN TURN TO KISS HER, but she turned her face away. I brushed her cheek. Her skin tasted strange. Like dusty Turkish delight.

'It's all over the place now,' she said.

'What is?'

'Garlic. They put it in everything. Even that.' She nodded at the screen. It was an advert for Heinz tomato ketchup. 'It isn't right,' she said. 'We're English.'

ON THE BUS, MUM TRIED TO LIGHT A CIGARETTE, BUT HER hands were shaking and the matches were damp. The rain had finally stopped, but everything was wrapped in it. In front of us two little girls tried to plait each other's hair while their mother put on her lipstick, smiling into her mirror. The lipstick was dark. It made her lips look cold.

'We shouldn't have gone,' I said. Mum looked tired; she was resting her head on the thin metal ledge by the window. 'What with the weather and everything.'

She shrugged. 'Oh, I know that. But well, she's old. She'd have been so disappointed,' she said.

WE PEERED DOWN THE BACKSTREET. WE STOPPED. IT looked like our house was on fire. The kitchen window had been pushed open and smoke was pouring out. Mum blinked, then started walking faster, breaking into a run. A cat slipped under the gate. Music. Dad was burning to death to Dean Martin records.

'It's a surprise,' he said, when we walked through the door, wafting our arms and trying to hold our breath. He was still alive. The curtains were singed. The grill pan had been thrown into the sink and had welded on to the bowl. 'Well, it was supposed to be.'

Dad was dressed up now. He had a new shirt on, and even through the smoke he smelled of Blue Stratos.

'I was trying to do us a bit of tea. I found some nice streaky bacon. I was going to do us some eggs.'

Mum looked at him incredulously. We'd never seen him cook. When she'd had pleurisy we'd lived on shop-bought sandwiches. He wouldn't heat up soup.

'I was peckish,' he grinned. 'But the bacon went whoosh. It should tell you that on the packet. It should have Danger written all over it, in big red letters.'

Through the glass door we could hear a stifled giggle. Mum looked alarmed. She stared down at her clothes and tried to brush them straight.

'Visitors? Who?'

'Maureen. She came back for her handbag.'

Mum dabbed her fringe with the tea towel. She spat and curled her lashes. In the front room, Maureen sat with her neck full of lovebites, giggling with her shoes off.

'I told him not to bother. He was showing me his new bit. That foreign record. That French one. Anyway, I think they'll like it,' she said. 'He can do the high notes, and everything.'

IT WAS LATE. PRESSING MYSELF TO THE GLASS I LISTENED to them laughing. Through the bumps I could see them. Maureen's sister had arrived with cans of Black Label. Terry. Someone else's in-law. Mum, in a dry pink dress, sat high on Dad's knee. He was singing. Bouncing. He was being 'the younger Elvis Presley'.

'Years before the rot set in.'

Maureen was dancing now. Wriggling in her tight black skirt. Snake-like. She had her eyes closed, her arms up, clapping.

DAD WAS OUT REHEARSING. MUM WAS IRONING, STANDING on the stool that her father had made for her in 1951. It had her name carved into the top and a little hollow heart.

'It only took me a couple of Sundays,' he'd told me. 'I made all sorts back then. Doorstops. Shelves. A realistic-looking apple. I nearly lost this, though.' And he'd hold up his thumb while I'd stare hard at the deformed half nail and the crooked ring-shaped scar. 'One little slip and you've had it.'

Mum pulled her sleeves, looking hot. For years she'd had bruises on her wrists the size of 5-pence pieces. 'It's those filing cabinets at work,' she'd say. 'When you bang them shut, they jump right back and hit you.' Her arm swished up and down the board. She smoothed out collars, cuffs, endless pants and dresses. Sighing, she picked up Dad's frilly show shirt, with its hundred tight ruffles down the front.

'I never thought that I'd marry a man who was into all this showbiz,' she said, pressing down the frill. 'I thought I'd marry a mechanic. You know, cars, machines, oily bits and pieces.'

'But you knew he was a singer.'

'I knew he liked a song. I thought he'd just grow out of it. When we were young, all the lads thought they were Elvis.'

'Do you think he'll do what Grandma says?'

'What's that?'

'Be a professional. Do singing full time.'

She slapped the iron down and the whole board rattled. Underneath, I could see stained black metal and some dodgy-looking wiring.

'I don't know. I don't think so. It's hard being a singer. It'd frighten me to death. And then there's the Hair Palace. They've always been good to him. It's steady. And let's face it, how could we manage without it?'

'He'll never give up the clubs.'

'I know that. And why on earth should he? He loves it. And you've seen how he is, once he gets going.'

ON CLUB NIGHTS, ALMOST AS SOON AS HE'D EATEN HE'D GO upstairs and change out of his charcoal Burton's suit. He'd wash and stretch himself in front of the long wardrobe mirror, rolling his shoulders, gargling loudly with lukewarm salty water. Then he'd sing a couple of bars, while pulling on his dinner suit.

He'd always been a singer. At school – 'when I bloody went' – he was teased by his mates, boys with stubble and hand-carved tattoos, for singing in the choir.

'Look at you,' they'd smirk. 'All girlie goody two shoes. Who do you think you are? Creep.'

In the house he'd sing along with his mother's favourite crooners. Bing Crosby. Perry Como. Rudee Vallee. And she would clap her wide pink hands and pour him glasses of warm milk and honey.

'They say that it's good for the voice.'

'Who does?' Dad winced. He could feel his throat clogging up.

'That Maurice Chevalier, he swears by it.'

'He does?'

Grandma looked at the hive-shaped jar. 'I'm sure it said honey.'

'Yes, Mother. Honey. But are you sure it said milk? It sticks to your throat like glue. And let's hope I haven't lost it.'

As soon as he was old enough, he'd go with his dad to pubs that had 'spots'. At The Olde White Swan you could sing with the band for as long as the audience let you. On Saturday nights, when his friends were queueing outside the Odeon, he'd be sat with his dad drinking shandy and waiting for the lights to go down. At first his legs would feel like jelly and his voice would start to waver when he heard it through the microphone, but as soon as the whistles started, and the applause, then he knew that he really had them. 'You were marvellous,' his dad would say, and women who were older than his mother would come and pat his head and tell him he was was better than the man they had playing at the Ritzy.

It was a long hot summer. The sun made him lazy. Restless. He worked in a petrol station and then got himself sacked for sunbathing on the roof of a broken transit van. He didn't want to be there anyway. He wanted to join a band. A real band, a band that played to rooms full of fainting girls, screaming, pawing his legs for more. He was skinny. Dark-haired. In the right kind of light he looked like Tom Jones. It was the way that he walked, moved. The way that he wore his clothes – his favourite drainpipe jeans and purple mohair sweater that a shy girl called Sandra had bought for him in Carnaby Street.

'The real one? Honest? So, did you see any Beatles walking about? Did you bump into Twiggy then, or what?'

All through August and into September he sang with a group called Mike West and the Panthers. Mike was in Australia, visiting his auntie in Sydney. When he came back, with his suntan and New Look hairstyle, they had a fight and Dad was thrown into the audience.

'They were crap anyway. Useless no-hopers. Fuck them. They couldn't write songs. They didn't even make it up to Christmas.'

He was nearly nineteen.

'You want to get yourself doing something,' his mother would tell him. 'Look at Frank. He can pull a car to pieces in a morning and have it back for teatime. People need cars,' she'd say. 'People will always need cars.'

But he'd already read an ad in a gauzy shop window. *Vincenzo's Hair Palace. Trainee Required. Enquire Within.* He went inside and drank tea that tasted like perfume. He said he liked people. He was hired. He combed out wigs and fitted them. He almost forgot what it was like, being in the limelight. He liked his new job. He was popular. He liked having money to spend on records, clothes and endless rounds of drinks at all the pubs in town. And when he did manage to grab hold of the microphone and do a few numbers, he was a star, the best they'd heard all week. There'd often be a whip-round, if there was no hint of a fight.

'There were fights then?'

'Oh, there were always the fights,' said Dad. 'And people are still like that. Back then it was worse. After a few too many drinks they goaded me all right. Wouldn't bloody stop. Said I was doing a queer's kind of a job. Started on about Vince, but I soon put them right. No one says that and goes home with their face in one piece.'

Then there were the parties. Anniversaries. Weddings. At his own wedding he sang, 'I'll Never Fall In Love Again'.

'And it was just like the record,' said Mum. 'People could hardly believe it.'

For years he carried on, singing whenever he could. Mum would stay at home, with me and her Alma Cogan records. Round and round we'd slowly spin, to 'Little Things Mean A Lot', and we'd take our time, getting dizzy round the furniture.

'She really does have it,' Mum would say, her soft hair flying. Her face turning pink in the firelight.

'What's that, Mum?'

'Just listen.'

'Listen to what?'

'Well, it's obvious. Can't you hear it?'

I could hear the words. I could pick out the violins in the orchestra. Loud. Soft. Loud again.

'I don't know.'

'Well, listen hard,' she said. 'She's the girl with the laugh in her voice. It's what they all say, and they're right. And doesn't it make all the difference?'

Then just before my ninth birthday, Dad came home from a night singing at the Catholic club. He was later than usual. Flushed. He'd fastened his coat up wrong.

'Just look at you,' said Mum, standing on tiptoe, gently undoing the buttons and slipping it off his shoulders.

'It was packed there, love. Standing room only. They were all in there tonight. You should have come. I went down a storm.'

'Well, I knew you would. We both did. Didn't we, Jack?'

'And I got paid,' he said, waving a small buff envelope. 'In real money. Not pints.'

'That's good,' she said, hanging up his coat. 'That's wonderful.'

'And I've decided. I'm going to change my name. That's the next thing. Now I'm a pro I want to be different.'

'But Joey Trench. It isn't bad.'

'It stinks.'

'It's all right.'

'No.'

'So, what about Joseph? It'll give you a bit more class. Like that singer, that opera singer. Joseph. Joseph Locke.'

'Joseph Trench? Don't be bloody stupid.'

'He's right, Mum. It sounds daft. Old-fashioned.'

Dad turned on his heels, swinging round. 'And what the hell do you know? You? You know nothing. And what are you doing down here at this time of night? You should have disappeared by now. So do yourself a favour, lad. Scram.'

All that night I could hear them through the wall. They were talking. Creaking. Moving things. Dad talked about Rolls-Royces with personalised number plates. Gold-coloured. The Talk Of The Town. Vegas! Mum's voice was piercing, croaking. Breathy.

You're the king, Joey. You are.

By the time I came down for breakfast, Dad had chosen his surname from a Thomson's travel brochure.

'From now on,' he said, 'I'll be Joey Seville.' He sniffed, lit a cigarette and pouted over his bacon. 'But I won't bother using it for everyday life,' he told us.

CLICKING OFF THE IRON, SHE BEGAN TO TIDY UP A BIT. AS soon as the *Coronation Street* theme tune wailed off she put a record on from her own special collection at the back. Alma. 'Dreamboat'.

Blanking out the words I started reading *Ghost Night*, the real

American comic that my grandpa had bought for me in town. 'Now that France is all sorted,' he'd said, 'I don't mind splashing out a bit.'

'Have you done your homework?' Mum asked.

'Yes.'

'When?'

'I did it after school.'

'Where?'

'In Queen's Park.'

'Oh,' she said. 'Well, all right then, if you're sure.'

She was dancing now. Moving in front of the gas fire with her invisible dancing partner. She said his name was Darren. He was dark-skinned, wide-shouldered, and just like Nat King Cole.

The ghost in *Ghost Night* was just a thin squiggly line, but the story seemed real. Not like the British comics with Dennis or those goody football heroes. In America it would have cost 25 cents. I liked looking at the ads. Over there you could buy real X-ray specs. Sea Monkeys. Wristwatches that recorded your voice – the kind detectives used. Old New Yorker ice cream came in a hundred different flavours, including bubble gum, cola and donut. 'Mom, make them smile!' said the ad.

My mum was sitting with her knees up now, swaying to the music. Curled in. Elf-like. All across the furniture shirts lay, flattened. Trousers. Blouses. Her best blue dress with the fancy Hi Society label.

'You can tell it's a good one,' she'd said. 'Because Mr Patel didn't waste his time cutting it out.'

The music got slower. Sad. Mum had her head down. It was like she couldn't swallow.

'What's the matter?'

'Nothing.' She jammed a cigarette into the gas fire.

'Dad said I could go with him on Saturday.'

'He did? God. Well, he must have been drunk.'

'Not really. He said it again this morning.'

'And what's so good about Saturday?'

'Nothing. I'd like to see him anyway.'

'Don't you get enough of it at home?'

'At home, it's different. At the club, well, it's where it's supposed to be.'

'It's full of old women.'

'Stuart's mum goes.'

'Exactly.'

We laughed and she went to put the kettle on. Dad wouldn't be home for hours. After singing and pacing the bouncy parquet stage floor, he'd be out somewhere with Pete, the organist. They'd go to pubs where people recognised them. Where women would blush and nudge, brushing his side at the bar.

'Would you like a glamorous job?' I asked. The room was filling with steam. Mum was sipping tea, scrunched, trying her best not to squash all the shirts.

'You mean, like Alma Cogan?'

'No, I mean like Dad.'

'Dad? Dad's job isn't glamorous. He fits wigs. Every Thursday afternoon he goes up and down the cancer ward with his display stand and order forms.'

'But the singing?'

'It's a hobby.'

'He could go and be a redcoat. We'd get loads of free holidays.'

Mum smiled. 'He's too old. They only take the young ones. And I think you have to be single. I don't know, Jack. If he'd wanted to do that, he should have done it years ago.'

'But he is a professional.'

'No.'

'But he gets paid.'

'Pin money.'

'So, he'll never be on telly?'

'Oh no,' she said. 'Mind you, I have seen worse, especially on that, what's it called? That *Wheel Tappers' and Shunters' Social Club* thing.'

'I bet Gran will miss it.'

'What?'

'Television. Her programmes. *Crossroads* and that.'

'She won't mind. They have things over there.'

'French things.'

'Yes. French things.'

She started folding some of the clothes and putting them into the pink plastic basket that was already stuffed with knickers and balled-up pairs of socks. I could see us all in France. Dad pretending he knew what people were saying. Singing. A kind of Sacha Distel. Mum would be in a bathing suit, striped, like the one I'd seen her wearing in a photograph. Her only visit. Evelyn 9, it said in the album. She was standing by a boat, a tiny silhouette against the floats and squares of fishing nets. She wasn't even smiling.

'Grandpa says you can see the sea from nearly all the windows. He says it sounds like thunder. Can we go? Can we visit in the holidays?'

'What with?'

'The fifth form are going to Marseilles. It's supposed to be cheaper than Blackpool.'

'We're going to Rhyl. Your dad's already booked it.'

'Rhyl? Again? But it's freezing.'

We were always going to Rhyl. Last year it had rained every day. The wind stung your face like a slap. We'd spent most of our time in a tiny amusement arcade that was packed with everyone else. Dad had won the bingo jackpot – £5 and a blue and white teddy. To celebrate he'd bought Bovril from the drinks machine and we went and sat on a bench, shivering, watching the sea, a fat grey slab in the distance.

'It was June last time. This time it's August, so there's bound to be a bit of sunshine. Anyway, from what I remember, Brittany isn't much better.'

'Do you want them to go?'

'They're excited. Like kids. Can't wait. Claudine will be here in a fortnight. She's coming to wave them bye-bye.'

She looked up at me, sad, with a smile on her face.

'What shall we have on now?' she asked, jumping up.

'Nothing?'

'Something to cheer us up. Something lively. Come on.'

Alma Cogan sang 'Mambo Italiano'. Mum danced a bit, then she got the photos out. Curled-up pictures of her parents. A cat. A house. Mum and Claudine as children.

'You could tell that she'd be clever,' she said, holding up a picture of a serious-looking schoolgirl. 'Even then, I knew.'

'How?'

'Oh, the way she looked at everything. Like she'd seen it all before.'

I left her with Alma and a bottle of Tia Maria.

In my bedroom I looked up Brittany on my Kellogg's map of the world. Finistère. It was all sticking out with sharp jagged edges. I couldn't imagine my grandparents living there. I knew they were French, of course. I'd heard them. I'd seen the looks from all the neighbours when they'd come and roll their eyes at the bottles of wine, garlic, the word Mai on the calendar that was spelt nearly right so they'd have to look twice to make sure that it really was foreign and not just a mistake that they'd made at the printers.

Lying on my bed I flicked through my homework. On the park bench things could get muddled. There was the strange thick scent from the flowers. Girls walking home with their hitched-up skirts and grass on their coats. Brown legs. Blowing hair. Insects.

Sometimes, if the weather was right, I'd close my eyes and

imagine I was in a garden. My garden. It had sloping lawns. An observatory. A flash silver Merc in the drive.

Chemistry. The diagrams were straight. Labelled. There were biscuit crumbs in the margin. Ginger Nuts. I shook them out but they left greasy dots on the paper. Mr Walker wouldn't notice. He'd just see all the writing and be glad that someone had bothered.

Maths. Some graphs were missing. Smudged red ink. My calculator needed new batteries. (Sit next to Nigel Taylor on the bus.)

English Lit. Pygmalion by George Bernard Shaw. I'd read most of it. *My Fair Lady* had been on telly recently and I'd watched until the races. I knew what would happen after that. There was a woman in Marks & Spencer who looked like Audrey Hepburn. Mum said she was Indian.

WITH THE CURTAIN CLOSED, MY BEDROOM LOOKED BLUE. Like I was lying underwater. With my Bolton Wanderers bobble hat pulled right down past my ears, the sounds were muffled. But this was cold water. It was more like Blackpool than the Med. I wore thick pyjamas, socks and my dressing gown in bed.

I could just about see to read.

The Milky Way. Known by the Mexicans as 'the little white sister of the many-coloured rainbow'.

Alma again.

It is a background formed of stars so distant, that we only ever see them as a crowd.

The door slammed.

Elvis. 'Mystery Train'. He was back.

A few seconds later, I could hear him snarling.

'What the fuck's all this about?'

'Nothing.'

'It's like a Chinese laundry. Look at it.'

'I was just going to—'

'And what's this here? Tia fucking Maria? Give me that.'

The music was loud. Even through the bobble hat I could hear it all. The voices. The same Elvis record, over and over again. I stared at the back of my book. Titles in the series: *Deserts. The Human Body. Prehistoric Life.* I gripped the cover hard and clutched it to my chest, and still their voices went on and on, screeching, whining, snapping.

Things were being moved. Scraped. Pulled.

'Stop, stop, stop it!'

The record jerked into silence, then started back up again. Was he going to hit her? He wouldn't. No, he wouldn't hit her. Why would he hit her for a few damp shirts?

I pulled in my legs. The book felt good on my face. I could smell the inky paper smell. Shiny. Smooth. Cold. Now they were laughing. Loud. Louder. It was like they just couldn't stop laughing.

Eyes tight shut. Squeezed until I could see red, then black, then little white stars. If I relaxed a bit, I could follow them. It was like moving through a galaxy.

4 A.M. DAD SNORING. MUM IN THE BATHROOM, RETCHING, coughing then retching again. There was light at the edge of the curtains. The street lamp was lit. The sky was getting paler. Mum crept softly across the landing, sniffing and blowing her nose. *Don't wake him up.* I whispered to myself. *Don't let him hear.*

I couldn't sleep. The house was full of noise. The sniffing, creaking, my UFO alarm clock with its whirr, tick, tick. So, wrapping myself in blankets, I sat with my book, Red Indian-style. Swaddled. Deaf. The planets. Pluto. Mars. Saturn.

Saturn's rings are made of many millions of tiny, ice-coated rock fragments.

Because Saturn is so massive, the pressure at its heart is

enough to turn hydrogen solid. That is why there is a layer of metallic hydrogen around the planet's inner core of rock.

Saturn is the queen of all the planets.

'YOU'RE LOOKING FORWARD TO RHYL, AREN'T YOU, LOVE?' Mum's voice was chirpy, chirpy, cheerful. She was wearing her apron and her next best dress. Her hair was up, full of clips and fancy hair slides. Lipstick. Shadow. Charlie. She'd made a real effort, but her face looked bashed.

Behind the sofa, last night's ironing had been thrown into a ball. Creased up. Trashed. It looked like Dad might have pissed on it.

'Rhyl?' He glanced up from page three. *Tina from Canvey Island. Brunette.* Likes Mike Oldfield. Jet skiing. Travel. She'd tucked her passport into her shiny tiny knickers. 'Well, I hope you're saving up. I'm not forking out for everything when we get there. I'm not made of money yet.'

'I know.' My voice was a squeak. I could see Mum through the kitchen door, swallowing aspirin and rubbing the side of her face.

'Hadn't you better be going?'

I looked at the clock. It was way too early but I nodded and put my coat on. When I went to kiss Mum, she flinched. I didn't look too closely. Her face smelled of Dettol.

Halfway down the street I looked back over my shoulder. I could see Dad upstairs, yawning and closing the curtains again. A van pulled up, the radio blasting.

'Can you tell me where St Jude Street is? It all looks the same. I've been going mad. Driving round in circles.'

I pointed towards the church and glanced back at the house where Mum was at the window with her eyes closed, walking backwards, slowly, into the cold grey light.

OUR SIX-WEEK SUMMER HOLIDAY CAME EARLY. WE couldn't believe it. Someone had burnt the school down in the night. You could smell it for miles. A TV crew appeared and the hard boys pulled faces and stuck two fingers up at the camera, but even they looked surprised to see the smouldering piles of bricks and the burnt-out yellow mini-bus. A blackboard with the words Five-Finger Exercise stood steaming in the rubble. Mrs Godfrey was crying.

'It's the shock,' someone said. 'Either that, or she's left something precious in the staff room,' and everyone burst out laughing.

Next to me, Stuart Harris just stared, rubbing at his glasses. Stuart was the fat boy of the class. He was all right. I'd known him since I was five. Some boys called him Play-Doh.

'Now what?' We'd been shepherded into groups and told to go home if we could. No one stayed, apart from a few of the swattiest first years.

'Shall we go into town then, or what?'

Stuart could hardly speak. His mouth slacked open. The police were sticking tape around the crime scene.

'I can't believe it,' I said. 'Look at the place.'

'I know. Isn't it great? It's fantastic. Best thing that's ever happened.'

'It wasn't you, was it?'

'Me? I'm not that bloody clever,' he said, pulling off his tie. 'I can't even get my mum's lighter to work.'

In town we went to the Easy Eats Café and bought a milkshake and a doughnut with our dinner money. We told all the waitresses that our school had burnt down, but none of them believed us. We soon got bored. We flicked through the records in WH Smith. Stuart liked Abba.

'The blonde. What a lovely arse,' he said, staring at 'Fernando'.

Aimlessly we walked around Woolworth's, our shoes sticking

to the black and red floor. It felt warm. Julie and Lesley from 2C were hovering by the make-up, smearing lipstick on to their hands and holding it into the light.

'Look at those dogs' dinners,' said Stuart. He was panting. He was talking like his seventeen-year-old brother who looked nothing like him. Neil was tall. Muscly. He worked in a garage and was a big success with the girls. 'It shouldn't be allowed.'

We shuffled past the girls. Julie giggled.

'Looking for lipstick, were you?' she said. 'I suppose you're into make-up and that?'

'What?' She was looking right at me.

'Well, your dad's on stage, isn't he? What shade does he use?' She held up a tin of something. 'Apricot Blush, or Dusky?'

I wanted to say something. A put down. Something funny. I could feel the heat in my face and my voice that was stuck like a huge great lump in my throat. Looking away, I stared at the Lucky Bags. Boiled sweets. Bubble gum. A woman in a blue gingham uniform stacked Love Hearts into rows.

'Come on.' Stuart walked past with his nose in the air. He couldn't think of anything either. Useless. Behind us they were sniggering. 'Let's go.'

Outside, I started breathing again.

'She's stupid, that Julie,' Stuart said. 'But her sister's nice. She won Miss Horwich last year, in a really small bikini.'

TOWN WAS FULL OF KIDS IN OUR SCHOOL UNIFORM. THE prefects and deputy head boy were smoking at the bus stop. Stuart dragged his feet.

'We might as well go back to my place,' he said. 'Mum can't really moan. It's not like we're skiving or anything.'

We went past the Hair Palace and I could see my dad leaning against the window and laughing with the girls. I felt sick. He looked smiley. Happy. Moving his arms about. I didn't look through the door. I just kept going with my head down, following the fag ends, the hard grey blobs of chewing gum that had stuck across the pavement.

'What do you think's going to happen?' Stuart asked.

My stomach jerked. 'What do you mean?'

'School. When do you think we'll have to go back?'

'When they build another one?'

'Yippee!'

We were walking past the market. The pavement was broken here, and strewn with dirty cabbage stalks. Rotten apples. Piles of chips with footprints skidding through them.

Behind the gate that said Fish in fancy wrought iron, I could see my grandpa sweeping round the stalls. He'd found a part-time job that would keep him a couple of weeks. 'I can't just sit around packing now, can I?' he'd said. 'That's your gran's job, that is.' And I could see her, wrapping her best ornaments inside sweaters, sure it was the last time that she'd see them all whole. 'You know what those ships are like. The Bay of Biscay. Waves the size of houses.'

The floor was wet and black. A man was throwing ice across a counter; he was whistling. His hair was covered in frost.

'What are you two doing, skulking round here?' Grandpa asked, leaning on his brush.

'The school's burnt down.'

'It has?' His eyes widened. 'Really?'

'Yes.'

'An accident?'

We shrugged.

'Well, the bloody little hooligans,' he said. 'They want locking up.'

'It's going to be on the news.'

'Yes? And what about you?'

'We weren't near the cameras.'

'I mean work. What about your work?'

'Oh, we're just waiting to hear.'

'Don't let this stop you,' he said. 'Don't get bone idle. Keep it up, boys. It's important. Remember. Whatever else is happening, always keep it up.'

Stuart choked a laugh.

Grandpa shook his head. 'Well, you'll both have to earn a living in the end.'

Someone shouted for him. A man in dirty white overalls took some lobsters out of a crate, their pincers tied with strips of yellow sticky tape.

'Keep out of trouble, boys. I've work to do. See you soon, Jack.'

We went outside and laughed with our hands on our knees.

'You have to keep it up,' Stuart panted. 'Jeeze.'

Over the road we went through a broken gate and down a cobbled alley. Across the disused viaduct someone had written Bev & Ajay 4 Eva! in wobbly white aerosol. Stuart tripped on an empty bottle of pop.

'Just think,' said Stuart, rubbing his knees. 'It'd be Chemistry now. Maybe that's where it started? One of Mr Walker's experiments goes wrong and whoosh!'

'In the middle of the night?'

'He might have had something rotting in a test tube. Too much gas.'

I shrugged. I wasn't that bothered anymore. I was thinking about Grandpa going all that way to France. The way he bent his head, letting his eyes drop down.

STUART LIVED IN A SMALL GREY COUNCIL HOUSE ON Violet Street. These were the houses that my Grandma Trench used to dream about in the fifties. They had bathrooms. Kitchens with new electric cookers. A tiny square of lawn at the back. 'The Garners got one,' she'd say. 'And they changed overnight. All lah-di-dahs and fancy airs and graces. Now look at them. They've gone back to being rough again.'

17a. The curtains were closed downstairs. The lounge all red and flickering black and white. His mum was lying on the sofa, huddled under a blanket. There was an old film on the telly.

'What are you doing back?' she said. As soon as she saw me, she pulled off the blanket, sitting up straight. Her stomach hung over her skirt. I could see her giant belly button squashed between its rolls. 'What time is it?' She scrambled round her feet for a packet of cigarettes.

'The school's burnt down. Honest. It's going to be on the telly.'

She flicked up her lighter and sucked the tip of her fag. In the darkness I could see the glowing orange end and a sheet of foggy smoke.

'To the ground?'

'Yes.'

'So, what are they going to do about it? You can't stay here all day.'

'Why not?'

She doubled over, coughing. 'You need to be out at your age,' she wheezed. 'Doing things. Learning. I hope they're making arrangements.'

'We don't know yet,' I told her. 'It only just happened last night.'

She gave me a look. 'Well, make yourself scarce, Stuart. I don't want you cluttering up.'

Blinking, she stretched to turn on a lamp. The room was full of carrier bags stuffed with things. Bottles. Newspapers. Bent-in half shoes. Mrs Harris saw me looking.

'I'm having a bit of a clear out,' she said, in a posh sounding voice. 'You can make us all a drink if you like, Stuart. I'll have tea.'

I followed him into the kitchen. He closed the door. On the back of it there was a giant white handbag and a picture of the Pope. The sink was full of dirty pots and pans. Mugs with tea still in them. Floating blobs of dimpled yellow fat were swimming by the glasses.

Next to the toaster there was a collection of prescription bags and small brown bottles.

'Mum's,' he said. 'Blood pressure. Heart and that. The asthma stuff's Dave the bastard's.'

'Who?'

'He's my new sort of stepdad.'

'What happened to the other one?'

'Colin? I haven't got a clue.'

We took our drinks upstairs. Stuart's room looked immaculate, but that's because it was empty, or nearly. At one side there were bunk beds, the bottom one stripped because his brother had just left home to live in a flat with his girlfriend.

'Lucky bastard,' said Stuart. 'Tracy's good-looking. Long black hair. Gorgeous you-know-whats.'

'Have you seen them?'

'Not exactly. But I found one of her bras under Neil's pillow. Huge it was. And see-through.'

I sat and stared through the window. The bit of lawn looked yellow. There were things thrown all over it. Rusty garden chairs. A paddling pool. An empty beer crate.

'The paddling pool's for Wendy,' Stuart said. He was trying to tune in his radio. Static. Crackles. Wheezing.

'Right.' I didn't ask who she was. She could have been his brother's, or one of his stepdad's kids.

He'd found something. Meat Loaf. 'Bat Out Of Hell'. The voice was going crazy, but we just sat there, staring at the small black box until it faded, and a man started talking about tailbacks on the M62.

'So, who do you think did it then?'

'The school? I don't know. Could have been anybody.'

'Someone who doesn't like it? But that's most people.

Someone who's in trouble? What about Woodsy? He was expelled last week for taking girls into the toilets.'

I shrugged.

'And what about all the animals?' he droned on. 'The mice. That rabbit. The angel fish in the library.'

'Dead. They must be.'

'The mice would have got it anyway.'

I nodded.

'And what about us?' he sniffed.

'What about us?'

'I left things in there. My PE kit. All those projects I sweated over. Shit.'

'Projects? What projects?'

'Well, you know. I did this really good painting of a rocket. Black and white. NASA. It took me bloody ages.'

'Right.'

The Police were singing 'Roxanne' and my chest began to ache. I swallowed. Roxanne. It was a girl's song. Pathetic. The walls were vibrating. A gust of wind came through the window and a giant Abba poster blew up at the edges. Agnetha was pointing at me.

'It's great this,' said Stuart. 'Doing nothing.'

'Yeah.'

We sat looking at the radio. I thought about Chemistry. Handing in my homework. Rinsing out test tubes. Arranging things.

'You know what's going to happen, don't you?' I said eventually. 'After summer we'll be sent to different schools. They'll just send us off. Anywhere.'

Stuart paled. 'Please don't let them send me to Kelby. It stinks. It's like a borstal. I wouldn't last five minutes.'

'You'll be okay.'

But I knew what he meant. I'd seen them coming out. Those Kelby boys looked hard.

'Stu-art!' His mum's voice screeched up the stairs. 'I need some errands doing.'

We went down. She was still in front of the telly. Next to her there was a bag of Liquorice Allsorts, and when she talked her teeth were black.

'Here,' she snapped open her purse. 'Three bottles of milk. Five pounds of spuds. And if it's Dot, ask nicely and she might let you get me some fags and half a bottle of Vlad.'

'Okay.' Stuart looked at the money in his hand. 'This won't be enough.'

'Tell her you'll owe them. Say my back's gone and I'll pay the rest on Friday.'

But then she sort of remembered I was standing there.

'It's just that you know what those queues are like in the Barclays,' she said. 'And my back isn't up to more than five minutes.'

I nodded enthusiastically. Her back looked hunched underneath her cardigan. She'd pulled her top over her skirt, but I could still see her stomach, trying to get out.

Red-faced, Stuart headed towards the corner shop. I dragged behind. I wanted to go home.

'I have to get back,' I told him.

'Why?'

'I said I'd help my gran,' I shuffled. 'They're emigrating.'

'But you're supposed to be at school.'

'Well.'

'Well, what about tomorrow?'

'Yes.'

'What?'

'We could go somewhere.'

'All right.'

'So, I'll come round to your house,' he said. 'Sometime in the morning.'

We were standing outside the shop. The bell rang and a

woman came out with a pools coupon. Stuart put his head around the door.

'It isn't Dot,' he sniffed. 'It's the other one.'

I walked home slowly. The sun felt warm across the back of my neck. Outside the newsagent's, the billboard said: School Torched. Pics. I wondered if Mum had seen the news. Had she been outside? My stomach ached.

On the corner a little boy ran past with his fingers pointing out at me.

'Duhduhduhduhdudh,' he droned. 'You're dead, you are. Dead.'

'Come here, Craig. You're a bloody little pest!' The boy pulled out his tongue and ran behind a wall.

Across the road some girls from our sixth form stood in a line with their boyfriends, all entwined, their hands in the boys' back pockets. Tight. Warm. One of the boys turned round, rubbing his hand through her hair; all messy, red, and I wondered what it felt like, to be up close like that.

When the street petered out into the narrow grassy lane, I kept my head busy by making up lists. The names of 1C. Girls first. Alphabetically. Christine Ackroyd, Sandra Bates, and so on. You could smell the gardens here. The close-cut hedges and smoothed-out lawns. Rotary lines squeaked. I could hear someone laughing. A dog behind a fence, scratching its way outside.

After Nigel Whittle I thought about the stars, invisible in the daytime. Infinity. It didn't seem real, but it was. Sean Murphy, the boy who lived next door, had an *I-Spy* book of the sky. He'd go out at night with his brothers and they'd stand in the backstreet, looking up until their necks ached, so they'd have to lie down on the tarmac.

'I was going to get a telescope,' he'd told me. 'But what's the point? I mean, you can either see them, or you can't.'

But I would have liked a telescope. I'd lean out of my window with it. Climb on to a roof. Anywhere. Stars are being born and dying all over the universe. In the pitch black quiet I could watch them all blinking up there. Mars. Jupiter. The craters all over the moon.

The house was empty. It was nearly half-past two. Even if Mum had gone to work, she should have been home by now. Where was she then? In the kitchen, the taps dripped and there was a half-drunk cup of coffee and a *Woman's Own* opened on My Man Ran Away With My Daughter. I left it there, even though my fingers were itching to find Dear Doctor, or whoever it was that you wrote to.

In the yard, the washing line was full again. It sagged in the middle with jeans and flapping shirts; Dad's leopard-print Y-fronts and socks that drip-dripped over the cracked black flags.

I sat in the lounge and listened. There was hardly any traffic. Next door were still in Ireland. The clock had a loud tick, tick, tock. I closed my eyes. I'd thought it would be great like this, but it wasn't. I didn't know what to do next, so I flicked through the paper, made some toast and went upstairs, dripping Blue Band on to the carpet.

For a few seconds I just stood on the landing, as I dared myself to look. One Thursday teatime, Nigel Whittle had found all his mum's things in three black bin bags. Her electric rollers, make-up and her huge collection of Whimsies had been left out for the bin men. That night, she went off on a coach down to London with his brother, and they didn't come back for a month. Now he only ever sees them in the holidays.

I looked around and pulled the wardrobe door. The handle felt loose but her clothes were still in it. Cardigans. Dresses. Three things on a hanger. I stood back, relieved. Of course she wouldn't go. She wouldn't leave me. She wouldn't just leave us for that.

In their bedroom everything looked neat and the bed had been made. Pink. Shiny. Smooth. On Dad's side there was a

crushed up packet of Embassy and a cheapo disposable lighter. A
racing form. Mum had an empty box of tissues and an Avon
catalogue from Christmas '78. Her strapless gold Sekonda sat in
its box, waiting to be fixed.

I lay on top of their bed, wiping my greasy fingers on the
wrong side of a pillow. The mattress felt soft. It was strange. It
was like being in somebody else's house. From here I looked at
everything. The ceiling. The fluffy pink light shade. Dust.

In the corner by the wardrobe, Dad had all his showbiz things
set out. He'd made it like a dressing room. 'Elbow room,' he'd
say. 'But you have to do things right.' His velvet bow tie dangled
from the back of an old dining chair. His suit was in polythene
on a polished wooden hanger, and on a narrow shelf he'd stood
a few cards, his purple gonk, and his treasured signed photo.
Tom Jones in a cat suit, with a huge gold medallion. 'For Joey.
You're the man! Best Wishes, Tom.' He touched it every night.
He closed his eyes and whispered something lucky.

'All the big stars do this kind of thing,' he'd said. 'It's
traditional. It shows you have respect.'

Respect. What a joke. I'd heard that song. 'R.E.S.P.E.C.T.' But
it was the, *sock it to me, sock it to me, sock it to me*, that got me
every time.

Mum was tiny. Weenie. Skinny though he was, he could lift
her with one hand. Her face, well, it was always looking up. No
wonder she'd say that her neck ached.

The back door clicked and she brought the washing in. It
wasn't quite dry but she folded some of it into piles and stuffed
them in the airing cupboard. She screamed when she saw me.

'The school burnt down.'

She smiled and shook her head, but then she looked worried.
'There wasn't anyone in there,' she said. 'Was there? I mean, it
was empty? Wasn't it?'

I helped her with the shirts. We draped them over chairs again
and hung them by the fire.

'I didn't go to work,' she said, saving a sleeve from scorching. 'I said I had the flu and it isn't exactly a lie because I feel like I've got it.'

'Are you all right?'

'I'm fine. I'm perfectly fine. Really.' But her face looked worse because the bruises had come out. There was a small scab of blood by her ear.

'So, where did you go?'

'I ran to the chemist's,' she said. 'We'd run out of Anadin.' She pressed her head, testing.

'Did he do it?' I asked. 'Dad?' Just saying the words made me sickly. I could feel myself blushing.

'This?' She put her hand up to her cheek. Her knuckles were scraped, purple-red.

'Oh, you know what we're like once we've had a few drinks. And I'd been drinking. God. Well, you saw. Daft. We fell into each other. I just kind of got in the way.'

'Again?'

'Oh, you know what I'm like,' she said. 'It's my size. I've always been clumsy.'

When the shirts were done, we sat and watched the news. There was the school. The firemen running through the playground. Mickey Roberts pulled faces until the games teacher jerked him away.

'Suspected arson,' said the newsreader.

'Suspected arson?' said Mum. 'Tell us something we don't know.'

WHEN DAD CAME HOME HE HAD A BUNCH OF PINK carnations for mum and a rugby annual for me. It was May, so it was marked Less Than Half Price! I hated rugby. I didn't even know how you played it. When we told him about the school he said, 'You lucky little bastard!'

Mum cooked eggs, chips and beans, but just before they were ready he told us to go and put our coats on.

'I'm taking you out,' he said. 'For a slap-up, top-notch meal.'

'But it's cooked,' said Mum. 'Look. I've done you two eggs and the plates are getting warm.'

'Well, I don't care, my sweet. Turn the bloody cooker off. Chuck the lot away. You deserve a treat.' He was grinning his extra-wide grin, like his teeth didn't fit.

'No, Joey,' she stammered. 'Not now. Not tonight. Please?'

'Sorry? What was that?' he stood back, cupping his ear, shuffling around like some stupid kind of dance.

Mum looked at me, blinked and nodded. 'Just get your coat on, love,' she said.

We walked to the Cosy Kitchen. It was a couple of blocks away. The lights were bright and it was more than half full with a crowd who'd just been shopping. Mum looked pale as she squinted and headed for the corner, stepping carefully over carrier bags. A baby was crying. I felt sick. I kept looking at the toilets and wondering if I'd have to make a dash for it.

'Come on then,' Dad said. 'At least have a look at the menu. We haven't got all night. *The Streets of San Francisco*'s on later.'

The menus were plastic-coated. Greasy. Mine had a fag burn in it. Mum kept smiling. Dad winked at the waitress and she turned her head away, blushing.

'Freya,' he said, looking at her badge. 'That's a very unusual name.'

Mum kept her head down when we ordered, pretending she was looking for something that was lost inside her handbag. We both had soup. Dad grinned and lit two cigarettes. Sucking on one, he handed Mum the other.

'Minestrone? That's nice and bloody cheap.'

'And for you?'

'Well, Freya, I'll have the double egg and chips,' he smirked, cocking back his chair.

I kept my head down, just in case he knew. *Double egg and chips?* Could he tell? Could he tell that I wanted to punch him? Looking into my bowl, I followed noodles, cabbage, bits of freeze-dried tomato until Dad was just a voice that blended with everyone else's. The soup was okay. Even though there were bits of powder left in it.

'MINE WAS A FAIRY-TALE WEDDING,' MUM WOULD SAY. Especially if she'd been looking at the photos in the *Bolton Evening News*. Little squares of couples, white-veiled and suited, looking startled, or all posed and lovey-dovey, blinking in the flash light. She loved this page. She'd comment on the dresses. The looks on the women's faces. Whether the groom was handsome or not.

'Acne,' she said. 'But he's tried to cover it up. Poor bloke. What a thing to wake up to on your wedding day.'

'So, why was yours a fairy tale?'

'It just was. Everything was perfect. The sun shone, in February, so that was like a miracle in itself. And I had a big white dress. A good one from Joan Barrie's – though it really came from the bridesmaid collection, aged thirteen, something like that. Anyway, my uncle Ernest drove me and my dad to the church, and he'd put flowers in his car. Pink plastic, but they looked real, with all the fancy satin ribbons. You'd never tell.'

'Were Gran and Grandpa pleased?'

'What do you mean? Pleased to get rid of me?'

'No. I mean, Dad. Did they like him?'

'Oh yes. They thought he was smart and polite, and every Friday night without fail he'd bring my dad a couple of bottles of beer and my mum a bar of Bourneville for a treat.'

They'd met in a pub called The Beehive. Dad was with his friends. She was with hers. They'd kept passing each other, going to the bar. He'd thrown his bag of crisps at her.

'Ready salted.'

'You remember?'

'Of course I remember. And that was that. You know.'

But I wasn't all that sure. Did Mum never really think about anyone else anymore? What about Mr Gentleman at the solicitor's? He was always giving Mum a lift home in his Midget. 'Just your mother's size, eh?' he'd say, opening the door, rolling his cigar between his short pink fingers. Then there were the men she dreamed about. Nat King Cole. Elvis. 'That lovely David Soul.'

The wedding was in February 1966. Grandad Trench had died the year before, so, although he'd enjoyed the engagement party, he'd missed it.

'But I bet he's up in heaven,' Dad said. 'And I bet he's having a whale of a time with all his favourite people.'

'What?'

'Well, he's bound to be hanging out with Al Jolson by now, and that bloke that he liked, that Harry Houdini. They'll be mates. They'll have all the best brandy and a crate of Havana cigars. *Hand bloody rolled.*'

'Is Al Jolson dead then?'

'Of course he's bloody dead,' said Dad. 'And if he isn't, then he should be.'

But Grandma Trench felt nervous without her husband on the ground.

'I'd never been to a foreign wedding before,' she said. 'And they do things different over there.'

But the wedding was in Bolton, in a brand-new church, St Martha's and All Souls. It had knotty pine pews, oatmeal carpet, and stained-glass windows that were full of modern art.

'So, where the hell's Jesus?' Grandma asked, in a hushed-up kind of voice. 'What kind of a church is this?'

The priest, Father Mitchell, was kind. He pretended that he knew everyone, though none of them went to his masses.

'We'd all been lapsed for years, and it showed. No one knew

where to put themselves. We had to have these lessons first,' said Mum.

'Lessons? What kind of lessons?'

'Faith. Making a home. Things like that. I really don't remember. I was trying not to laugh. Especially when he said "let's all kneel down and pray". Oh, we got the giggles all right, kneeling there in his tiny little office, nudging all his books. And then he kept asking me how old I was. It was as if he couldn't believe it. I think he liked me though. I was wearing my plainest dress and my mother's best crucifix on a real gold chain.'

After the service – 'it was far too long and my new satin-look heels were killing me' – they went to The Olde Red Lion for drinks and a running finger buffet.

'Your gran, my mum, did most of it,' she said. 'And it was lovely. Cakes. Pink salmon. Little whist pies. People took photos. You should have seen it. Grandma Trench didn't eat, she just kept peering inside the sandwiches and sniffing. Then later, there was dancing. Your dad sang, of course. Everyone loved him.'

'They did?'

'Yes. Even aunt Claudine. And she didn't believe in marriage then, though of course she soon changed her mind when she met posh Gerald, the big London dentist.'

And then I'd try and imagine it. Dad, all fresh faced and loving. Soft. Did he keep his arms around her? Say things? Say nice things? Things that made her feel good, like her Alma Cogan records?

'Oh, it was a wonderful day,' she said, flattening the paper. 'Now, look at these two here. What a pair. And have you seen the size of that groom? Honeymoon in Majorca? Lovely. Lucky them. They look happy though. Don't you think they look happy, Jack?'

'I don't know.'

'Well, I do. Look. Look here. See that sparkle? You can see it in their eyes.'

I LIKED TO THINK OF HAPPY. WHEN I WAS ON MY OWN, I could close my eyes and feel it, and I'd slip right back in time. Wrapped up warm in a scratchy yellow blanket. The itching didn't matter. I was on the back seat of the car and they were singing their heads off to the radio. Both of them. Sunny. Sand all over. Mum's long hair streaming through the window.

Then what? A summer. A birthday party. Mine. A tinkling kind of record player with a red leather lid. We all clapped hands and passed the giant parcel. Games. *Can you do it? Go on. Try.* Mum in the corner with the blue iced cake. The candles lit. Smiling. I could see her face through the tiny yellow flames. 'Come on, precious. Come and blow. It's wish time. Come and make a wish.' Then I'd take a breath. One huge breath. Puff out my cheeks until I could feel something popping, blowing hard until they vanished, wishing, wishing, wishing twice over, just in case it worked.

But what was it I wished for?

Anything? Sometimes. But then I had it all planned. Four quick things. It was nearly always the same. Peace to All Men (amen). An Action Man. Long quiet nights. And a brand-new house on the Sycamore Barratt Estate.

THE SUN WAS OUT. A WOBBLY YELLOW LINE. DUST RAIN ON the wedding portrait. Claudine's graduation.

As soon as Dad left for work, Mum put her sunglasses on to do the washing-up.

'Are you going into work?'

'The flu lasts longer than a day. Ask anyone.'

She was listening to *The Love Hour*, and she soon started sniffing at Marvin Gaye, 'It Takes Two', her arms in suds, staring through the window.

But her face looked better. Less puffed out. She hadn't put her make-up on.

'I'm not going out today,' she said. 'So it's just you, me and the telly.'

'But why don't you go and see Gran? Help her with the packing. She won't be here much longer, and you could talk. You know.'

She dried her hands on a scorched bit of tea towel, a remnant from Dad's bacon. She moved away. The front of her dress was dripping.

'No, love. I phoned last night and nearly all the packing's done. Most of the boxes have been taken away by the shipping company. Grandpa's at the market and your gran's gone to work for that Shona today.'

'Who?'

'Shona. She runs the Battered Cod. You could go and get our dinner. I bet she'd give you extra chips and gravy.'

'But I said I'd meet Stuart. He's coming round this morning.'

'He's coming here? When?'

'I don't know.'

'Well, don't let him in,' she said. 'And get your coat on, ready.'

I sat for an hour in my anorak, folding the clothes that she'd ironed again last night. Some of them still looked creased, but I didn't say anything.

Mum hummed. She was checking all the buttons.

'He said he'd found one loose. You haven't seen it. Have you?'

The doorbell rang, but I didn't want to move.

'Will you be all right?'

'Fine. I'll be fine,' she said, pulling bits of thread. 'And there's a western on later.'

In the pale sunshine, Stuart looked grey. His clothes were too tight, and he hadn't brushed his hair so it stuck out in all directions like next door's fancy guinea pig.

'We're free. Free! Free! Free! Free! Free!'

'Okay,' I said. 'Don't get carried away.'

It wasn't really warm, but it felt a bit like summer. People had their doors open. Buzzing flies banged into the side of my face. Bluebottles. A dog rolled around outside Mrs O'Connor's. It had tiny slavering teeth and a bald patch.

'Mange,' said Stuart. 'Either that or rabies.'

We walked to the end of the block.

'Where to?' Stuart asked, rubbing round his glasses.

'Jasper Street.'

'Too far.'

'We could take a short cut,' I said. 'Go over to Mattie's if we get too knackered.'

'Oh, all right,' he sniffed. 'But only if we're desperate.'

On the corner of Jasper Street, Matthew Freeman lived with his older brother John, his girlfriend Candice, and a pair of German shepherd dogs. A couple of years earlier their parents had died in a motorbike crash. One of the many reasons why their house was usually avoided was the way they kept the smashed-up Triumph under some tarpaulin at the bottom of their yard. On windy days, the cover would blow and the flattened half of the sidecar creaked, as if someone lay moaning inside. At school, a girl called Pauline Macy had bet any boy a free date at the pictures if he'd touch it with his hands.

'And they have to be bare,' she'd said. 'No gloves allowed.'

'But why?' we all asked. 'And why on earth would you want to go out with anyone who'd touched it anyway? That's sick, that is.'

'Well,' she'd said, hands on hips, eyeing us up and down. 'I like my lads to have a bit of bloody dare about them. So?'

So, we all agreed that Pauline Macy was pretty, with her long fair hair and bumps in her blouse.

'But it's a hell of a long way to Jasper Street,' we said. 'And anyway, there's nothing much on at the pictures.'

We were panting when we got there. Stuart's hair was flat. His face was covered in sweat.

'Christ, I told you. We should have gone into town. Sat in the Wimpy or something.'

'Nah,' I said, trying not to sound too puffed. 'That costs.'

'Yeah. But it's worth it.' He rubbed his steamy glasses and we breathed against a wall, hands on our knees, panting, thinking about warm burger smells and frothy pink milkshakes. 'And I bet it's packed with other kids from our school. It would have been a laugh.'

'I haven't any money. And we're here now, anyway.'

Stuart looked up, and pulled a sweaty face. 'Great,' he said. 'It's a beauty spot. Well worth the hike.'

Jasper Street had a row of tatty terraced houses on one side, and a patch of old allotments on the other. The allotments hadn't been used for at least ten years. Everything had been left. The numbered sheds. Benches. Rusting tea caddies and broken-up tools. The council had been planning to build houses on the site, but they soon found that the land was sliding towards the railway embankment, and worthless. Now there were barbed-wire fences and signs that said, Keep Out! No Trespassing! Danger!

We ducked through the fence and headed down towards the sheds. The ground was covered. Weeds. Bricks. Broken bottle ends. Stuart looked like he was limping.

'But it's the way I always walk,' he said.

At the back of the first shed there was a dead black cat. It had been there for months. Whenever we came we always checked on its state of deterioration. Now the ears had gone. Its jaw was all over the place. There wasn't much left of the tail.

'It doesn't look real anymore,' Stuart said. 'You can see its skull. Look.'

I stared at it. The skull showed up white through the shrivelled black face. I could see a couple of whiskers.

'Here, kitty, kitty, kitty,' Stuart called, rubbing his fingers together.

'I thought black cats were supposed to be lucky.'

'Didn't help that one much. Look at the state. Very fucking fortunate.' And it might just have been the tone of his voice, but we both cracked up laughing.

It felt strange in the sheds. Dark with all the dust and boarded windows. We left the door open. Stuart was wheezing still, and dying for a sit-down, but I liked looking around, wondering what it had been like.

On the wall there was an old Sutton calendar. August 1970. On one of the squares it said: Sweet peas all dead. No more pink cupid. Tell Noreen bye bye.

On the blackened table there were empty Schweppes bottles. Raspberryade. Real lemonade. A tin of Golden Virginia. I took off the lid. Dust and three dead beetles.

'Don't you think it's weird?' I was trying to pull a notebook apart.

'What do you mean?'

'Well, why is all this stuff still here? Why hasn't the whole place been trashed? It looks like nothing's been touched. You'd have thought some gang or other would have taken the place over by now. Or torched it. God. They haven't even written their names on anything.'

'I don't think it's weird. It's because it's so bloody boring here. I don't know why we came all this way just so we could sit in some crappy old shed. Shit. And there's nothing worth nicking anyway.'

'I suppose not.'

'So let's go round to Mattie's. I dare you.'

'No way.'

'I bet he torched the school.'

'He might have, with his brother.'

'Come on. At least we'll get a brew.'

'Will we?'

'Course.'

'You go.'

'No.'

'You wanted a drink.'

'So? We'll go together then.'

On our way out, I stuffed the notebook into my pocket. Halfway through the fence, Stuart snagged his jacket on the wire.

'My mother's going to kill me.'

'Don't let her see it.'

'But look at it.'

It was hanging. It looked like he'd been knifed.

'You'll have to take up sewing.'

'Oh yes,' he breathed. 'You're very fucking right.'

We were quiet outside Mattie's house. On a dusty square pane, a sticker said: Dogs Running Free. Enter At Your Own Risk. We could hear the TV behind the door, and someone moving about.

'He's in then.'

'Well, something is.'

Before we could think too much about it, Stuart was already knocking. I felt nervous. My legs were clacking together, but when he opened the door, Mattie looked so ordinary that we both began to grin.

'Come in,' he said. 'The dogs aren't here. John's got them with him in the van.'

The dogs weren't there, but the house still reeked of them. The furniture was chewed. There were claw marks on the walls. When I went to sit down there was a marrow bone on the cushion. It looked brown. Gooey. I didn't want to touch it, so I stood by the door instead.

'So, what are you two doing round here?' Mattie asked. He was wearing a T-shirt and dirty jogging bottoms. Bare feet. I looked down at my gym shoes and wondered what it must be like with no mum and dad. His nails were black. You could see a clean bit, where his shoes had been. Could he do what he liked all the time?

'We were at the allotments,' said Stuart. 'We only stayed five minutes.'

'Why?'

'That's what I said.' Stuart stretched his legs out, looking expectantly round at the kitchen.

'I'll make us all a brew then.'

'Great.'

He seemed to take ages, so I sat on a clean bit of carpet. On the telly there was a rerun of *Randall and Hopkirk (Deceased)*. The picture was fuzzy. It looked like double vision in a snowstorm. Over the fire there was a dartboard and a David Bowie poster. On Saturday nights his brother went into town, dressed like Ziggy Stardust.

When the tea came it looked all right, but it tasted funny with its globby sterilised milk.

'Do you want some whisky in it?' he asked, in a normal-sounding voice.

'What?'

'Whisky. Do you want some whisky in your tea?'

We both kind of shrugged.

'I'm not that keen on whisky,' Stuart said, but Mattie had already got the bottle out and was sloshing some into his own.

'It tastes different in tea,' he said.

He came and poured us each a glug. It smelled strong. My mouth didn't need to touch the cup. I could taste it already.

'It's great about school,' Mattie said. 'Now there's no going back.'

'Do you know who did it?' Stuart gagged.

'No.'

'Well, we thought that you wouldn't. We knew it. Didn't we, Jack?'

Mattie gave him a look. 'Come upstairs,' he said.

We followed him. I left my cup on the side. My mouth felt awful.

'Come and see this.'

At the top of the stairs, with its thin bit of carpet, he turned into his brother's room. The curtains were half closed so it took us a little while just to figure out what we were looking at.

'Jeeze,' panted Stuart.

Plastered across the walls there were pictures of nude women. Really nude. With everything open. Not like page three.

I followed Stuart, who was going from picture to picture, jiggling his glasses, getting a closer look.

'Wow, look at this.' On a fur rug, Tanya from Moscow was doing the splits, holding on to her ankles. She was pouting at us.

'Doesn't Candice mind?' I peered at the pictures. I'd always wanted to see everything like this, but not at Mattie Freeman's. Not here. No way. I felt stupid going round. Having a gawp. What was I supposed to say?

'She lives here for free. She hasn't got a choice.'

'Wow.' Stuart couldn't get over his luck. Whisky and dirty pictures. He flopped on to the side of the bed, exhausted.

'They do all sorts of things in here,' Mattie said. Stuart looked startled. He sat up, then down again, looking at the bed. 'You should hear them.'

'No?'

'Yes. And Candice is a screamer.'

Draped across the floor I could see bits of women's clothes. A skirt. Sandals. A thin floaty blouse.

'Oh, that's our John's,' said Mattie, picking it up. 'He's a right gender bender, but he's only into girls.'

I kind of croaked. I wasn't even sure what he meant. Stuart looked green. He'd been gulping down his tea.

'It's an education,' said Mattie. 'Just listening.'

It felt dirty in the room. Grimy. I could feel it on my hands. I didn't want to touch the bed, so I slid to the floor and sat hunched against the wall.

Stuart shook his head. 'Excellent.'

Underneath the bed I could see some dumbbells, weights, and a fluffy hot-water bottle. There were piles of girlie magazines and grubby bike manuals.

'Now try this.'

Stuart looked worried until Mattie found some glasses and poured in something else.

'It's foreign,' he said. 'Even John doesn't know what it is. It's from Greece. Spain. Somewhere like that.'

I took a sip. It tasted okay. Like the boxes of liqueurs that Dad always got at Christmas. We didn't say anything. We just sipped and stared at the posters. The girls were starting to look a bit nicer. Jackie was my favourite.

'I hear your dad's a bit of a goer,' Mattie slunk across the room.

My head jerked. I'd only had a thimbleful, but the room was starting to tilt.

'What?'

'You heard. Your dad and the ladies. You know,' he winked. 'I bet there's a dozen of his kids right across town. Little Joey lookalikes. Ahhhh ... '

I felt cold. I could see all the goose bumps springing up my arms. I didn't know what to say, so I sniffed and curled in my shoulders.

'Mind you, Candice has seen his act and she says she's not surprised. Says he has all the women swooning.'

Stuart giggled.

'You must be bloody joking,' I sniffed, staring at my feet. My old white gym shoes with the blue Biro stars. I tried to blank him out, counting all the ridges, the stars, the six metal holes until they blurred into nothing.

'I bet your mum hates all the groupies.'

Stuart snorted.

'Or is she just used to them? Do they turn up at the house wanting autographs and bits of his clothes?'

'Oh, his mum,' blurted Stuart. 'She's nice, she is. Mind you. She's little.'

'What do you mean?' Mattie pulled out his T-shirt. Two little points at the top. 'You mean she's got no tits?'

'Oh no. I mean, she's little all over.'

'A doll. A Barbie? Very nice.' Mattie came and sat with me. 'Yes. It must be nice to have a mum.'

My head sprang up and I looked straight into his face. Red-rimmed eyes. Dirty-looking freckles. He looked old. What now? What was I supposed to say?

'I'm sorry,' I mumbled.

'You want to look after her.' He was pulling at the cord on his pants, winding it tight around his knuckles. 'We weren't that careful. We let them go to Llandudno on the bike.'

'It wasn't your fault.'

'We were supposed to be trading it in. Getting a car. A Beetle. John said he wouldn't be seen dead in a Beetle. He said they were teachers' cars. I said he was right. So they went and kept the bike.'

I looked at the window, and through the dark red curtains and down, I imagined the bike. A big black lump in the corner.

'Mind you,' he said, pulling down his T-shirt. 'I still think a Beetle's a poof's kind of a car. The bike was better any day. Even the sidecar was cool. John had put a transfer on it. A wolf.'

'A wolf,' repeated Stuart. His eyes were dropping now.

'You know,' said Mattie. 'I'd let you go and see it, but it got scraped off when that lorry hit it. You can just about see the fangs.'

STUART WAS QUIET WALKING HOME. HIS LIPS KEPT puffing out, like he was doing silent belches. At the bus stop, he said, 'I've got 10p. I can't face walking it.'

I leant on the wall. My mouth was dry and my teeth felt coated. Metallic. I wished I had a Polo.

'Do we smell like we've been boozing?' he asked.

'Nah.'

'We only had a bit.'

'Yeah.'

'Do you feel all right?'

'Course I do.'

'Right.'

'So, what did you think of those women?'

'Great,' I said. 'Gorgeous.' Jackie had thick black hair, and, although she didn't quite show everything, she was pretty.

'It must be great,' said Stuart. 'Living there.' But I could tell he didn't mean it. He stumbled on to the bus. The rip in his coat was like a big blue tail, blowing in the wind. Through the window he pouted his lips, made the V sign at me, and burped.

IT WAS DOWNHILL HOME. THE SUN WAS MOTTLED NOW, and cold. In front of me, two girls walked together, sharing a coat, shivering, their heels scraping hard across the pavement. Down past the infirmary. The kebab shop and diner. The club.

By the club, with its dead neon sign, I walked slower, then stopped. In the windows there were posters for bingo, and a pie and peas quiz night. *Tetley on Tap. Watney's Red Barrel.* There was Dad grinning down, frozen in a black and white photograph – that was another thing he did when he started getting paid. He'd found an ad in the back of *The Stage* for a theatrical photographer. *Goldman & Son, Manchester.* A younger Bruce Forsyth stood and pointed a finger. 'For that professional touch!' it said. We couldn't believe the prices. There was no Rhyl that year.

'You have to speculate to accumulate,' he'd grinned, practising his autograph.

Now I'd seen that photo all over the place. Stuck behind the counter of the fish shop. *With love to Lil and Bobby xxx* In the newspaper, in Friday's weekend showbiz section. On the back seat of a bus. I'd taken that one home. Those pictures cost a packet, and he wouldn't have wanted to waste it. For a while, Stuart's mum had one taped across her fridge. It said, 'Howdy, Jean!' and 'Thanks'.

So what was Mattie saying? It couldn't be right. No way. Had he seen those women? Groupies? More like grab a granny. Most of them were pensioners. Thick legs. Beads. A few of them had whiskers. Not like Mum. Mum looked pretty. All dressed up. Lipstick. High shoes. Mattie wasn't right. Mum would know. She'd find out. She'd know something was up. She'd know on the nights that she went down to the club.

'I don't go often, because it makes it more special,' she'd say. 'And I'm not a big drinker.' But on her birthday, or something, Dad might take her out afterwards. He knew a bar that had a special late-night licence. In Lowther Street. Somewhere.

The air felt dusty. Thick with revving cars. Some men were digging up the road again, spreading showers of grit and bitter black tar. In the distance I could see a flag and the town-hall clock. Is that all the time it is? What would it be? Break time, then Biology. Mrs Summers. Lungs.

I kept walking round, but my feet were getting sore. I sat in Queen's Park. A girl in a T-shirt dress threw something for her dog. It yelped. Jumping high in circles. Mad. The dress looked stupid. It made her look like she'd forgotten to put her trousers on, or something.

Radios blared from everwhere. Indian music. Queen. At the pond a mother lifted her little girl over the railings so her bread would reach the ducks. 'Say quack, quack, quack,' she said.

The grit made my eyes water as I walked past all the Asian

shops, their doors wide open, the windows full of film posters and gold-edged saris. A handwritten sign said: Phone Pakistan From Here. Very Cheap Rates!

'You want to look after her,' a voice came through an open window, over the flour sacks and the giant tins of ghee. 'The ladies are different. They're not like you and me. They don't think the way we do. They don't think that way at all.'

'I know. I know. I'm listening,' said a voice. 'And I do know all about it.'

I dug my nails into my hand. I screwed up my toes until they felt worse, walking faster, singing pop songs in my head, new ones, not oldies, but I couldn't remember the words.

A woman walked past with a toddler. Black hair. Fast brown eyes. He looked back at me, staring, pulling hard at her hand.

Then over the football pitch, with its single bent goalpost. The mud squelched over my shoes and the wind was getting up. A boy with his arm in a sling kicked a shrunken orange ball. From the corner someone shouted, 'It's bloody Man United.'

'Piss off.'

'It's Inter Milan!'

'Piss off, will ya?'

'You're fucking crap, you one-armed wonder. You're shite.'

I kept going. I didn't look. I knew these boys from school. They had loads of brothers and sisters. Big dads and dogs that ate their clothes. These boys were always outside, hanging about, looking like they were freezing to death, even in July.

Mum was still at home. I wanted to hug her, but I couldn't get near. She was watching a cowboy film, putting rollers in her hair. They looked tight. Spiky. I could see her forehead stretching and her eyebrows going up. Her face looked better. She was smiling now. Happy.

'Are you all right, love? I was wondering where you were.'

'I was with Stuart.'

'All this time? God, you must be starving. Do you want to eat?'

'Okay.'

She jabbed in a hair clip. 'We're going out,' she said, blowing on her nails, checking to see if they'd smudged. There was a pear-drop smell. Bright blood red.

'Who?'

'Me and your dad. Go on. Eat. There's some tuna in the fridge.'

But I didn't want to move. I was warm. Standing behind the sofa, my muddy shoes sticking softly to the carpet as John Wayne shot a magazine of bullets into the pale grey sky. In the hazy background a man cracked a whip and a hundred white horses went flying through the dust. Someone drawled something. The phone rang, and Mum stood with her back to me, playing with her earrings.

'Who was it?' I asked.

'Your dad.'

'Well?'

'Well, we're not going out. But he said he'd bring me back some nice cod and chips.'

THEY WERE LAUGHING. THROUGH THE MUSIC AND *DALLAS*, I could hear Mum saying, *'Oh Joey, you crack me up, you do.'*

WRAPPING UP WARM, I WENT TO BED EARLY. I LISTENED to a man talking about London on my old transistor radio. He was an artist. He painted people's portraits in his high-roofed attic. It didn't sound like London. The way that he talked about light. Sky. The trees he could see from his windows. I looked out. The houses behind had their lights on. I could see Mrs Crompton washing up. A fag in her mouth. Staring. The man in London had a tiny bit of garden. He said he liked orchids, but all he could manage were some hardy red geraniums. We'd done orchids in Biology (term one). The orchid is a monocot. Two Australian orchids bloom underground. No one knows how they pollenate. Then I remembered the notebook in my coat pocket. The one that I'd taken from the old allotment shed.

Victor Braid. 27, Parkway. A red cover. Lion Brand. Musty. The pages had stuck. There were plant names. Antirrhinum chimes. Show angels. Sanvitalia little sun. There were weather reports. Birds spotted. Goldfinch. Blackbird. Jackdaw. *Plant out potatoes.* Ratte and King Edward. (Friday). Buy N Something nice.

N? Who? Noreen? Was that it? So, what did he buy? I rolled towards the wall, thinking. Chocolates? Flowers? Perfume? The writing was spiky, like an old man's writing, but in my head Noreen wasn't old. She was young. Slim and curvy. A nurse. A bank cashier. Pretty. An actress. She was the girl that I liked in *Man About The House.* She was Jackie on the poster. Mine.

Downstairs, the music was turning slightly slushy, and with all that I'd seen, Jackie, Trudi from Helsinki and Tanya on the rug, I was sure that I'd dream. I'd better. So, pushing on my hat, I closed my eyes tight and imagined them here, crossing all my fingers before I fell asleep.

'THE PEOPLE OF LOWER BRITTANY ARE AS LIVELY AS broomsticks,' I read, while my dad hit the table, bouncing the plates up, laughing. There was a picture of a fishing fleet, and Mont-Saint-Michel. Some old men in caps smiled outside a church, and if it wasn't for the one in the daft-looking beret, they could easily be standing in Bolton.

Gran was too busy to come round, but she'd posted us some tourist-board leaflets and a picture of the house where they'd be living. It was small and white. It had a bright green door and shutters at the windows. Mum had read it twice over, but now she wasn't looking.

'So, that's where the old witch will be in a fortnight,' Dad sniffed, holding up the picture. 'Well, they won't last long in that. Have you seen it? It's on a hill for Christ's sake. Talk about steep. And I bet there's no heating. They'll freeze their bloody bums off in that.'

Mum took the leaflets and threw them into a drawer.

'Oh, they'll be fine,' she said, straightening her cushions. 'They're used to roughing it. They like it like that.'

But Dad had already lost interest. He was on his after-breakfast fag and his giant mug of tea. As usual, the radio was on, but it wasn't quite in tune, so we got Gary Numan with a whistle.

'Are friends bloody electric? What's that supposed to mean?'

I shrugged. My cornflakes were from the bottom of the packet, so they looked like biscuit crumbs floating on top of the milk.

'And what are you up to today? No school again?'

'How can he? There's nothing left of the place.'

'We're going to be moved. After the summer holidays.'

'Moved? You've only just started,' said Dad. 'What a bloody waste.'

Stuart had been talking to Jill, the secretary's daughter. We might be going to St Stephen's. It seemed all right, and not too far away, but his mum wasn't keen. 'Our Kenny's Sharon went there,' she'd said. 'And she's never been off the social.'

'Well, that's something,' said Mum. 'At least they're making plans.'

Dad picked up the *Sun* and rattled it.

'It says here, Elvis stayed up all night and slept all day. No wonder he was fucked.'

'No?'

'Yes.'

'Well, that's funny, because Robbie looks all right.'

'Who?' Dad coughed and narrowed his eyes.

'Robbie. Robbie Preston. You know. Scammy Rob? He's at Warburton's now. He's been on nights for months. Pat says it's the best thing that's ever happened to her; mind you, she can never do the Hoovering.'

'Well, I'm sure it was the same for Priscilla,' he said. 'Christ.'

He was looking for the ashtray, and when he couldn't find it he dipped his fag into his tea. 'So Jack-the-lad, you'll be doing nothing but moping then, will you? If I were you I'd get myself a girlfriend. I'd make the bloody most of it.'

'Joey . . .'

'Well, now the school's gone, those girls will want something to do.'

Mum closed her eyes and swivelled them up to the ceiling. Dad was still on page three, his fingers leaving grease marks on the nipples. 'Wash and bloody shave time,' he said. 'I've someone in at nine.'

He went towards the door. The back of his Noël Coward dressing gown was sticking in his bum.

'And you can get dressed with me,' he said. 'No use staying here all day when I can find some decent work for you to do.'

'Me? Are you sure?'

'Of course I'm bloody sure. Come on. Make a move. Now. We'll be off in ten minutes.'

THE CAR FELT ICY. IT TOOK A FEW GOES BEFORE IT started properly. It was an ancient Hillman Minx with a do-it-yourself respray and an iffy kind of engine. Dad wasn't bothered. It happened every day. I looked round the street. Could all the neighbours hear? Mrs Dawson was always complaining. Her husband worked in Planning.

Dad set off singing, drumming on the steering wheel. The sun made me squint until the road was just a line. He didn't talk much. He just sang along to the radio, getting the words mixed up. Inventing new lyrics to 'Staying Alive'.

'I'm a bit like him, you know.'

'Who?'

'Tony Manero.'

'Who?'

'Him. That bloke from *Saturday Night Fever*. John Travolta. White suit. You know.'

'But you said Tony.'

'That's the part. The dancer. By day he worked in a crappy little shop, by night he was a dance star.'

'When do you go dancing?' Did he go to Scamps? Stuart's real dad went there every Thursday night. It was dancing at Scamps that had put him off his marriage.

He looked at me. 'When do I go dancing? Christ. You're just like your mother. Don't you see? Don't you bloody get anything?' We swerved around a brick. 'I bloody give up on the pair of you.'

I felt nervous somehow. I'd dressed half smart. Proper shoes. Pressed jeans. A light blue shirt that I'd once got for a christening.

'This is the way to do it,' Dad mumbled, nipping down a backstreet. He ignored the One Way signs and scraped on to the pavement when other cars came our way. 'No point sitting in traffic.'

Vincenzo's Hair Palace was in a tall Victorian building. In the fancy red brickwork there were chipped angelic faces and a crushed three-legged lamb. A stone said: Opened by Alderman Finch in this year of our Lord, 1889. There was a boot scraper. Pot plants. A bright gold awning and silhouettes of women with wide full lips and small pert noses. They had locks of flowing hair.

Vincenzo was nice. He was skinny thin and at least sixty-five. He had silver blue hair, flashy-looking ties and silk cravats that he'd tuck down his shirt, like an old-fashioned actor. He'd been born in Rome, and I'd often heard him, whispering things in Italian. *Dove chi troviamo?* Dad had been there for years, and he'd never bad-mouthed Vince.

'Don't you think he's funny?' I asked.

'Funny ha ha, or funny hee hee?'

I shrugged. I didn't know the difference.

'Vince isn't funny,' said Dad. 'So, he might be a bit of a Quentin Crisp, but he pays all our bills, so we can't bloody argue with that.'

'Who's Quentin Crisp?'

'Never you mind,' he said, parking down the backstreet. 'Come on. Let's go and sell some hair.'

Ruby was downstairs. She was drinking frothy coffee and checking her appointments.

'Good morning, sunshine.'

She looked up at me and winked. Her hair was real but it looked like moulded plastic. I knew Ruby. She came to all our parties. Her husband was ex-navy and a professional arm wrestler. He was always in the paper. His actual name was Reg, but Dad just called him Popeye.

'You've brought your lad in then?'

'I'm keeping him out of trouble.'

'You? You wouldn't know where to start.'

Dad cracked his knuckles and she winced as *The Best of Broadway* started humming through the speakers.

'Vince?'

'Oh, he's been here for ages,' she said. 'He's sorting through the costumes.'

'Come on then,' he said, swiping me on the head. 'Up we bloody well go.'

The Gentleman Only Salon was up two steep flights of lino-covered stairs. Past the costume store and the staff room, with its Baby Belling, sour milk bottles and a long beaded curtain that had come all the way from Morocco.

'I feel like that Madame Petulengro.' Vince appeared, parting the beads and then letting them drop behind him. 'And who do we have here? Hello, Jack.'

'I thought he might be useful,' said Dad. 'His school burnt down this week.'

His eyes widened. 'Really? Was it arson? Or simply sheer neglect?'

'Oh, we don't know yet,' I told him. 'They're investigating.'

'Do you have a job for him then?' Dad squeezed my shoulder hard, jabbing in his nails.

'I'll think of something,' he said. 'Come and find me later.'

We went into the showroom with its creaking floorboards and dark old-fashioned tables that held all the stands for the toupees and whole head wigs made from real hair or nylon. From wide glass cases you could buy fixing tape, lotions and a special dry shampoo that looked like dirty talcum powder. Across the walls glossy posters showed men with bouncing fringes, laughing, playing tennis, an arm around a girlfriend. *A New Look! The Real New You! Hair You Can Really Wear!*

'Sit behind the counter for now,' said Dad. 'You can start pricing combs.'

There were boxes of them. Hundreds.

'Will you sell all these?' I asked.

'There was a special deal on at the warehouse. I know what I'm bloody doing you know.'

'I know.'

'So shut it.'

He lit a cigarette, staring out of the window. Flat grey buildings. A pink neon sign. *Gold Bought.* Pigeons. He hovered in front of the mirrors. Yawning. Stretching. Pulling something out from the bottom of his teeth.

At five to nine, my hand was already aching when a man shuffled in with his wife. He had a puffy red face and a bright orange wig. The hair was stiff and fraying. It lifted when he talked.

'Morning.'

The wife took off her coat and settled in a chair. Dad swaggered in. He had a giant false grin on his face.

'Mr Parker? A pleasure as always. Follow me, sir.' Dad led him through the curtains. 'And Jack will make us all a nice cup of tea. If he can manage it.'

'What?'

'I'll have mine weak,' said the woman. 'And we both like plenty of sugar.'

She slurped. She checked the magazine rack. Wig catalogues. The *Weekly News. Titbits.* Then she put them all back, as if her hands were dirty.

'Is child labour back in then?'

'No, I'm with my dad,' I said. 'I'm only helping out.'

'We've been coming twenty years,' she told me. 'Hair loss runs in the family. My son's at it now.'

The boxes of combs were endless. I kept slipping off the stool. Black plastic. Green plastic. Coated aluminium. 30p. 50p. £1.10 for the deluxe handi-preener.

'That tea tasted lovely,' she said. 'And I bet it wasn't cheap.'

When her husband came out he was smiling, but he looked exactly the same.

'All done and dusted,' he said, writing out a cheque. He had a row of cheap Biros in his pocket. Ink stains on his hands. 'Look at me,' he said. 'I've been paying bloody bills all morning.'

'Well, that should last you a while.' Dad handed him a small white box. It had Easy Care, written all over it. Sandy Sunset. 100% Man Made.

'Just look at that,' said the man, ducking in front of the mirror. 'I know I'll look smashing, and it's all down to you.'

'Well ... *thankyouverymuch*,' said Dad, in his best Elvis voice. The woman giggled.

'Oh, we'll be there on Saturday. We never miss a show.'

I grinned. Dad flashed her a smile and a wink.

'I'm one of your greatest fans,' she said. 'Well, we both are. Aren't we, Fred?'

'Too bloody right. You do a great "American Trilogy".'

'What are you looking so flaming chuffed about?' Dad said

when they'd gone. 'Go and find Vince. Go on. Piss off. Skedaddle. I've other fish to fry.'

'COME TO GIVE ME A HAND?'

Vince was on the floor in the costume store. The room was full of dusty plastic bags and piles of crumpled clothes.

'Yes. Dad said to come and find you.'

'Well, you can start with the historicals. They're over in the corner. It's just folding up and packing. That one's Julius Caesar.'

It was warm. There were piles and piles of costumes. Theatre posters. Stephen Sondheim. *A Little Night Music.*

'What are you going to do with them all?'

'I'm selling them,' he said. 'Getting rid. The theatres don't need me anymore. They run their own things up. And look at the Octagon. It's all modern dress. And then of course there's Harlequin's, the new cheapo hire place down the road. Have you seen it? Windows full of Wombles and Worzel, and *The Muppet Show*, tat.' He held up a blouse. It was embroidered. It had tiny birds down the front. 'Now, that's what I call class,' he said. 'And it's versatile. It's been used for Anne of Cleves. Ophelia. And it's done a couple of weddings.'

I tucked in the arms of Julius Caesar. It felt like a thin cotton sheet.

'Looks lovely with a pair of Clarks sandals,' Vince smiled. 'And a few shiny leaves round the hair.'

'Laurel.'

'Oh,' he smiled. 'Well, you're nothing like your dad.'

He hummed. He wriggled his shoulders. He rolled his pale blue eyes and pulled at a couple of lashes.

'It breaks my heart to do this,' he said. 'I've had some of these for donkey's years. Sometimes I'd buy them from the theatres. Or Berman's. That was in the good old days of course. That was when I did all the shows. Operetta. Pantomime. I've done a dozen bad *Mikados*. Oh, the wigs I did for that one. All blue-black. And all of them looking the same.'

'So, where will these go?'

He stopped what he was doing, rocking on his ankles.

'Who knows? A school down the road might be interested. But they've never any money and everything will have to be altered. Mind you, children are tall these days, aren't they? And most of them don't even look like children anymore.'

Through the door I could hear some girls laughing. A voice said, 'You can't wear that. It makes you look like Sid Vicious.'

I swallowed. My throat felt dry and my fingers were starting to ache, from all the tiny buttons.

'Are you all right there?'

'Yes.'

'So. Are you missing school?'

'Missing it? Kind of. Yes.'

'You know, that's the thing. It's like that with anything. Once it's taken away . . .' he zipped up a flapper dress. 'So, what is it you like? Art? PE? What?'

'Science.'

'Oh? And why science?'

I thought about it. The rows of wooden stools. Work benches. Lab coats. The hissing Bunsen burners. Mr Walker had singes in his pockets. He wore baggy tweed trousers and a Chelsea Football Club badge.

'Well?'

'Well, you can't really argue with science,' I told him.

Vince looked at me and nodded, then he raised his eyebrows, and patted down his hair.

'Well, yes,' he said. 'When you put it that way, I can certainly see the attraction.'

AT DINNERTIME I WENT TO FIND DAD. HE WAS SELLING A toupee to the Chinese man from Water Street. His name was Mr

Ho. He worked on the market and wore flip-flops every day. In winter he wore them with socks.

'This one's called Viva,' he was saying. 'It's top of the range. I mean, just look how it moves.'

'How much?'

'Thirty-three pounds.'

'Too much.'

'We do have cheaper lines.'

'How much cheaper?'

'Twenty?' He held out another toupee. It was a different shade of brown. Mr Ho had jet-black hair. Did he really want it two-tone?

'We have this.' He dusted off the label. 'It's called Frederick.'

'Who's Frederick?'

'I don't know,' said Dad. 'It's just the name of the wig.'

'So, is this Frederick famous for his hair?'

Dad narrowed his eyes and looked on the side of the box. 'Well, yes,' he said. 'It certainly looks that way.' The silhouette showed a cross between Tony Curtis and Louis XIV.

'Frederick's too dear,' he said. 'I don't need Frederick. I'm not that bald.'

'What about Rhapsody?'

Rhapsody was black, but it was curly at the edges.

'The wife wouldn't like it.'

'No?'

'No.'

'Well, would the wife like "discontinued?"' asked Dad, scrabbling through the boxes.

'How much?'

'A tenner.'

'Then she'd like it very much.'

'You get no guarantee.'

'What can happen to a piece of false hair?' said Mr Ho. 'I'll take it.'

'Bloody tight git,' Dad said, as he flip-flopped down the stairs. 'His wife works all hours in her sister-in-law's chippy. His money stinks of that chicken chow mein. I can smell it on my fingers.'

'He knows Grandpa.'

'He does?'

'Yes.'

'Well, I thought he bloody might,' he said. 'They stick together, that lot.'

'What lot?'

'Immigrants.'

'THEY'LL BE BETTER OFF THERE,' SAID DAD. 'THERE THEY can eat all those frogs' legs and whatnot. Snails.'

We were in the hospital car park eating pasties. Dad had parked next to a van with a Trust In The Good Lord bumper sticker and three flat tyres.

'Don't you like them then?'

I couldn't imagine them going, and not just for a holiday. They'd never been away. Mum had already bought a stationery set, stamps and a sheet of Air Mail stickers.

'Oh, they're all right,' he said. 'I tried my bloody best to like them but they never really grew on me. They're just too different. You know, too foreign.'

'Elvis was a foreigner.'

'No he wasn't,' said Dad. 'He was a bloody American.'

We sat and watched people going in and out of the doorway. Some women carried flowers, fruit. Tupperware boxes.

'Feeding time at the zoo,' said Dad. 'Still, anything's better than the muck that they give you in there.'

'How do you know? Have you been in?' I couldn't remember him ill. Not proper ill. Dad only ever had illnesses that needed Rennies, or extra-strength aspirin. He'd once sprained his ankle on the way home from the pub. For at least a month, he'd worn a support bandage, and he'd done most of his act sitting down.

'I'm here now, aren't I?' he said. 'I'm here every bloody Thursday. I can see what they give them you know, and it's nothing like this.' He held up his half-eaten pastie, dropping crust over his trousers. 'Shit.'

An ambulance sidled past us. A small black van.

'There's bodies in that,' he said.

The sun looked pale. It moved behind a cloud, and I could feel us both shivering. Some nurses walked past, laughing. Dad leant over the steering wheel, grinning at them.

'Oh very nice,' he said. 'There's nothing like a nurse. Mind you, most of them only look nice from the back. You can usually tell.'

'How?'

'You just look at the state of their legs. See her?'

I nodded. She was dawdling, hanging on to the back of her cap.

'Legs like bloody tree trunks. I bet her face isn't all that much better.'

'She might be good at looking after people, though.'

'She might. Still, when you're in hospital you need more than just that to get you through the day. Bloody long days you get in hospitals,' he said. 'And they only ever have BBC2, or *The Jimmy Young Show.*'

'They have hospital radio.'

'Yes, but have you heard it? It's "Onward, Christian Soldiers", or "Chirpy Chirpy Cheep Cheep". There's nothing in between.'

'You could go in. Why don't you? You'd be great! You could do them your act.'

He sniffed long and hard through the window. 'I did ask once, you know. It was sometime near Christmas.'

'What did they say? Did they let you?'

'They said that I'd bugger up their equipment.'

'What?'

'With the amp and that. They said their machines might go bang, and then where would they be?'

Leaning back, he stuck out his lips, brooding, then he started checking through his folder. He looked in his old black notebook, circling times and names and dates.

'You stay in the car,' he said.

'But I want to come in.'

'It's a hospital. It's not a bloody sideshow. You have to be discreet.'

'I am discreet.' I wanted to go in. I wanted to see the rows of beds and feel safe because I wasn't in one, and I didn't know anyone who was – apart from Grandma Trench, and she didn't really count.

'They don't let children in.'

'Why not?'

'It's the rules.'

My stomach sank. 'But you said.'

'I know.' He clicked down the lock on his case. 'But I forgot. You'll be all right. I'll leave the bloody radio on.'

He went, wheeling in the case, stumbling over the step. His hair blew back. He tried to push it down, looking small and crumpled in his shiny grey jacket and his cheapo slip-on shoes.

A woman came out and mouthed to a man in a car. 'I was in the wrong department,' she shrugged. 'It isn't you-know-what.'

The sky had grey and blue streaks that pushed hard against the chimney. I wondered what they burnt in there. Bloody bandages. Gore. Amputated fingers. Streams of thick black smoke belched every now and then. I saw some white bits scattering, snowing flakes of shattered bone.

I listened to the radio. I moved the dial and found a man in Scotland talking about his trout farm. He'd made a small fortune. He smoked them. His wife made pâté and sent it all around the world in bubble-wrap parcels and picnic baskets. The

Japanese lapped it up. You could tickle trout. He said it was better than salmon.

In the glove compartment I found a packet of melting Toffos and an *AA Guide to Britain*. I read about places that still had thatched cottages and duck ponds. Expensive four-star hotels. I read about Bolton. They'd made it look good with some painted-on sky. They only showed the nice bits, like Samuel Crompton's birthplace and Jumbles reservoir. The shopping precinct was over the page. A brand-new-looking Arndale. Litter-free fountains. *A bustling town centre. Come and find a bargain.* Timpson's. Well, that should get the crowds in. £2.50 off a pair of patent shoes.

I read about Rhyl. They hadn't bothered with a picture. The best hotel was called The Wellington. Great steaks in the restaurant. Sea-view rooms. *Dancing 'til Late.* When we were in Rhyl we stayed at Mrs Hopkins' guesthouse. The rooms looked on to other rooms. A black and red fire escape. Last year I'd seen a woman in a bra. She was closing the curtains. She didn't look bothered. I'd looked out for her every day after that. I'd seen her on the prom. She looked different with her clothes on. Bigger. Someone had shouted 'Vanessa!'

Under the book there was an advert for a car wash. Jimmy's Keep-U-Clean! A dirty scrunched-up tissue had a sticky boiled sweet in it. I leant against the door, the handle sticking into my back. I spread my legs across the seats and looked up at the windows. Imagining. Wards with flowery curtains. Stainless-steel instruments. There'd be women stood around with their clothes off, just waiting to be looked at. I was good at science. Biology. I could be a doctor. Wear a white coat. See things.

I was bored now and cold. I couldn't stop yawning. How many wigs could you sell every week? Surely some people were still in there from the week before? Some people didn't bother. Why should they? They liked the Kojak look.

I flicked through his notebook. Order more tape. New

American lines? Ward F1. Michael Dixon (9). Robert Mace (12). Bethany-Ann Taylor (5).

There were a few leaflets. Pictures of smiling children wearing 'Princess', 'Domino', 'Sonny'. I pulled at my own hair. I liked to feel the tug. I couldn't imagine having one of those wigs stuck on to my head. They looked real, but that was in the photograph. Studio-session photographs didn't show the real false shine of the hair. The way the fringe would lift and tuft after only a couple of wears. The way the hair looked exactly like a doll's. Even for the boys.

On the radio there was a play on. Someone called Peggy had fallen in love with a trapeze artist called Carlos. It was funny. Carlos could hardly speak English. He didn't know what she was on about half the time. There were crossed wires. Mistakes. They kept getting the words wrong like that man in *Fawlty Towers*. Peggy sounded confused, and when you really listened it wasn't all that funny.

Towards the end of the play I began to panic a bit. What if Dad came back now and Radio One had been lost for ever? I turned the dial. The news? Was that on Radio One? I waited until after the weather. Mild. Westerly winds. 'Now back to Jonathan in the studio . . .' Jonathan coughed a bit and laughed about the tickle in his throat. I turned the dial further. Irish dancing music. Opera. Something that was foreign. Suddenly Dad was tapping on the window. I moved over. Blood rushing. I was in for it. The woman's voice went on and on. Faster and faster. I didn't know what she was talking in.

Dad heaved his things over the seat. He rubbed his arms, looking puzzled at the radio while the woman jabbered on without ever taking breaths. Then he sat back and shrugged, before reaching and turning it off.

'You're a good lad, son,' he said.

'What?'

'You heard.'

His hands looked cold as he pulled out his fags, rooting through his matches for one that wasn't spent. He shrunk into his jacket and the car was filled with sulphur, smoke and the rattling engine noise. We sat there, staring at a man in a sling, leaning on some crutches. A nurse ran after a taxi, her hair coming loose. Dad set off, saying nothing.

'I'm sorry about the radio,' I mumbled, when we stopped at some lights.

'You were only having a listen,' he said. 'Where's the harm in that?'

Outside the house, we jumped high on to the pavement. The street was empty. A bike had been left. One broken roller skate. The end of the curtain was blowing through the window. Green stitching. Shiny. We sat in the car for a minute, Dad not moving, just staring at the house, as if he'd never seen it. He looked lost. I sat with him. I didn't know whether to go.

'Dad?'

He turned. He was chewing his lips up, thinking.

'I was bloody right.'

'Right about what?'

'Nothing,' he sniffed, getting out. 'Well, you know, it's just been one of those days.'

THERE'D ALWAYS BEEN JUST ME.

'You're all we can afford,' said Dad. 'And that's bloody stretching it.'

Mum would look embarrassed. 'We don't need any more,' she'd say. 'We're all right as we are. Well? Aren't we?'

'Oh yes. Too bloody right,' said Dad.

NEXT DOOR, THERE WERE SIX OF THEM, BUT THERE should have been seven. They had a girl. They called her Niamh, an Irish name, and none of us knew how to say it. Dad would grunt, and Mum just called her 'the baby'. She was tiny. She had a thin grey face. Mrs Murphy would often stand with her on the front step, 'to bring a bit of colour to her cheeks'. And she looked like a doll, wrapped tight in a lacy white shawl.

'I always did want a girl,' she said. 'Four boys and Gerard, well, it gets a bit much with their football, and all their filthy clothes just lying about. Now I can buy dresses. Bonnets. Little frilly things.'

Niamh died when she was three months old. She had something wrong with her heart. Sean said it was the wrong way round, or upside down, or something. Mum said she'd heard all the screams and commotion. 'But I thought it was only the telly. I thought it was *The Professionals.*'

It was a cold spring day. We weren't exactly invited to the funeral, but Mum took me along to the cemetery with a bunch of limp pink tulips.

'They're not exactly lilies,' she said. 'But this kind of flower, well, I think it's more suited to a baby.'

We stood at the back, watching Gerard Murphy sobbing over a coffin the size of a shoe box. Sean kicked his heels and pulled at his stiff black tie. Every so often, his mum would rush to wrap her arms around her boys, scooping them into her, pulling their faces until it looked like they'd just about suffocate.

'Look at it,' Mum choked. 'That box. It must be as light as a feather.'

There was a big black circle round the grave. The priest's robes kept flapping up. He was wearing blue trousers underneath. 'Turn-ups,' I said. But Mum didn't hear. She was crossing herself for the first time in years and mumbling little prayers into the collar of her coat.

I was cold. The wind sifted through the trees at the back of us, it crept into my clothes and one of our tulips had lost all its petals.

'I think they'll appreciate the gesture,' Mum said, when most of them had gone, laying our flowers next to heart-shaped wreaths and a silver teddy rattle.

'Solid sterling,' she mouthed. 'Well, that won't last long. I bet it's gone by morning.'

Dad was home early that night. He didn't ask about the funeral, but he didn't play his music all that loud. Elvis ballads. Perry. 'It's Impossible' His voice was barely a whisper. Through the joining wall we could hear something clattering.

'I don't know why you moan,' he said suddenly. 'Brothers. Sisters. They're a lot more trouble than they're worth.'

'Why?'

'Well, they are. Look at me and your mum. We don't get on with ours.'

'But uncle Frank's in Canada. Claudine's in London. You never see each other.'

'Yes,' he said. 'And that's just the way we like it.'

SATURDAY. CLUB NIGHT. AND I COULD GO, HE'D SAID. Had he remembered? Eating his bacon he hadn't said anything. He was sorting through his contract, pretending it was complicated. He had sheet music by his plate. Elvis in sunglasses. 'I Just Can't Help Believing' (1971). He mumbled the words, moving his finger up and down the notes as if he could read music, pausing, stopping, getting it right.

'Will you be home for your dinner?'

Dad ignored her, his hands around his ears. Now he was louder. Snarling it.

'Right,' whispered Mum. 'Just forget it.'

DAD HAD TO WORK. 'I'VE GOT A REP IN. I DON'T KNOW. He's coming all the way from Croydon just to sell me roll-on wig glue.'

'Well, we might be back at dinner, but we have things to do.'

'Like what?'

'Shopping.'

'Well, don't spend money that you haven't even got.'

Mum dragged me round town, looking for candles, place mats, doilies. 'I need to be prepared,' she said, holding up a packet of lacy white snowflakes. Luxury size. Four hundred for 29p. 'Claudine has all the fancy stuff in London. Well, she's bound to, isn't she? They've got Harrods there.'

'I thought they were staying in a hotel?'

'I don't know what they're doing,' she said. 'You just never know with them. And I'd feel awful if I didn't have them in.'

She bought them. She bought two pink candles and a packet of serviettes. Gel stick freshener and padded toilet roll. Then she hovered by the toothpaste counter, picking up toothpaste, brushes and some bright green minty mouthwash.

'We all should get new,' she said. 'You know what dentists are like, and Gerald's bound to use the toilet.'

With our bulging plastic bags, we walked all the way up to Gran's. Past Kwik-Save, where a boy sat cross-legged in a trolley, eating Golden Nuggets from the box. A poster in the window said: Hai Karate and Pagan Man. All At Half Price.

'It'd have to be,' said Mum. 'No one can afford those kind of prices round here.'

The sky was murky. It was dropping on the house that looked empty already, the Sold sign falling into next door's rhododendrons.

'Come in then, and don't mind the mess.' In the bare front room there were three metal deck chairs and an upturned cardboard box they were using as a coffee table. 'Your dad's at the market,' she said. 'It's a busy day, Saturday.'

Grandma Keldiles was half an inch taller than Mum. When I was younger I'd spend hours in my room doing stretching exercises. Arms. Legs. Toes. Weightlessness makes astronauts grow several centimetres during long missions. But would they stay that tall when they came back down again? A person's height is usually four times the length of his or her femur.

I'd thought about it. I was always thinking about it. Would I be like Mum? Would I be called Titch and have to wear blocks in my shoes? Small women were okay, they were fragile, but men just looked stupid. And I'd never get a girlfriend. Mum told me not to worry. 'Just look at Roman Polanski.' But I didn't know what he looked like. I just pictured Ronnie Corbett. By the time I was ten my worries were over. I was already taller. I could feel my bones aching. I could link my mum's arm and see over the top of her hair style.

'Just like your dad,' she'd said.

But I knew it was the stretching.

In the kitchen, most of the things were in boxes with different coloured labels.

'*Woman's Realm*,' smiled Gran. 'The handy hints page.'

But her old tin coffee pot was still on the go. A tin of Dark French Roast with a Pierrot on the front. We drank it with Ideal, from chipped red mugs.

'I'm using these up,' she said. 'I'm just taking the best ones with me.'

We sat on the deck chairs and she looked at us. I could see her, staring at Mum from her shoes to the top of her head.

'Are you all right, Evie? Are you keeping well?'

'I'm fine, Mum,' she said. 'I'm always fine.'

'No one's always fine. Not even your father.'

'My school burnt down,' I told her.

'I know. I could hardly believe it. Terrible.'

'It might have been an accident.'

'It might,' she said. 'Who knows.'

Mum got up and started rinsing out the cups and emptying the coffee pot on some old sheets of newspaper. Her footsteps clattered. Gran sat back with her hands locked, and smiled.

'It'll be funny,' I said. 'You going back.' My voice bounced off the walls. You could see where their paper didn't match. Torn strips. Five grey rectangles where their pictures used to be.

'I suppose it will,' she said. 'At first.'

'So, why are you going?'

Mum looked over her shoulder: she was shaking her head, and frowning, but I pretended not to notice.

'It's where we come from, Jack. It's where we both belong.'

'But you've lived here longer than you ever lived there.'

'Yes, but it isn't the same. I don't know. It's just never felt right.'

'Why?'

'I don't know. The place. The people. Their ways.'

I swallowed. What did she mean? The people? What about me and Mum? We were here, weren't we?

'So, who's over there?'

'Jack . . .' Mum said, but she didn't look round. She was busy straightening things. Folding all the towels into neat little squares.

'People. Family. My sisters. Brothers. Cousins. Your grandpa's. Your grandpa's brother, Peter, is really very old.'

'Peter? Don't you mean Pierre?'

'Well.'

'Well, why don't you just go and see them? Grandma Trench went to Canada a couple of years ago. She stayed for nearly a month. She said a month was plenty.'

'Jack. Why are you being like this? You know how long we've waited for this day. All that scrimping. All that saving up. Remember when I had that awful job at Radley's? It's what we've always worked for.'

'Will you miss us?'

'Of course they'll miss us,' said Mum. 'Now go and find a biscuit.'

I walked around the kitchen with a Kit-Kat (all damaged stock from the market). I read a recipe for a double baked chocolate cake that was stuck on to the defrosted, unplugged fridge. *Show them that you care!* I looked at the calendar. Three red fish and some spiky-looking coral. *Louis J. Malgorn. Electricitie Générale.*

I could hear them muttering. Mum just managed to laugh. Through the wet window I could see the blurs of flowers that my grandpa had planted and my grandma liked to fuss over. Yellow. Red. She pruned them. She looked up their names in catalogues and gave them damp tea leaves to eat.

'It's nice to have an interest,' she'd say. 'And we get the cuttings for free.'

The rain trickled under the door, making a small grey pool on the lino.

'No one had a boat quite like it,' Grandma was saying. 'Terrible, really. So why should I be so surprised?'

They were talking about old times, fishing, and someone called Edouard who owed somebody money.

'You remember?' Grandma asked.

'Not really,' said Mum. 'No way. It was donkey's years ago. Of course I've forgotten. I'm not Leslie Welch.'

'Who?'

'Leslie Welch, Mother. The memory man.'

'Oh? Well, your father hasn't forgotten,' she said. 'He hasn't forgotten a thing.'

In the front room, I sat and watched the rain streaming down the window. I breathed on it and wrote a wobbly Jack. Across the road a car backfired and a woman tottered past, with a carrier bag over her hair.

'Marks & Spencer's,' said Mum. 'And it's dripping down the back. Poor thing. I wonder if she's noticed?'

When it slackened off, Grandma waved to us through the raindrops that had just begun to glisten. A rainbow appeared over Ali's Cash and Carry. Mum's four bags slapped against her legs and my teeth began to chatter.

'I wish they'd just go,' she said as she stepped over puddles and a stream of murky water shot out from a grid. 'You know, I'm just sick of all this waiting. This forever hanging around.'

THE AFTERNOON DRAGGED. I READ ABOUT ECLIPSES. IN China people thought that a dragon was eating the sun, so they banged gongs and drums to frighten the dragon away. In 585 BC, two fighting armies made peace. In a total lunar eclipse, the moon turns rust red. Solar eclipses are possible because the moon is four hundred times smaller than the sun, and is also four hundred times closer to the earth. This means the sun and the moon appear to be the same size in the sky.

Stuart phoned. He was staying with his dad on the other side of town. Since his dance days at Scamps, he'd been living in a tiny rented bedsit over an all-night laundrette,

'You can come round if you like,' said Stuart. 'Dad drinks beer and he usually lets me have some. Last time, his mate turned up and we watched vampire films all night.'

But I told him I was busy. Yuri Gagarin was in the next chapter.

Downstairs Mum was cleaning again. She was arranging red chrysanthemums, her bunch of weekend flowers that might just last till Wednesday. I kept reading. Yuri Gagarin showed no fear in his photograph. His arm in a casual wave. But how would he go to the toilet? (See page fifty-nine – 'the urine collection device'.)

In the pictures, the astronauts all looked the same. As time went on I found it hard to concentrate. I kept thinking. Tonight's the night. Dad up there, singing. Me sat there, watching. And there'd be no sign of a rug.

I kept checking the clock, and every so often I'd nip into Mum and Dad's bedroom, looking closely at the gonk, the plastic-covered show suit. I imagined Dad in it. Sneering. Snarling. The audience turning their heads away. 'Just who the hell does he think that he is?'

WHENEVER DAD WAS SINGING, HE'D EAT A LIGHT SUPPER, already rolling his shoulders, doing facial exercises that he'd read about in *Variety*. 'It's a bloody film stars' paper,' he'd said, when we'd laughed. 'It's how they get into their part.'

I sat on one hand, my stomach churning, pushing my fork around.

'Nice sardines,' he said.

'You haven't eaten much.' Mum was sat in her rollers, her skin glistening with face cream.

'I've got the heebie-jeebie's,' he said, rolling up his sleeves, flexing his hands, his thin white muscles. 'I'm trying the new routine out tonight. Pete thinks it's great, but you know what it's like.'

'You'll be fine,' said Mum.

'Fine?'

'Great. You'll be wonderful. You know you always are.'

Dad screwed up his face and his knife clattered down, splashing the back of his hand with bright tomato ketchup. He licked it, then sniffed and narrowed his eyes.

'You're not saying much,' he said. 'Cat got your tongue?'

'He's coming tonight, isn't he?'

I held my breath until he nodded, holding out his fork, studying a flake of sardine with its dripping silver back.

'Well, what a bloody night this is going to be,' he said. 'Still, I did say. Didn't I say, son? Didn't I give you my word?'

'Yes. And you'll be fantastic,' I swallowed. 'People are always saying how fantastic you are.'

Dad grinned widely, crunching his way through the bones.

'That's my boy!' he winked. 'Did you hear that, Evie? Did you hear? We'll show 'em. We'll knock 'em bloody dead!' he laughed, slapping down his hand.

WE WALKED DOWN TO THE CLUB. DAD HAD LEFT BEFORE us, his hair puffed out, his suit immaculate, his cuff links polished in spit. Mum kept running up and down the stairs, changing her shoes, spraying her neck, forgetting things.

It had just turned dark. The shop signs were lit. Bargains. Pizza. Flashing fish and chips. In a doorway, a couple stood snogging. I couldn't see the man, but the woman had her eyes closed and Anarchy In The UK scrawled on the back of her jacket.

Mum shivered. 'True love,' she said. 'Oh, I know that. Me and your dad. We spent hours in doorways. And we never felt the cold.'

The Albemarle Club was on the corner of Western Road and Caxton Street. To join you had to be proposed by other members, then there were the rules, meetings and subscription funds, because here you could buy extra-cheap booze, play bingo, hear Dad (or other, visiting artistes), and on Sunday nights you could dance to Keith Biloxi and his Wild West Band.

We weren't members.

'We're with the act,' Mum said, swallowing nervously into her handbag.

A man called Bert signed us in, coughing. He was wearing a soft cloth cap and a tightly knotted scarf.

'I won't bother with you,' he choked, clipping me round the ear with his yellow-tipped fingers. 'We don't want to lose the bloody licence.'

The room was warm. Bright. Full. Maureen waltzed past. She was drinking Cinzano and wearing shocking pink.

'Well, I'm that depressed,' she said to Mum. 'And you have to do something to cheer yourself up.'

I felt strange. Wobbly. Usually, I'd be home now, watching telly, reading about Orion with a lukewarm can of shandy and some salt and vinegar crisps. My heart thudded. It felt like my shirt was moving with it, and everyone turned to look as we made our way up to the bar. I read the posters. Tonite at 8.30. Club Favourite. The Popular Local Vocalist. Mr Joey Seville!

What if something went wrong? What if Dad started coughing or forgetting all the words, like that boy in morning assembly?

Mum introduced me to the bar staff. She barely reached the top of the counter, even in her highest-heeled shoes, so she went round the side and clambered on to a bar stool. Over all the heads I could see Dad at the side of the dance floor. He looked different already. Laughing. He was moving his hands when he talked.

'Right then, son,' said the barman. 'What'll it be? Pint of best bitter?'

Mum giggled. 'Now, Ron,' she said. 'Give the lad a Pepsi. And thanks for letting him in.'

I sat on my stool watching all the people drinking at the small round tables. Some were eating pies. The bingo was over. Between two fat women there was a bottle of ribboned Pomagne.

'They went and won the jackpot,' said Ron. 'Mind you, there wasn't much in it.'

The women looked tired. Sometimes they shivered, pulling their cardigans tight round their shoulders, covering yawns with the curled-up backs of their hands. The couple from Vincenzo's were sitting near the toilets. They were smiling at the wall, his head like a bright Jaffa orange.

Mum sat next to me, smoking, sipping gin and tonic and clinking round the ice. Everyone was talking. The women at the front. The men with their backs to the dance floor. All the serious drinkers stood around the back. I liked watching. Hearing what they were saying. The women were the best.

'Connie goes to that spiritualist church. Says she can hear Freddy.'

'Freddy isn't dead. Is he?'

'No. He's in Australia with that Joan from Haslam Park.'

'No?'

'Yes. They've been there twenty years now. Mind you, she can't get a divorce from her first. Can't or won't. Two sons and a daughter with Fred. The daughter looks nice in the pictures. Blonde. She looks just like Hayley Mills.'

'So Connie, she can hear him then?'

'Says so. And why not?'

'Well, yes,' said the woman. 'Australia's nearer than heaven.'

I COULD TASTE BEER. THE FAGS MADE MY EYES WATER. I felt light-headed, like I'd smoked at least a hundred. At half-past eight, Sammy Nash came out, blinking. He was the fat comedian/compere. He was neckless. Bulging in a purple suit and a green bow tie. Coughing, he flicked up the microphone and sauntered to the edge.

'Can we have something done with these lights?' he pointed at the ceiling and someone scuttled out from underneath the bar. I blushed. Across the room, people glanced up from their drinks. Dad didn't look scared. He was laughing and moving his hips as the lights dimmed and changed. 'He's warming up,' I thought. 'He's started.'

Chewing on a fag, Sammy told jokes that I didn't understand. Mum shook her head and hissed under her breath. From inside my stomach I could feel my Pepsi bubbling. I wanted to get off the stool, to walk about and fart, but there was nowhere to go, and anyway, I was stuck to the dents in the vinyl.

In the background, the music started, a quiet shushing sound. The floor turned pink and people stopped muttering. When Sammy said, 'And now here he is ladies and gentleman. From our side of town. For your eyes only, Mr Jo-ey Se-ville,' everyone put their fags down, or tucked them into their lips, clapping. I clapped with them, my hands limp and clammy, biting the side of my mouth. I felt sick. I could smell Mum's perfume, then someone whistled and a door slammed shut.

Dad sauntered on, grinning. Pouting. So here he was. The Great I Am.

Mum looked down, she was winding her watch, tapping on the glass.

Come on, you know the start of this one ... but as soon as he started, Dad wasn't Dad anymore. He moved like he did at home to 'Suspicious Minds', only bigger. He swivelled. He swept up the air with his hands. Women started swaying and mouthing all the words. At first I felt embarrassed. His trousers looked tight, you could almost see everything. A woman squirmed and giggled into her girlfriend's podgy shoulder.

'Kathy,' she mouthed. 'Just look at him ...'

But by the time he was singing 'Love Me Tender' to Mrs Price from Dalton Street, I'd forgotten to be bothered. I turned to look at Mum. She was smiling, but she was looking somewhere else. My heart kind of sank, then bubbled up again. He was good. Really. I could hardly believe it. So why was he still fitting wigs?

During 'That's Amore', when everyone was swaying and clapping along, I slid off my stool to get a closer look. Leaning against a post, my legs had turned to jelly. I felt strange. It was like I didn't know him. He looked, well, different. Bigger. And his eyes were all sparkly, like someone off the telly.

Finally, he wiggled up his arm and dropped his hand with a flourish. The applause was like thunder, all around the room. Dad nodded his head, a quick sort of bow.

'Now there'll be a short break,' he said. 'So don't you all go leaving me now.' Even his voice sounded different, with its vague American drawl.

The lights came up slowly and people headed for the bar. Ron gave Mum a bottle of orangeade and she poured it into a glass.

'I'm taking this round to your dad,' she said. 'I shan't be a tick.'

'Where is he?'

'Oh, he'll be in his dressing room,' she said, 'washing off the sweat.'

She slid from her stool and disappeared quickly into the

crowd. Through the crush of people I followed her. Men were blowing smoke rings. Laughing. 'He's got a Harley–Davidson. Bastard. He's always been flash.' Women giggled with bright red faces, blowing up their fringes. It was warm. 'Can't somebody open a window?'

Mum, with hunched-up shoulders and her wobbly high heels, made her way past the Gents and knocked on a door that said Private.

'Oh,' she said, when she saw me. 'I thought you'd be wanting a Pepsi.'

'No. I want to see Dad.'

'Don't we all? Come on!' she yelled. 'Open the door up, Joey. We're getting crushed to bits out here.'

The door swung back and Dad was there, bare-chested, wiping under his armpits. He was dripping.

'All right,' he said. 'All right. I was only having a wash.'

The room had strip lighting. Fluorescent. It was piled high with boxes. Crisps. Peanuts. Jars of cocktail cherries. *Menthol maraschino.*

'Welcome to Caesar's Palace,' he said. 'It's all glamour here.'

We sat on a couple of plastic chairs while he put his shirt back on. Behind him, a creased topless model held some lager to her breasts. Ice Cold When You're Hot! Mum fanned her face, then stared into her compact.

'It's melted,' she said. 'I look awful in these lights.'

Dad looked at me and raised a single eyebrow. I smiled with him, because he still wasn't Dad. Then he cracked his knuckles.

'I don't know why you bother,' he said. 'That cheap stuff gives you spots.'

Mum looked closer, pressing down her chin.

'I can't see any.'

'You can't? You need bloody specs.'

She looked again, wiping it off with a tissue.

'You liked it out there?'

'Yes,' I told him. 'You were great. Fantastic.'

'I'm on a bloody roll,' he said. 'I've got them eating out of my hand.'

He walked around the crates, flexing his hands, hitting the air, ecstatic. On the wall there was an ultra-violet fly catcher.

'They're new these things,' he said. 'They're great. Listen. Pop, pop, pop. You can hear the buggers frying.'

I looked up. I could only hear it whirring through the bright blue light that was jumping from the bars. Black spots. Nothing.

'You two still here?' he turned sharply on his heels. 'I've drunk all the orange now. I've had my refreshment. So could you both please piss off? I need some time. Alone.'

We went back through the crush. I felt disappointed. I'd imagined Dad's dressing room, and even though it couldn't have been true, I'd seen it with those mirrors that had light bulbs stuck around them. Soft carpet. A drinks cabinet full of champagne.

It felt even hotter in the bar. Ron had saved us some stools.

'He's doing all right,' said Mum, feeling her chin that was red from all the scrubbing. 'He's right about this make-up. My skin feels raw. Like I've been standing in the wind.'

But I was looking at my own face in between the optics. Long nose. Small lips. Thick brown hair. I turned sideways. One of the mirrors had cracks that curled like broken fingers.

'This isn't how I thought,' I said, as someone pushed behind me.

'Well, I did warn you.'

'What?'

'I warned you. I told you. I said it wasn't, you know, Saturday night at the Mecca.' Two women walked past. They looked about fifty, clutching Dad's picture, full of smudgy felt tip where he'd signed it. 'There's no one trendy here.'

'But it doesn't matter. Trendy doesn't matter.'

'Look at it,' said Ron, holding up his watch. 'It's always the same. Every week I just know I'm going to miss it.'

'Miss what?'

'*Match of the Day*. It's bloody Notts Forest.'

'Oh?' Mum looked over her shoulder and yawned into a smoke cloud. The lights had dimmed. There was hush. People scraped back their chairs leaving thick black marks on the floor. 'Here we go again.'

In the pale pink light, his face looked softer. When he touched his ear, I touched mine. Maybe he'd changed? In real life. He might have. He might stay like this for ever.

I could feel the blood thumping. It was hot. The music was getting slower. He walked around the room, stroking women's cheeks. Winking. He didn't care what they looked like. 'I Just Can't Help Believin''. Mum didn't care. She just laughed to herself and circled the rim of her glass.

'Oh, he's bloody got them now,' she said.

Above the swaying heads, smoke curled in and out of the light shades. Dad moved around the fog. Slinking his hips. His narrow, velvety shoulders. He found a pretty woman. She was wearing a long green dress and granny boots. She looked young, with dark cropped hair, and earrings. He sang her a line and the woman looked away, blushing. She put down her drink and headed for the toilets. Dad shrugged and moved on to the next. A blonde who'd kept her coat on.

'Look at him,' said Ron. 'He's in his bloody element.'

He ended with his great 'American Trilogy'. Stuart's mum was there, nodding her head, looking serious. She looked different. Her clothes were all glittery and she'd put a lot of make-up on that ended in a circle, halfway round her neck. Dave the bastard wasn't with her. She was sat on her own, with rows of empty glasses and a white plastic handbag.

I clapped hard. I could feel the bones vibrating in my hands. Mum was talking. 'Here,' she said, handing me a bottle. 'The bar will be packed in a minute.' But I didn't care. I didn't want a drink.

I went and stood by the wall where I could just about see him. He was wiping his forehead and patting Pete on the shoulders. He looked pleased. He waved to someone, puffing out his chest. 'You all right, love? Great.'

The woman in the green dress walked past. She looked at me, smiled, and went out of the door. The cold blew in. Drizzle. The bright round headlights of a car. 'Taxi for Ashton? Can someone give them a shout?'

Dad had seen me, he was striding over. As he got nearer I could feel the heat as he moved, escaping, like steam through his jacket.

'Well?'

'You were ... excellent,' I mumbled, stuffing my hands in my pockets. People were looking. It was as if I didn't know him.

'You liked it then?'

I nodded. 'You were better.'

'Better? Better? Better than what?'

'Better than anything.'

'Anything?'

'Yes. You even sounded better than the records.'

'That's my boy,' he said, cracking me on the shoulder. '*Better than the records.*'

DRINKING, HE HAD A CROWD WRAPPED ROUND HIM. Mum's red dress was lost in the jackets, coats; the wide-backed women with stiff short hair and necks the colour of sherry. The bar was emptying slowly. People hung around, then started moving on. Next door, someone said, the landlord was a pushover, that he'd soon be closing curtains and dimming all the lights.

'What about us?' Mum asked.

'What about us? Just get a few more drinks in before they go and put the shutters down.'

Mum looked pale without her blusher. She was rubbing her eyes and checking through her purse. In her handbag there was a zip compartment. She turned her back and took a fiver out of the gas bill envelope. Dad was smiling, waving his fag about. He was wearing his glasses now. Elvis glasses. Dark lenses. Gold frames. Holes punched out of the sides.

'These lock-ins are fine,' he drawled, 'but you still have to pay the man. So, when these are all gone, we've plenty of drink back at home.'

'We haven't,' Mum muttered.

Dad shot her a look.

'I could nip home,' said a woman. 'Pick a few cans up. And I've half a bottle of rum that's sitting, doing nothing.'

'Right ho, Brenda, we'll see you back at ours.'

Glasses clattered. The table was full. Sticky. Through the torn net curtains I could see the slow blue flash of an ambulance on its way to the infirmary. On Caxton Street there were fights every night, and the A and E nurses darned tears with dull hooked needles and extra-strength catgut that would run out after midnight. Especially at New Year. A boy in my class had a dad that held the record. Twelve fights in a night. Three hundred stitches. 'You can't beat that,' he'd said. 'Look. I'm all scar, me.'

We walked home in a group. Dad linked arms with two of the women, but they were old, with wobbly legs and the rain had made an ice rink of the pavement. Dad sang an extra loud, *'that's amore!'* They giggled. They were lapping it up. 'What will our Janey say?' one said. 'She'll be green with bloody envy.'

Mum walked with me. She slunk into the side of my coat. The rain was fine. It was like walking through cobwebs.

'WHAT ARE YOU DOING HERE?' GRANDMA ASKED. 'IS IT Sunday?'

'Monday.'

'Oh? Have I missed something?'

I shook my head and sat in front of the telly. The sound was off. A couple were arguing in silence, their faces twisting as they smashed up quiet plates.

'I was having a bit of a nod,' she said. 'I was up late last night. The woman next door was crying over something. They sent out for her daughter. The clever one. They couldn't shut her up.'

The room was hot. Boiling. The radiators had tape, melting round the pipes.

'Broken,' Grandma said. 'It's been like this for days. I don't feel it anymore, but when they get them mended, if they get them mended, we'll all be freezing cold.'

Outside, a nurse was guiding a woman in a long pink dressing gown. 'I can't see my feet,' she was saying. 'I don't know where I'm going.'

'Are your mum and dad at home?'

'They're at work.'

'Both of them?'

'It's Monday.'

'Is it?'

'We couldn't come yesterday.'

'You couldn't? Why not? What else can you do on a Sunday?'

I shrugged. I didn't know what to say. In the middle of the party, the Murphys had appeared on the late-night coach from Ireland. Gerard had threatened to call the police when he heard all the commotion, but Dad had calmed him down, invited him in, and they'd sat on the sofa together, drinking Irish whiskey and singing Gene Pitney songs.

'I've always been a fan,' said Gerard. 'He's got a voice that sears the heart.'

Mrs Murphy, bleary-eyed, took her four boys into bed. 'Let's hope we just pass out,' she'd said. 'We've been travelling twenty hours.'

Mum and Dad had slept all of Sunday. I'd moved some of the mess about. Stuart came round and we'd watched the afternoon thriller with Mum and Dad upstairs.

'Oh, they won't be sleeping,' he said. 'No way. It's Sunday. They'll be shagging themselves silly.'

GRANDMA LOOKED CONFUSED.

'So what was it you did?'

'The car broke down,' I lied. 'We couldn't get it started.'

'That old banger? Well, what do you expect? He could be driving a Cadillac by now. One of those long fancy things. They don't break down. I don't know why he just doesn't go and get himself a ticket.'

'A ticket? What kind of a ticket?'

'Any ticket.'

'I saw him on Saturday night. He was singing at the club.'

'You did?' She sat up straight now. Interested. 'What was he like? I haven't heard him sing a song in years.'

'But he sang here at Christmas. Remember? All those carols with the church brass band. They didn't have a singer at the time, so they said he could just join in.'

'Yes. But carols aren't "with it". And they always sound the same. Not to mention the trumpets.'

'What?'

'The trumpets. They were all out of tune, and then they went and drowned him, showing off.'

'He was good,' I told her. 'The place was packed.'

She nodded, straightening her blankets. 'You should have heard him in the old days. I could get about a bit then. I went to see him in Sheffield. I don't know what they called the place, but it was big. Huge. They had a stage, plush velvet seats and girls to take your tickets. It was amateur night, but he was on the same bill as someone who got famous.'

'Who?'

'Oh, I don't know. Some man. Good-looking. He lives in Hollywood now with a guitar-shaped swimming pool. That could have been your dad, but then, you know.'

'Know what?'

'He went and got married. No one likes a pop star with a wife.'

I laughed. I couldn't even begin to imagine my dad as a pop star. Dad lived in the past. No one cool liked Elvis. Unless it was Elvis Costello. To get on *Top of the Pops* you had to be different. Strange. Look at Gary Numan. And I pictured my dad with flat black hair and lipstick, scowling at the camera.

Grandma licked her lips. They looked cracked. Dry. In all that heat it must have been like sleeping in a desert. She rummaged through her drawer and brought out a picture.

'Frank sent me this,' she said. 'It's my grandson.'

I looked at it. It was a girl in dungarees, playing in a garden. She looked about six. Pretty, with short curly hair and a little red necklace.

'It's a girl, Grandma.' I turned the picture over. On the back someone had written, Kelly in the Garden. The garden looked huge. They had trees.

'A girl? That's not a girl. Look. He's wearing trousers.'

'Girls wear trousers.'

'Not that kind.'

'Course they do, Grandma. It's the fashion. Oh yes, she looks very trendy.' I said it gently, joking, but Grandma looked upset.

'But I've told them. I've told all the nurses. Now they'll be thinking that I'm mad.'

I held the picture up and screwed my eyes a bit.

'You know,' I said, 'she does look like a boy. Anyone can see that. If it wasn't for the name on the back, I wouldn't have known the difference.'

'What name?'

'Kelly.'

'Kelly? That's an Irish name. It isn't a Christian name, Kelly.'

'Yes. It's a girl's name, Grandma.'

'Where?'

'Everywhere.'

'In Bolton?'

'I suppose so.'

'I don't know any Kellys,' she said.

I was sweating now. I could smell Grandma's dinner, stewing in the kitchen. A man came past, whistling down the corridor.

'That's Ronnie. He's always here, doing little bits and pieces. Mind you,' she said, nodding at the radiator, 'those pipes are beyond him. He's Sister Elizabeth's husband.'

'But she's a nun. Nun's are married to Christ. You know that.'

'All of them?'

'Yes.'

'Oh. Well, I suppose Ronnie might be a friend, doing her a favour. It must be hard work being married to Jesus. I mean, where's Jesus Christ when you want a bit of paint work doing? Ronnie's very handy. He's doing everything magnolia.'

Grandma looked tired. I wanted to go, but I wasn't sure how to say it. It wasn't dinnertime for at least another half hour, and I didn't know if I could manage that long in the heat.

'Your dad,' she said. 'I don't know. He's just like my Arthur. You didn't know Arthur, did you?'

I shook my head, sneaking a look at my watch. Her Our Lady of Lourdes alarm clock had stopped altogether. Even Mary was wilting.

'Arthur was a shy man on the outside. Hardworking. He didn't like a fuss, but he certainly knew how to enjoy himself, when the time was right. Birthdays. Christmas. You know. He used to take me dancing. Proper dancing at the Savoy Ballroom in Oldham. He was very good-looking. A bit like Des O'Connor. Older, of course. But he had that twinkle in his eye, like Des has with the ladies. You've seen Des O'Connor, haven't you, Jack?'

'Yes.'

'And you've seen that little twinkle?'

I nodded. I kind of knew what she meant.

'Just like your dad, eh?' she said. 'And Arthur. He had it. Though they're nothing like you. No. I don't know where you come from.'

She started yawning, patting down her hands.

'You have another sleep,' I told her. 'Catch up. I'd better be going now, anyway.'

'Does your mum know that you're here?'

I shook my head. It had been a spur of the moment thing. There was nothing else to do and I knew that she'd be wondering.

'I like having visitors.' She looked around her room, sighing at the walls, the silent television. A woman in a long flowing dress was running down a beach with a sliced white Nimble.

'We could have all retired,' Grandma said. 'I could have been in paradise now. Phyllis Granger says they have it all in Florida. Sunshine. Palm trees. And her house is painted pink.'

'They have Disney World there.'

'But no National Health.'

I started fastening my coat, the zip almost melting. Then I remembered. 'Gran and Grandpa are moving to France.'

'For good?'

'Yes.'

'Have they been deported?'

'No. They want to go back.'

Grandma closed her eyes, then opened one of them.

'So, they came all that way, all those years ago,' she said. 'Just to give us you.'

I FROZE OUTSIDE, WATCHING A DOG AS IT TIED ITSELF IN knots, wrapping its way around a lamp post. The owner was in the fish and chip shop. He looked like a skinhead, but when he came out, he was only going bald. He bought a fish and gave half to the dog. Everything else looked closed. I was bored again. Worn out. Without money, there was only so much you could do without school, so I walked around the block. Past the street where Stuart said the prostitutes hung out, a cobbled back lane full of empty cardboard boxes. I didn't see anyone, but he might have been right because there was a silver high-heeled shoe stuck on top of a grid.

I walked through town. The fountains were bubbling with washing-up liquid and empty Coke cans. The Wimpy was packed and the shops were full of Sale signs. No Better Offers! – they were closing down again. Stretch jeans. Gold belts. A one-legged man played the harmonica, but no one was giving him money. He sounded too sad, and the women walked past him with their heads down, looking disappointed.

Outside the Electricity Board, I saw Mr Walker. He was flicking through a brochure.

'The old cooker's had it,' he said. 'It's grilled its final sausage.'

'Have they found out who did the school?' My cheeks were burning; it felt strange, talking to a teacher like this in the street.

'It was probably an accident. Gas pipes or something. No one can do that much damage on purpose. Unless they're in the IRA. You should see the place now,' he said. 'There's almost nothing left.'

I walked back that way. In the air you could still smell smoke and behind the wall JCBs scraped up bricks and men in hard hats shovelled their way through the grime. I tried to remember what it had looked like. The dining room. Cloakrooms. The hall with its stage, the plaster Virgin Mary with the paint chipping off, and on Fridays, if it was raining, you could pay 5p and go and listen to a fifth former playing scratched records.

A man came out of a house.

'You know what they've gone and done, don't you?' he said, folding his arms and leaning on the gate.

'No. What?'

'It's only been down five minutes and they've sold the land off to Barratt's. We're having a bloody housing estate here now. Bungalows. Flats. Three-bedroomed semis.'

'Already?'

'Well, that's what it said in the paper. Said they had to sell up to pay for something new. Though where they're going to build a new school, I've really no idea.'

I felt sad somehow. Lost. Where would I end up? Would I need a new school uniform? At Kelby all the hard lads beat you up if you went in it. I shuffled to the railings. The playground was still there under all the stacks of rubble. Smouldering white lines. Tarmac that was so old and broken, it had sliced through the leg of a small clumsy first-year. Through the empty windows someone shouted, 'It's still bloody burning in here. I can see it. I can feel it through my boots. Jesus fucking Christ!' A man in luminous orange pants came past with a twisted netball post. He was singing 'Jerusalem', smiling.

'I DON'T LIKE IRELAND,' SAID SEAN. 'WELL, I DO. I JUST don't like going all that much. It's weird. It's like another country.'

'It is another country.'

'You know what I mean. And my uncle Patrick is a git. He's always going on. He drowned a sack of kittens last week because they'd scratched the settee. Tiny things. Crying. God, it was terrible.'

'He didn't?'

'Yes. And they live out in the wilds. My cousins have to walk over a mountain just to get to school. Well, okay, so it isn't really a mountain, but it looks like one. They have to get up at five every morning and set off in the dark.'

'Don't they have a car?'

'Uncle Patrick's got a van, but he says it's in no fit state to take children anywhere.'

'Right.'

We were in the kitchen. I'd heard Sean in the yard next door, banging a tennis ball about. He was on his own. His brothers were all at the Infants.

Sean was in the class above me. He was gangly. Pointed. He was the best runner they'd ever had in the Lower School. Mr Hunter, the PE teacher, wanted to train him up. 'Cross-country. Long distance. We could go to the trials. We could win something.' But Sean never turned up for the training sessions. He was always in the library or chatting round the benches with the Maths Club boys. 'Okay, so I can run,' he'd told me once. 'But it doesn't mean to say that I like it.'

He tipped his chair back. 'My uncle has a farm,' he said. 'Well, they call it a farm, but it's just a patch of mud with some chickens on it. Oh, they did have a cow last time, but I don't know where that went.'

'The freezer?'

He laughed. 'They don't even have a fridge, never mind a freezer.'

'So, you had a crap time then?'

'Sort of. Our Matthew got hit. Right across the face and he's only just turned six. My dad went mad and Mam was crying her eyes out.'

'Who hit him then? Why?'

'Patrick, of course. Said he was being lazy. I don't remember what he should have been doing, but whatever it was, he wasn't doing it fast enough.'

'But I thought you were on holiday?'

'They call it that,' he said. 'Just to get us over there. Mind you, the stars were bloody magnificent.'

Magnificent. The word sounded great the way Sean said it.

'They were? It's been all cloud here. Nothing.'

'I went up that mountain with Stacey-Ann Maguire. We lay flat on our backs. It was like being on the moon.'

'Stacey-Ann Maguire? Who's Stacey-Ann Maguire?'

'My cousin.'

'So, why do you say her whole name out like that?'

'I don't know. They all do over there. It sounds better.'

'Right.' And I could easily imagine her. Fifteen. Dark black curls. Like the girl on the Skytrain poster.

'Anyway. The sky was something else. You've never seen anything like it. Clear as crystal. Honest. Orion. Taurus. Hyades. We stayed there all night, well, nearly all night. It was cold, though. Freezing.'

'Did Stacey-Ann Maguire like the stars?'

'She said she did, but then she didn't say much at all.'

We sat drinking coffee, eating stale digestives, sniffing over his old *Sky at Night* annual.

'You wouldn't think it, would you?' said Sean.

'What?'

'That the dirty sea at Blackpool is pulled in by the moon.'

I shook my head.

'It's full of sewage you know. Shit and stuff. Our Michael was sick in it last year.'

I looked at the picture. It was the one the astronauts on the *Apollo 10* craft had taken. The far side of the moon looked like a dried-up Christmas pudding.

'Would you like to go into space?'

'Nice idea,' said Sean. 'But not really. No. I get claustrophobic sharing a bedroom, never mind a rocket.'

Through the kitchen window I could see Mum in the back yard, bringing washing in. She still had her work clothes on, her good black coat. Her arms were full of it, dangling. She waved.

'I'm going,' said Sean. 'I'm meeting my brothers at half past. Mam doesn't trust the lollipop lady, she says she's always too busy talking to notice any traffic.' He turned at the door, hesitating. 'You know, Ireland wasn't all that bad. It was okay. Different. And you can marry your cousin, you know.'

'How old is she then?'

'Thirteen,' he said. 'Well, nearly.'

MUM WAS QUIET AT TEATIME. DAD TRIED TO GET HER talking by flicking peas at her.

'Have I got news for you,' he kept saying, but he wouldn't say what it was.

'Good or bad?'

'Do I look in the slightest bit miserable?'

'Well, no.'

'So?'

'So, good news then?'

Another forkful of peas flew Mum's way.

'Have I got news for you,' he grinned.

'What is it, Joey?' she asked, wiping down her blouse. 'You might as well tell us.'

'Okay, okay, okay. I thought you'd drag it out of me.'

'What?'

He banged down his fork. 'Ladies and gentlemen, this coming Saturday night, I've got my big chance, if I play my cards right.'

Mum looked worried. 'What do you mean, you've got your big chance?'

'I mean, I've got a bloody agent coming up to the club, so you'd better make yourself scarce. It doesn't look professional having your wife in the audience, making up the numbers.'

'But I don't—'

'Whatever. You can stay here with Jack. I'll get you a box of chocolates.'

'How did you get an agent?' I asked. 'Was it Grandma?' She was the only person I knew who was always going on about agents.

'Grandma? How on earth can a woman my mother's age,

confused and confined to a nursing home, get me a fucking agent? You have completely lost the plot, boy.'

'It's just that—'

'Shut it. I thought you wanted to hear?'

Mum turned white, reaching for her fags.

'All day I've had people nipping in the shop just to tell me how great it was on Saturday. And not just people I know. Maureen came in with a woman I'd never seen before. Said her name was Lindsey and she'd been at the club and thought I was a real class act, blah, blah, blah, blah, blah. And they weren't the only ones. A bloke who works at C&A popped in. Smart he was, too. Manager of kids' clothes, something like that – might be able to get you a few bargains there, Evie – anyway, he said I was wasting myself fitting wigs, and let's face it, now you can buy wigs anywhere who knows how long Vince is going to last. I mean, now the costumes have gone and he's thinking of selling upstairs to a jeans shop.'

'So, where is all this leading?' Mum asked, pushing her plate away.

'Well, at long last, after all this flamin' time, I phoned somebody.'

'Who?'

Dad scraped back his chair, looking chuffed.

'Mr Max Lexington of the Lexington Talent Agency.'

'Max Lexington? That's a mouthful.'

'Will you fucking shut up? What do you know? He's a bloody top agent is Max.'

'So, he's coming then?'

'Definitely. He was very interested. His secretary put me right through and we had a bit of a chat. As it happens, he's up this way on Saturday, so it must be bloody fate or something.'

Mum looked dumbstruck.

'Well, that's just great,' I said. 'You might be discovered.'

'So, what if he takes you on?' Mum asked. Her voice was quiet now. Slow.

'Then I'll jack the wig job in. Probably even get a nice bit of a bonus after all my years of service. Then, I'll take to the road.'

'You will?'

'Yes. You can't be fussy when you're just starting out.'

'Just starting out? But Joey. You're forty-one. You've got responsibilities.'

'I'll get bloody paid.'

'How much?'

'I don't fucking know.' He banged his fist on the table. 'Look. This is my big news. I should have done this years ago. Be excited. This time next year I could be on the *QEII* singing in the lounge bar with all the fancy nobs. I'll be singing "Delilah" with the world sliding by.'

'But what about us?'

'What about you? Don't you want me to make something of myself?'

'Yes.' Mum's voice was a squeak. She looked completely worn out.

'So? Just. What. Is. Your. Problem?'

She looked at him. She could see his face was set. His hands were in big clumpy fists by the ashtray.

'Well, I think it's great, honest, but of course I'm worried, it's a very big change, and I've a lot on my plate right now, what with tomorrow and everything and Claudine rang and she isn't going to stay. She said it's no big deal on the phone. She says that London's nothing but a train ride away.'

'She did?' He softened. 'Well, she doesn't say that at Christmas. It's more than a train ride then.'

Mum sniffed. It looked like she was going to start crying. 'And with Mum and Dad going. Now you . . .'

'Me? I've got the little Minx. I'll be back after the shows.

Apparently, most of the best gigs are in Yorkshire and Yorkshire's just a spit away.'

'But what if the weather gets bad?' She was biting her nails into splinters.

'Come on, little girl,' he said. 'Come on. Let's have a drink.' And he brought out the cans from the back of the fridge, wet and smeared with spilt cottage cheese.

'We'll make a toast to new starts. Me. Us. Your mam and dad. And there's no need to be sad on their account. They can't bloody wait to piss off.'

Mum tried a smile. 'All right,' she said, picking up a can. 'I'll have a couple with you.'

I stayed in the kitchen reading *Ghost Night* again. On page twenty-five there was an alternative, mystery ending. I cleared the table and washed up because it was my turn anyway and I couldn't face the lounge. Mum was crying. Laughing. Alma Cogan was on. Dad must have been in a very good mood. 'Mambo Italiano'. 'Bell Bottom Blues'. 'Little Things Mean A Lot'.

Through the frosted window I could see Mum sitting on his knee. She looked sunk in. Like his legs were swallowing her up.

When Tom Jones started, I walked with Sean to the park, where we sat on the swings in the dark, squeaking and blowing cold breath. The trees were full of tom cats, moaning.

'So, what's she like?' I asked. 'Your cousin. Is she nice looking?'

'She looks older than thirteen.'

'Thirteen's old enough,' I said. 'Thirteen's plenty.'

Girls who were thirteen wouldn't even look at me, let alone lie with me on a mountain in the pitch-black night, looking at the stars.

'She has a bit of a chest — you know.'

If he couldn't bring himself to say the word tits, then he must be really keen on her.

'So, what happened?'

'Not a lot. I put my hand on her knee and we brushed up against each other a couple of times. Our faces got close. I could smell her toothpaste, we were that close sometimes.'

'Right. So, what are you going to do now?'

'I might send her a postcard or something. I could send her one of Bolton, just for a laugh. Girls like letters, don't they?'

I nodded. My mum had a tin of old letters stuffed under the bed. I'd read them all once. Dad had called her 'my kitten'. She'd kept everything. A Babycham beer mat. A key ring. A tatty piece of paper with directions pencilled on it.

'If I had a sister, I might know a bit more about girls,' he said.

'Me too. My cousin's coming tomorrow.'

'A girl?'

'A boy.'

'Oh.'

We sat with our hands frozen to the chains, our gym shoes dragging on the cinders.

'They get stuck sometimes, you know.'

'What do?'

'Tom cats. Once they get it in they can't get it out. They have to be helped or something. They can get stuck in there for days.'

We walked back listening to them howling through the leaves. When we noticed the sky, we walked with our necks flicked back. The moon was like a coin over Palma Street. A thousand sparkling stars.

'Venus,' said Sean.

I looked at the brightest, and the stars that went and curved in between like a big silver necklace. I'd read all the books, but my mind had gone blank. I didn't know what they were called.

'Can you see it?' said Sean.

'Yes.'

'The thing is, without the blue lines in the book, it doesn't really look like a plough, does it?'

And then I saw it. The two pointer stars and the Pole Star. North.

'I'd like to go up a mountain,' I said. 'See them all properly with nothing in the way.'

'There aren't any mountains round here.'

'There's Winter Hill.'

'The walk up there would kill us.'

'We'd have to dress for it. Be prepared.'

I shivered. I was freezing cold in my anorak. I could smell Sean's Vick.

'I suppose we could,' he said. 'But we'd have to make sure that the sky was right. No point going all that way to look at some big black clouds in the rain.'

We stopped at our back gates and leant against the wall.

'Dad had some news for us tonight,' I told him. 'He says he's leaving the wig shop. He's going to be a professional singer. An agent's coming down on Saturday to watch him do his act.'

'Is that good or bad?'

'I don't know yet,' I said. 'Could go either way.'

From the back yard I could hear Sean as he opened up his door. Guinea pigs squeaking. His brothers were laughing and his mum was shouting for peace. 'Get inside, quick, you're bringing all the draught in with you. Sean! Shut the door now, will you, love?'

Curled inside my pockets, my hands were like stones. My nose was running. Through our jammed back window the Mystery Train was winding its way through the curtains. The voice was long and hollow. Strange. It didn't sound like Elvis. Inside, the fire was out cold and they were upstairs, rattling. Moaning. The furniture going bang, bang, bang on the floorboards. I kept my coat on, and wrapping my football scarf tight around my ears I sat and read a gardening magazine that had been sent to the house by mistake. *Annuals. Biennials.* The Royal Botanic Gardens. Above me, the light shade swayed a bit, then stopped. I kept my head down, just following the words, the shiny bright pictures of other people's gardens. *A peach tree is a good container candidate. Apple canker is a killer. 'Meyer's Lemon will fill your conservatory with heavenly scent, as well as fruit for a lovely gin and tonic.'*

ON THE MORNING THAT MY GRANDPARENTS WENT BACK TO their homeland, the weathergirl in the nice red jumper had promised a sharp cold spell, then cloud, with occasional drizzle. She was wrong. Mum stood tight-lipped on the back step, worrying about what she was going to wear now that the sun had made an appearance, and everywhere was blue.

'She said it was going to be bad. She promised. I had it all planned. Cold, she said. I was going to wear that big sweater with these new pants. Nothing else matches. I don't know. I suppose I could just keep my coat on.'

'Just keep your coat on? It'll be boiling at the airport. They always have the heating turned up. It's the oldest trick in the book.'

'What is?'

'The heat. It's so you'll buy more drinks at their inflated prices.' Dad rattled the paper, hissing, as if he knew these things. Like he was always jetting off. 'Bastards.'

'I don't know.' Mum carried on cleaning while deciding what to do. 'Useless English springtime. Cold. Warm. You never know where you are with this weather. Easy for you two,' she sniffed. I was in half school uniform. Dad was in his work suit.

'I'm only having a few hours off,' he'd said. 'That's all I can manage. I might be handing my notice in next week. If I start messing Vince about we can wave bye-bye to the bonus.'

'Well, I'm not a hot person,' said Mum. 'I could say I had a chill or something.'

'Wear what you like. No one's going to notice.'

She ran upstairs. She was ages. When she came back down, she looked close to tears. She was wearing the woolly trousers and a fluffy green sweater.

'They'll just have to do,' she said, peering through the curtains. 'They're what I had planned.'

We were early. Claudine, Gerald and nine-year-old Timothy were meeting us at the airport.

'The train has a connection,' she'd said. 'If we came to you then we'd be way off route. Pointless.'

Claudine was an expert on routes. She talked French all day in a smoked-glass office, arranging itineraries for people travelling through Europe. She studied new maps and decided how many stars certain guesthouses should have in the brochure.

'They're not called guesthouses,' she'd giggled. 'Come on. Surely, you know that much, Evie?'

But Mum had never really spoken any French, and no one had ever pushed her.

'It says here cloud.' Dad held up the paper.

'And they're always right in there.' Mum dabbed her face with a tissue, then gave the telly a quick wipe down.

'Go on then,' said Dad. 'You can turn the fire off for a bit if you like. I don't mind. I'm sweating.'

By the time we went to pick up Gran and Grandpa, she'd changed and changed her mind a few times, so she was wearing the original outfit, only she looked a lot hotter. In the car Mum kept shuffling as we passed people without coats, in thin cotton dresses. Mrs Murphy had her shorts on.

'She hasn't got the legs for them,' said Dad. 'She'd be better off like that lot.' He waved to a group of women in flowing black purdah. 'She'd look a lot more exciting covered up.'

'She's had five children.'

'Well, they don't come out of your legs.'

'Joey . . .' Mum reddened.

'Well, not that part of your legs. They come out of – well, you know what I mean, so shut it.'

My grandparents were stood at the door with small blue suitcases.

'Look at them,' said Dad. 'Very British Airways.'

He smashed out his fag and went to open the car door, not because he was being polite, but because there was a knack to it.

'Hop in the back you two,' he said, giving the side a kick. 'You can have your last look at Merrie Olde England with our Jack here. Would you like a farewell tour? We could go the long way round.'

'They'll see England again. Don't be morbid, Joe.'

'Oh no, love, he's right,' Grandpa said. 'We won't be coming here again. Not at our age. And think of the expense.'

We crushed up, with the cases on our knees.

'Won't they go in the boot?'

'Well, they would,' said Dad. 'If I could open it.'

When no one was talking, he put the radio on.

'Find them a station they'll like,' he told Mum. 'Something nice and gentle. They don't want their ears blasting off.' He was smiling. He was in a holiday mood. Mum turned the knob, but the music was hissy.

'Don't worry about us,' Gran said. 'We like looking out of the window.'

At the airport, Dad got lost. We circled several roundabouts over and over again. We went down one-way roads and nearly got flattened by a coach full of Japanese students.

'It's like a bloody city,' said Dad. 'Why can't they put up proper signposts? Look at it. Terminal this way and that. Everything looks the same. They must be taking the piss.'

Mum looked worried, but Gran and Grandpa were enjoying themselves.

'It's all changed,' said Grandpa. 'Look how many floors they've got in the car park. It's huge.'

'Yes,' said Dad. 'But how do you get in it?'

Eventually, he was stopped at Pilots Only and had to ask directions.

'Know-all,' said Dad, turning round, banging the car on the pavement.

Claudine, Gerald and Timothy were already in the Take-Off Café. They stood when they saw us, and Claudine held out her arms, like someone doing ballet.

'Hello you lot,' she said. 'We're on our third muddy coffee.'

Aunt Claudine looked nothing like Mum. She was olive-skinned, with bobbed brown hair that swished whenever she moved. She was almost the same height, but she seemed a lot taller. She'd once told Mum that she hadn't actually grown, but an expert in a run-of-the-mill department store had shown her how to put her clothes together, so it just looked like she had.

'You should try it. Treat yourself. It makes such a difference, and I bet they have someone in your Lewis's.'

'I'll bet they have,' said Mum.

Today, she was wearing black pyjamas.

'Linen. And they're ever so cool.'

'Well, I've had the flu,' Mum said. 'And it's lingered.'

'Look at you,' said Gerald, slapping me on the shoulder. 'You're quite the young man now.' And the light bounced off his perfect even teeth and reflected in his smooth, denim-coloured eyes. He looked like the Blue Stratos man. 'Joey,' he said. 'It's been too long.'

'It's the signposts,' said Dad. 'They might as well be in foreign.'

We pulled up more chairs and squashed around the table. Gran and Grandpa sorted through their tickets. Mum couldn't keep still; she kept touching Gran's arm, her back, patting her bony knees that stuck out from her trousers.

Claudine gave out parcels. Mum blushed. We hadn't brought anything. We weren't expecting presents.

'They're nothing much anyway,' Claudine said. 'Just some

things we picked up on the way. You know. Gifty things. Some preserves and some smellies in baskets.'

Dad looked pleased. Expensive-looking aftershave and a soap-on-a-rope microphone.

'We thought that you'd like it,' said Claudine. 'And the soap's a bit of fun.'

Mum and Gran got perfume and jars of cherry jam. Grandpa got shaving things that must have cost a packet.

'I'll make it last,' he said. 'It's the way you squeeze out the tube.'

My basket was full of car-shaped soaps and a Man United deodorant.

'They're hard to buy for at that age,' said Claudine. 'We had it made up. And everyone likes United.'

I didn't. United were cocky. And the soaps looked more like Noddy cars. Pale green and yellow. Pink. I had a basket full of baby soap.

Timothy was even quieter than me. He sat there with his book open, and when he thought no one was looking he'd go back to reading it. He looked sun-tanned, like he'd just been on holiday. He looked tall for his age; and glossy.

'We've got an hour before book-in,' said Grandpa, filling his pockets with sugar cubes.

'Check-in, Dad.' Claudine kept looking round whenever anyone spoke. 'Now, have you got all your documents handy?'

Grandpa showed her the red plastic wallet that the airline had provided.

'And the good thing is,' he said, 'we can keep it.'

Claudine smiled. 'You should see what you get when you travel first class,' she said. 'You wouldn't believe what they give you for free. I got a dinky little make-up bag, full of stuff, chocolates, and a pair of cotton slippers.'

'They're not free,' said Grandpa. 'They're all in with the price of the ticket. You just think that you're getting them free.'

'Too bloody right,' Dad piped up. 'They're full of scams, these places.'

Mum, Claudine, Gran and Grandpa went off for a walkabout. Grandpa wanted to see exactly where it was they were supposed to be going. They had linking arms. Dad queued for drinks.

'Oh, I've had enough caffeine,' said Gerald. 'My head's already buzzing.'

Timothy wanted milk.

'I'll have the same.'

'Milk?' said Dad. 'Milk? Bloody hell. Don't you want a Coca-Cola?'

I shook my head. I knew what dentists thought about it. You could polish your money with Coke.

Through the long wide windows you could see planes taking off. I wouldn't have minded a look, but Timothy didn't seem interested.

'How's everyone been doing?' Gerald asked.

'Okay.'

'It's been a hard year. Difficult. We just couldn't get down. Pity. We just haven't had a minute to ourselves. Where does the time go to, I wonder?'

Timothy looked up. 'We've moved,' he said. His voice sounded girlie, soft, and I wondered if he ever got picked on, with such a soppy name as Timothy.

'Yes. Tim's right. We've moved to a bigger place. We've even got a garden.'

I looked at him, puzzled. What did he mean, they've even got a garden? I thought that they were rich.

'But we haven't got a games room anymore.'

'Like I said, you have to compromise, Tim. It's all give and take when you move to a better area.'

'Isn't London just London?'

Gerald laughed at me. 'It's all to do with your postcode,' he said, as Dad sidled up with a tray of splashing tea; some of it had gone into the milk, so I picked the glass that had taken the most, but Tim didn't look too impressed.

'So,' said Gerald. 'Are you still singing?'

Dad nodded. He looked proud. Nervous. 'And I might be going pro.'

'Really?' Gerald's eyes widened. 'Covers or originals?'

Dad stiffened and lit a cigarette. 'I do original covers,' he said, puffing out a smoke ring.

'That's it. Of course you do. Right. And are you still giving them, what? — is it Elvis Presley?'

'He's part of the act. Well, his bloody songs are. I don't just take him off.'

'No. No. I've heard that you're great. And I'm sure you have them just rocking in the aisles. What's it been like then, now that he's, you know, dead? Is he still just as popular?'

'Yes. Too right. And he always will be.'

'So, just what is it that you like about him?'

'Elvis?' Dad looked amazed. Didn't Gerald know? 'Elvis is the King,' said Dad, saved by the rearrival of the Keldines gang.

'We couldn't find the toilet,' said Mum. 'We were dying.'

We sat in a circle, no one saying much. Grandpa kept getting out the wallet, checking the passports and admiring it. 'It looks like leather,' he said. 'It smells like leather. Look at it. You can hardly tell the difference.'

'Well, you both look nice for the trip. Don't they look nice? Gerald? Tim?'

They nodded without looking.

'It's a good-quality suit, this is,' said Grandpa, feeling the lapel. 'When I get off the plane I want them to see that it wasn't all wasted. That I've worked hard over here, and made something of my life.'

'Oh, you've certainly done that,' said Gerald, as Timothy snorted a laugh.

Gerald stood up, stretching. I'd forgotten how tall he was.

Compared to aunt Claudine he looked like a giant. He looked more like a Viking than a dentist. I tried to picture him in a white coat, doing extractions. I looked at his hands. They were huge. Wouldn't they just make you choke?

'We'd better go,' said Gran. 'I don't want to miss it. I don't want anything to go wrong. Not at this late stage.'

'It won't,' said Claudine. 'And they say check-in time's two hours, but when you travel regularly, you know it isn't really necessary. They're only being cautious.'

'But it says so on the ticket.'

'If it makes you feel any better, you go,' said Claudine. 'But we've come all this way to spend some time with you.'

'You do what you like,' said Dad. 'It's your bloody ticket.'

As soon as we started walking to Departures, Mum began to sniff, her hands went white and she couldn't let go of Gran's jacket.

'We're waiting here,' she said. 'I want to stay right here till that plane's up in the clouds and safe.'

'Aeroplane statistics are always very good,' said Timothy.

Dad checked his watch. 'I've a toupee in at three. And no one else can do it.'

Mum swallowed.

'Okay, okay. I'll go and give them a ring,' he said.

She was biting the sides of her hands. Nibbling. I couldn't understand it. I knew that she would miss them, we all would. But this? They'd never seemed all that close.

'At last,' said Grandma, handing in her ticket. 'Home.'

Claudine said something in quick-fire French. Mum's lips began to go.

'We'll call as soon as we're sorted. We'll be fine.'

Everyone hugged and kissed, and Mum gripped my hand as their cases sailed into the tunnel.

'Just think,' said Dad. 'You'll be there in a couple of hours. Let's hope that your furniture makes it.'

We had plenty of time to kill. I liked watching the boards, pretending it was me who was going to Dubai, New York, Berlin. Dad tried out his new aftershave. 'It's nice,' he whispered. 'But it isn't quite as classy as Vince's Aramis Devin.'

Gerald and Tim wandered off after a while; they just didn't seem all that interested in talking to us. They were looking at train timetables, checking which ones had a sit-down restaurant as well as a buffet car. Mum and Claudine sat huddled drinking coffee. Sometimes Mum was smiling and holding Claudine's hand. It was strange, seeing them together like this, looking like they belonged.

'She's landed on her feet,' whispered Dad. 'When I first knew Claud she was nothing but a hippie.'

14.35. Rennes. On Time.

'Now would you look at that.'

'What?'

'Well, that's a bloody miracle, that is,' said Dad. 'There's normally a five-hour delay at this time of year.'

'Five hours?' Gerald smirked.

'Easy. I've been told it's a good idea to come prepared. To have your sleeping bags all packed and ready.'

'You have? Who by?'

'The paper. And you should bring your own refreshments.'

Fuzzy with the heat, the hours of waiting around, we stood with our foreheads pressed hard against the glass. On the tarmac we could see Gran and Grandpa, tiny, smart, in a line of baggy tracksuits and stone-washed denim. Grandpa was clutching the wallet. Happy. They were looking round, straining their necks, but they couldn't see where we were.

'I don't know what all the fuss is about,' said Timothy. 'They're only going to France. We're always in France. It isn't exactly Australia.'

When we'd manoeuvred out of the car park, backed out of Immigration and used the wrong slip road (twice), Mum rolled the window down. Her face was red. Sweating. She'd been chewing the tips of her fingers.

'I thought Claudine looked nicer. Young. How come she looks so young? She's put a bit of weight on, but it suits her. She's told me she's even thinking of having another baby, now that they've got the bigger place, and I'm sure she already is. She just didn't say it.'

'Is what?'

'Expecting a baby. I don't know why, I just think it. Her face was rosy.'

'Blood pressure.'

'Well, that's all part of it, isn't it?'

'Well, it was with you, and I couldn't go through all that bloody palaver again.'

'And Mum looked sweet in her pink trouser suit, though she's had it for donkey's years. I think she got it for Kenny's wedding. Remember?'

'Kenny with the stutter, or Kenny with the eye?'

'The eye,' said Mum.

'Right.'

'Kenny with the stutter didn't get married. He looked after his Mum.'

By the time we got home, she was almost losing her voice.

'I'm not disappointed that they didn't come back,' she said. 'But it would have been nice. I had everything in.'

'Well, never mind,' said Dad. 'I like tinned salmon and cake. You're not saving it, are you?'

'No,' she yawned, resting her head on the window. 'You have it. Have it all. I couldn't eat a thing.'

DAD WENT BACK TO WORK. 'I'LL DO A BIT OF OVERTIME,' he said. 'I want to butter him up.'

SHE MADE ME AN EASY TEA. IT WAS LIKE A PARTY. THERE
were sandwiches. Jam and cream sponge. Her favourite chocolate biscuits. But Mum didn't eat. She sat hunched up, half
watching the news, half looking at the picture of herself in
France, aged nine.

'They'll be there now,' she said, squinting, trying to make
things out in the hazy grey background. 'Well, nearly.'

'What was it like? Can you remember?'

She shrugged. 'Well, there was fish,' she said. 'It was
everywhere. Claudine was sick on the oysters. No wonder. She'd
never had them before. But oysters are normal over there. In
India, they give babies curry. Honest. Sita told me. *Oysters*. Well,
we were supposed to be staying with an uncle, but something
happened, I don't know what, and we had to go and stay in a
little hotel. It was lovely. All blue and gold. The Hôtel de la
Marine. See, I've not forgotten that. Dad went mad. He argued
with the owner about something. Mum didn't speak to him for
days.'

She swallowed and pretended she was listening to the
newsreader. She tutted. Yawned. Milk was going up to 15p a pint.

'You'll see them again you know. Don't look so worried.'

'Will I?'

'Course. And if dad gets rich with his singing, he could take
us. We could even stay in that same hotel. It'll be great.'

'No,' she sniffed. 'Well, I don't know. Maybe.'

'Wouldn't you like to?'

'Yes.'

'So?'

'So what? Look, Jack, they've only been gone five minutes.'

'But we could. It would be something to look forward to. We
could get the ferry. I've half worked it out, and it's only a bit
more expensive than Rhyl, especially as we'd be staying with
them. We would be staying with them, wouldn't we? They
wouldn't mind. Is there any room?'

'Christ. Questions, questions, questions. I don't know. I haven't the faintest, foggiest idea. God.'

'What?'

'Nothing.'

'Well, what do you mean then, nothing?'

'I mean, go upstairs, Jack, just shut up for once and stop being such a bloody little smart arse.'

IN THE TAKE-OFF CAFÉ, OVER ANOTHER ROUND OF MILK, Timothy had told me that his suntan was over a month old and it had come from Cannes.

'What?'

'You mean, "where?" Cannes. It's in southern France. It's where they show all the films, but we don't go then, of course. Mum says it's madness.'

'So, what was it like?'

'Hot. Well, warm. We stayed in a place with a balcony and I sat on it all day.'

'Don't they have a beach?'

'Well, yes. But Mum was busy working. The balcony was nice.'

'Didn't you get fed up?'

'Not really.'

'I've never been to France,' I told him, and he didn't look surprised.

'We're always there. It's like we're never away. Mum gets cheap deals and freebies. I like it of course, but then, I wouldn't mind trying Florida. Now that would make a change.'

'I wouldn't mind trying anywhere,' I'd said. 'We go to Rhyl.'

'Rhyl? As in Wales?'

'Yes.'

'Ah,' he said. 'Right.'

So, they were always in France. Never away. They'd been all over. And France was a big place. Bigger than England. You could be skiing in one bit, freezing to death and sunburnt in another.

'Have you been to Finistère?'

'Yes,' he'd shrugged. He was bored of this now, he was even blowing bubbles in his milk dregs.

'And?'

'Well, it's rocky. Windy. It's the end of the world,' he'd said. 'And, boy, does it look like it is.'

I COULDN'T GET TO SLEEP. I COULDN'T STOP THINKING. If Claudine could get freebies, maybe she could get Mum some freebies too? Then she could go over there at Christmas, and if there was only one ticket, then I'd stay here, with Dad. It wouldn't be that bad. I could do the cooking. In Asda you could buy meals-on-a-plate, frozen. They even had gravy, stuffing. All the trimmings. Easy. I wouldn't mind. Really. And I supposed it would be worth it.

DAD WAS HAPPY NOW. HE COULDN'T STOP THINKING about Saturday. He'd bought a new bow tie. Smaller. Velvet. Bottle-green. Smart. He was always covered in aftershave. He'd had his suit dry-cleaned.

'This is it!' He went around the house, singing, giving Mum a rotten headache, dancing, his fist shooting up in the air. 'This is it!'

On Thursday morning Mum dragged herself down to pour tea and fry a bit of bacon, but as soon as Dad had left for work, and she'd heard the car as it spluttered round the corner, she went upstairs, slipped her nightie back on and hid under the covers.

'What's the matter?' I stood in the doorway, talking to a lump.

'I'm tired.'

'But you're supposed to be at work.'

'I'm tired. I'm not going in. Now go and give me some peace.'

All day she was up there, occasionally coming down for a cup of sweet tea and a fistful of biscuits. Then there'd be silence, sniffing, and shuffles to the toilet. At four o'clock she had a long bubble bath, cried, did her hair, then got herself dressed. Then she fiddled in the kitchen cupboard, finding something for Dad's tea. She hadn't been shopping but there were plenty of tins in there. New potatoes. Peas. A Fray Bentos steak pie.

When Dad appeared, she didn't say anything about her day up in bed. When he said, 'You been all right then?' she nodded, then listened to him talking about a man they both knew, a real ladies' man, who was starting to lose his hair.

'He's as sick as a parrot,' said Dad. 'I was trying not to laugh. Mind you, he's ordered Raphael, our most expensive new line. Blond of course. I told him it looked great with his suntan.'

Friday was the same. Mr Gentleman phoned.

'Is your mother sick?' he asked. 'She's left me high and dry. Again. She could have told us. She knows that I'm amenable.'

'She's, well, she's had a lot on her mind,' I stuttered. What was I supposed to tell him?

'And how long do you think this new illness will last? She's only just back from the flu.'

My stomach fizzed and spluttered. I could hear her flushing the toilet.

'I'm not sure. A couple of days at the most?'

'A couple of days?'

'Yes.'

'Has she seen a doctor?'

'I think she knows what it is.' I knew that if I brought the doctor into it, he'd be wanting to see a sick note.

'Right then. Well, I'd better call again tomorrow, if I don't see her first.'

I stared at the telephone. It was a grey trim phone that Mum had set her heart on in 1973. Now it looked old-fashioned and the ring always got on my nerves. I unplugged it. What if he called again? What could I say? What if she lost her job? It wasn't really much, a few hours filing and answering the phone, but I was sure that Dad would kill her.

I padded upstairs. Silence. I peered through the crack in the door. She was lying with her eyes open, staring at the ceiling.

'That was your office.'

'Oh.'

'Mr Gentleman. He's going to ring tomorrow.'

'Oh.'

'So what should I tell him.'

'I don't know.'

'Shall I get the doctor?'

'I'm not ill.'

'So why are you in bed?'

She closed her eyes. Rubbed them. 'I've had it.'

'You've had it? What's that supposed to mean?' I sat on the edge of the bed. The quilt was covered in tissues.

'I don't know what it means. Why does everything have to mean something to you, Jack?'

'Well, you're just lying there. I'm worried.'

'I'm just having a bit of a rest.'

'So, what shall I tell Mr Gentleman?'

'I don't know. Tell him what you like.'

'You might lose your job.'

'I might,' she said. 'But I won't.'

I went outside. My legs were full of cramp and my muscles ached from worry. Mum hardly moved all day. She didn't watch telly or read her *Woman's Own*. She just lay there. Staring. What if she really was ill, and I didn't know it? I'd read about cancer. We'd talked about it in Biology because the teacher's mum had it. Cancer wore you out and people had no idea. Sometimes there weren't even lumps. Mum could have leukaemia.

Mattie was on the park, and for a second I forgot about Mum, and I thought of his brother's bedroom. Those pictures. The booze. The smell. I could have walked past, but he'd seen me. He was lounging on the roundabout with his jeans caked in mud.

'I'm whacked,' he said. 'I'm having a little lie down.'

He looked worn out. Pale. Was it catching?

I sat on the swings and moved a bit. It was warm, and over the wall I could hear children playing, chasing through the lamp posts.

'I've been here for hours,' said Mattie. 'I was going to come to your house, but I couldn't remember the number. Red door?'

'Green. 59. My mum's ill, though.'

'Bad?'

'Not really.'

'What then?'

I shrugged.

'Women's troubles?' he said.

'Maybe.'

'Candice gets that. She won't do now though. Not for a bit, anyway.'

I looked at him. His face was white and patchy grey. His nose was full of snot.

'What are you on about?'

'She's pregnant.'

'Crikey. How old is she?'

'Sixteen. And she's pleased all right. She wanted a baby. Looks like she had it all planned.'

'What about your brother?'

'He's not bothered. John doesn't mind either way.'

We sat for a bit, trying not to look at each other. I couldn't imagine a baby in his house. A nice clean baby rolling around with the marrow bones.

'What will you do with the dogs?'

'Candice wants rid already, but we've told her to piss off.'

'You're keeping them?'

'Too right.'

'They can kill babies. You're always reading, Pet Kills Kid In Pram.'

'I love them dogs,' he said, wiping his nose on his sleeve.

We walked to get Stuart. My legs felt heavy and when we went past my house I looked up to see if the curtains were closed, but Mum had left them open, just to fool the neighbours.

Stuart looked surprised to see me and Mattie standing there.

'I found him in the park,' I said.

Stuart's house was empty. His mum had gone to bingo. We shuffled over the step.

'You can come in for half an hour. Then she'll be back.'

The front room was still full of bags of things thrown all over the carpet, Mattie couldn't stop looking at the cabinet full of ornaments, the palm-tree standard lamp and the big colour telly.

'All this stuff,' he said. 'Shit.'

'She gets it all on tick.' Stuart came in with three mugs of tea. 'She's been paying for that lamp for the past three years. It's nearly had it now.'

We sat in a row watching *Love Boat*.

'Candice is pregnant,' I said.

'Oh?' Stuart looked up. 'Well, I'm not surprised. Are you?' Then he looked at Mattie. 'That's great,' he said. 'I wouldn't mind being an uncle. I bet it's a laugh.'

'Well, I wouldn't mind, but I'm only bloody twelve.'

We didn't say anything. I could hear Mattie breathing. Sniffing. We just kept looking at the boat, waiting for the pretty girl to put on her bikini.

'My dad might be going on one of those things,' I told them. 'A liner.'

'No way.'

'Yes. It's true. He might get a job as a lounge singer.'

'Good one. Right. A new job in the middle of the Pacific Ocean? Well, you can't get much further away than that. So, what's brought this on? Is he running away from a few of his little mistakes then? He's not been with our Candice now, has he?'

Mattie and Stuart were killing themselves laughing. Then Stuart looked at the clock.

'It's time to piss off,' he said. 'She'll be back in ten minutes.'

We went outside. Across the road a woman was shaking out a big tartan blanket. It caught on a rose bush. The air was full of dust, you could see it, blowing upwards in the sunshine.

Stuart's mum appeared, huffing round the corner. She was wearing gold slippers and an Elizabeth Taylor caftan. Mattie sniggered.

'Boys,' she said. 'Why don't you go down to the library or something? Educate yourselves.'

'It's closed. They're painting it.'

'Typical.'

'How was the bingo?' Mattie asked.

She pulled up her handbag and hugged it.

'It was fine. I didn't win the jackpot, but then I never do. It's a social occasion. It's nice to get out.'

The handbag was wide. It was full of pads, felt-tip pens and a gonk that was the same as my dad's, with its long purple hair and crazy plastic eyes.

'Is that your lucky mascot?' Mattie asked.

'Yes. That and my Silver Jubilee snowstorm.' And she pulled it out. The queen in coronation robes. 1952–1977. She shook it, and the snow poured down, landing on the royal shoulders, like giant flakes of dandruff.

'Does it work?'

'Only on Tuesdays. Now get lost, the three of you. I'm off to make a cuppa.'

We shuffled a bit as she turned into her path. Mattie made faces and Stuart looked worried. As she opened her door, the gonk fell out of her bag and it landed on the soil, like a strange exotic flower.

'She'll be giving it a bath tonight,' said Stuart. 'She loves that stupid gonk.'

'Where did she get it from? Blackpool?'

'No,' he said. 'Well, I don't know. She came home with it one night. I pulled the eyes off, but she went and glued them on again.'

MUM LOOKED BETTER. SHE WAS DRESSED AND DOWN-stairs. She was cooking. The house smelled like a bakery, with a whiff of something burning. The kitchen was covered in flour.

'I've decided to give it another go,' she said, chopping up an apple.

'Give what another go?'

'Life. But I need some more butter.' She ran her finger down the grease-stained recipe. 'Two packets. Just to be on the safe side. And see if they do powdered cinnamon, you know, in those little glass jars.'

'What are you making?'

'Pompe aux pommes.'

'What?'

'Pompe aux pommes.'

'Right,' I said. 'Sounds great.'

'I HAVEN'T MENTIONED IT AT WORK,' DAD SAID, DOLLOP-ing on his custard. 'I want to tell them when it's final. When I can turn round and say, I told you that I'd do it. And now I bloody have. You get the picture?'

Mum nodded, smiling.

'Bloody great pie,' he said.

'It's French.'

'Get away, Evie. It's apple pie. You can't get more English than good old apple pie. It's traditional.'

'You're right,' she said. 'It is.'

'Like bangers and mash.'

'Hotpot.'

'Roast beef and gravy.'

'Fried egg and chips.'

'Apple pie,' laughed Dad. 'French. Now I've heard it all.'

HE WAS SICK ON SATURDAY MORNING. I COULD HEAR HIM. Belching. Groaning. It splashed hard and fast in the toilet. It was early. Pale outside. Mum stood in her dressing gown and shivered on the landing.

'It's nerves,' she said.

'No it's not. It's that bloody apple pie. Come in here and look at it. Look down there. Can't you see? All that green stuff's apple. It must have gone off.'

I rubbed my eyes. I was still half asleep. My bobble hat drowned out some of the sound, but I could still hear his moaning.

'And here I go again.' The toilet flushed. He was whimpering.

People often got sick in space. The Russian cosmonaut Gherman Titov suffered space sickness. And was it any wonder? Think of all the people who get travel sick just on their way to Blackpool. Then think of space. All that way up. Exactly. The weightlessness affects the balancing mechanism inside the ears. Not to mention the sight of it. No horizon. Panic. But that was in the sixties. They'd have drugs for it now.

Dad sipped Milk of Magnesia in between his tea.

'Great timing,' he said. 'If I'm like this tonight, you've had it.'

'You'll be fine,' I told him. 'And it couldn't have been the pie, because we had the pie and we haven't been sick.'

'Not yet you haven't.'

'Well, I don't feel sick,' I said. 'It must be something else.'

'Like what?'

'Something that you ate, that we didn't. What did you have for your dinner?'

'I don't know. Chips.'

'It could have been the chips.'

'Not bloody likely.'

'It must be nerves then.'

'I don't get nervous. I get a buzz. A little bit of stage fright just before I'm on. *Just before I'm on.* I don't throw up all day.'

'But Dad. It's a big day. A big night. You've got that Lex man coming to see you.'

Suddenly he paled. He looked like he was going to spew, right there across the table. Then he swallowed, coughed a bit, and took a gulp of tea.

'Jack,' he said. 'You think I don't know? You think I don't know that this is the big one? Of course I fucking know. I dreamt about it. Now just go and put a record on, and shut it.'

Mum hummed around to Shirley Bassey. I'd been warned off the male vocalists. Even Frank Sinatra. Dad said he wanted to relax a bit first. It was Saturday morning. It was too early to be thinking about the hard-work side of show business.

'Even Tom Jones gets to chill,' he said. 'So Jack, forget "Wooden Heart". Forget "Delilah". Shirley will be fine.'

HE STAYED IN THE HOUSE ALL DAY STRETCHED IN FRONT of the gas fire. He read the *Daily Mail* (another mistake they'd delivered).

'It makes a change,' he said. 'The writing's smaller.' He rattled it. 'Does it make me look clever?'

Every so often, he'd disappear into the bathroom, checking his face, 'to see if I'm still looking sickly'.

Dad was pale anyway. Milk-bottle white that looked even worse because his hair was so dark. In the summer (if the sun ever came to this side of Manchester), he turned a streaky pink. Once he'd borrowed a sun lamp. He'd been told that if he used the special cream he wouldn't go red. He did it all in secret. Okay, so he was in showbiz, and showbiz people did this kind of thing all the time, but they'd hardly ever admit to it, especially not in Bolton.

Dad had closed the curtains, smeared his face with cold white cream and waited for the lamp to turn him into the nice olive shade of Englebert Humperdinck. The goggles hurt his eyes. Then the heat made him drowsy. He only dropped off for a minute. 'Okay, okay, then. Two minutes. Two bloody minutes at the most.' His face had been grilled. Mum heard him shout, then quickly found the burns section in the first-aid book.

'Oh, look at this poor chap,' she'd said, holding up a picture. 'Well, you know where he went wrong, don't you?'

'Where?' Dad groaned. He could barely open his mouth. He'd developed new red wrinkles.

Mum tutted. 'Well, everyone knows that burns and water don't mix.'

Dad's faded after a day or two. A few weeks later, he discovered Mum's Max Factor, and an hour or two before he was due on stage he'd apply the greasy beige liquid for an instant pain-free tan.

'I don't care what people think,' he said, trying to look manly as he dabbed it round his eyes. 'Okay, okay, so it might be bloody women's stuff. But all the actors use it. And anything's better than frying. I couldn't go through that again. No way.'

SEAN WAS OUTSIDE WITH HIS BROTHER AND THE GUINEA pigs. I escaped for ten minutes, away from Mum's frenzied kitchen cleaning and Dad's raw nerves.

'It might be germs,' Mum had whispered, scrubbing down the table. 'He might have picked something up.'

'Like what? When?'

'I don't know. When we were having our tea. And those burgers,' she'd said. 'Did they seem cooked? They weren't a bit raw in the middle?'

'But he hasn't been sick for hours.'

'Well, I know,' she'd said, sprinkling on some Ajax. 'But I'd better not take any chances.'

We stamped around outside. The guinea pigs raced across the yard. Hairy. Squeaking. Ginger.

'They're getting too fat,' said Sean. 'They need more exercise.'

'Don't let them escape,' cried his brother. 'Please don't let them escape!'

'Michael. They will not escape.'

'They will, they will. They might go under the gate.'

'Under the gate? Have you seen the size of the gap?'

'Yes.'

'And have you seen the size of the guinea pigs?'

'They might squeeze out.'

'They will not squeeze out. Anyway, why would they want to escape? They love it here. They get all the carrots and the lettuce leaves they want. Look at their cage. Two rooms and some ladders. They're in guinea-pig heaven.'

'Well . . .'

We watched them scamper round, then huddle in a corner.

'Look at them,' said Sean, poking them with a stick. 'The fat lazy bastards.'

'Mam!' Michael wailed, running in. 'Sean's being cruel. He's poking them. He's poking Patch and Pickles!'

'Bloody stupid things,' said Sean, scooping them up, throwing them into the hay. His shirt was covered in hairs. 'They do nothing but eat, sleep and shit. You can't even train them. Not like rabbits.'

We sat on the step. His brother was still going on, but we could hear his mum just laughing.

'Cry, cry, cry,' said Sean. 'But it's not his fault. It's just his disposition. Mam says. He's been like this for years.'

BY TEATIME, DAD'S NERVES HAD BROKEN A COFFEE JAR, two cups and three glass ornaments.

'Well, you shouldn't have put them there,' he'd snapped. 'They were bound to get in the way.'

Mum swept the pieces with her face drawn in. She looked at the clock. Only another three hours and fifteen minutes to go. She rummaged for some aspirin. She had a headache coming on.

Suddenly, Dad livened up. He bounced out of his chair, flexed his knees and started doing high karate chops.

'Oh look,' said Mum. 'It's Bruce Lee.'

'I think it's time. Time to get with it. However I might feel,' he said. 'Whatever that apple pie has gone and done to my insides, I'll just have to snap out of it.'

So he snapped. He closed the front-room curtains and did a warm-up on the floor. Sit-ups. Arms out. Head rolls.

'He's going to kill himself,' Mum whispered. 'I wish he'd just sit down.'

We were at the kitchen table, with the door just an inch or two ajar. Now you see him, now you don't. Through the frosted glass he was a blur of squats and stretches. The music started slow. The male vocalists were back and I could see him, miming on the rug, overemphasising the movements, as if he was playing at Wembley.

Mum had her hands under her chin. She was pulling in her lips and making little sniffing sounds.

'I don't know whether to laugh,' she said. 'Maybe I should. Maybe I'd be better off laughing.' We looked at each other and collapsed into giggles, swaying our shoulders with him, flapping our hands to the music.

'We'll look on this and laugh,' Mum said. 'Have you seen that daft expression?'

I peered around the door. He looked like Mike Yarwood, doing Shirley Bassey. Surely he couldn't be serious?

IT TOOK TWO HOURS FOR HIM TO GET DRESSED. FIRST THE bath was filled. Bubbly. Nice and hot. Orange Aqua Manda with the dust blown off from Christmas. Then the soap-on-a-rope microphone appeared, for the early vocal warm-up.

Through the steam-edged door, he appeared in his leopard-print Y-fronts and vest. His hair flopping over. His top lip snagging. Now it was time to show his respect. It was stroke the gonk, whisper to Tom time.

WE DIDN'T SAY 'GOOD LUCK', BECAUSE WE KNEW IT wasn't lucky. We didn't even say 'break a leg', because Dad wouldn't let us. 'It isn't lucky. It can't be lucky.' And he could prove it. Look at Donny Lester who sang down at the Legion. He'd broken his leg getting out of the car at a gig. 'A double fracture. Complications. Painful. He was off the circuit for months. And he was never the same after that. No. He just couldn't get the moves right.' So we hugged him. 'Not too bloody close, or you'll crease me.' And we waved until he just wasn't looking anymore.

'Well,' shrugged Mum, lighting up a fag. 'That's it then. He's gone.'

'GRANDMA WILL BE PLEASED,' I SAID. 'IF IT ALL TURNS out. She'll be that excited. I should have gone to tell her.'

'Nothing's happened yet.'

We were sat watching telly. Mum kept getting up, doing things, pretending everything was normal, and she didn't have a picked, blood-bitten lip and one eye on the clock.

'I hope he turns up.'

'Jack,' she said, 'not another bloody word. Crikey. What are you trying to do to me? I'm bad enough as it is.'

WE DIDN'T EAT ANY SUPPER. WE JUST SAT DRINKING CUP after cup of extra-sweet tea while Mum chain-smoked her extra-strength Regal. We tried talking about other things. School. Rhyl. Mrs Dawson's fruit tree. We talked about Grandma Trench, and how she moaned and stayed up in her room with the door clamped shut.

'Waste of bloody money that place,' said Mum. 'She's paying for the rest of it, you know. It's all included. The recreation room. Morning coffee. The little games of bingo. They even give them a bit of something for a prize. God. Wouldn't you think that she'd put her dressing gown on now and then, just to have a little mingle?'

We edged around Brittany.

'Funny,' said Mum. 'I thought they'd have phoned by now.'

We tried following the story on *The Sweeney*.

'Was that the man who left the gun then?'

'No, that's his brother.'

'What brother?'

'You know, the one that killed the woman.'

'He killed the woman? What woman?'

It was hopeless.

At ten past ten, when Dad opened the door, we shot right out of our seats. He'd surprised us all right. He was over an hour early. But it was okay. It looked okay. He was smiling.

'What happened?' Mum asked. 'We thought you'd be later than this.'

He plopped slowly into the cushions and Mum quickly disappeared, getting him a beer.

'I've had it waiting for you. Feel how it's all nice and cold from the fridge. So?'

'Well, I was a star,' he beamed. 'Yes. They loved it. Clap? Their hands were sparking they clapped that much. On and on, they just couldn't get enough, so I gave Pete the eye and we put an extra one in at the end.'

'An encore.'

'That's right. An encore. Smart arse.'

'And he came?'

'Oh, he came all right. He came. He saw. I conquered.'

'What did he say then? Go on, Joe, tell us.'

Dad took a long slow drink of beer. His head back. His Adam's apple bobbing.

'Max Lexington said I was marvellous. That the world was my oyster. Rotherham would probably be a good place to start, he said. He knows a little club there. Not too classy, not too rough. But he's a top agent. He needs to mull it over. Said he'd have a think driving back in his car. And what a car. You should have seen his car, Evie. It was a Jag.'

'A Jag?'

'God's honest. A big red Jag. And when he opened the door there was all this wood panelling and the smell of leather seats.'

'He must be good then.'

'Of course he's good. I said he was good, didn't I?'

'So, why does he have to go and think it over?'

'It's business. It's the way it all works. He can't sign me up there and then at the back of the club. No way. He also has a partner. A Mr Sammy Rose. He needs to enquire if there's a space on their books for a vocalist. They're selective. They don't just take anyone.'

'So, why don't you look all that worried?'

Dad grinned and wiped a fleck of foam from the corner of his lip.

'Well ... you know ... Max gave me the nod. Said it's practically in the bag, my contract. Said he thought I was a genuine new talent. Yup. Those were his exact words, "a genuine new talent". And the club couldn't keep his eyes off him.'

'I thought they were looking at you?' I snapped my mouth shut. I'd said it. But he didn't seem to mind. He just went on.

'They couldn't stop looking because he was different to the regulars. Completely bloody different. And he didn't half stand out. He looked, well, he looked well off. He knew how to act, standing right at the back in his long camel coat. Classy. He didn't drink. He ordered lemonade.'

'Lemonade?'

'What's wrong with lemonade? He has to keep his head straight, Evie. After all, he's working.'

'I suppose so.'

'And he's going to tell me tonight.'

'What?' Mum looked at the clock. It was nearly half-past ten.

'He said he was going to phone with a definite answer, tonight.'

'But look how late it is. Where's he driving to?'

'Hyde. And they work late hours these agents. It's when it all happens, night time. Some acts don't even come on until well after midnight in these classy cabaret joints. It's another world, Evie. Another world.'

After his third can of beer, he decided to slow down. 'I'll have to keep my head straight. You never know. We might be doing deals.' He'd already sharpened a pencil and found himself a notepad. 'It'll look bad if I'm slurring. It wouldn't look pro.'

I kept quiet. I didn't like to mention all the showbiz stars I'd read about, who regularly drank until they dropped after every live performance. The drugs. Mum would only start worrying.

He put some records on. There was a party atmosphere. We danced on the rug again, all of us, and he didn't mind me miming.

'All the stars do it,' he said. 'Every now and then. It's still entertaining, and it gives their voice a rest.'

When 'King Creole' had scraped into fade we sat and watched the telephone. It was ten to twelve.

'Late,' said Dad. 'But not too late.'

We didn't change the record. We sat and listened to the cars outside, and a man shouting, 'Kathy! Kathy! Let me in Kathy! I love you!' Someone ran past the window. Close. We could hear him panting. Then nothing. Even the cars petered out.

Dad cracked his knuckles. Mum was turning white. Rigid. Nothing. Tick, tick, tock.
Silence.

You must never look at the sun directly, either with the naked eye or through binoculars or a telescope. Observing the sun is potentially very dangerous and can result in irreparable eye damage or blindness. Children are particularly at risk.

SHE LET ME OPEN THE CURTAINS.

'Just a crack,' she said. 'I don't want full-blown daylight.'

I was careful. I pulled slowly, just a few centimetres. The sun blazed. We could feel it, warming through the glass. It made us blink, squint, and we both turned our heads away, amazed.

'Look at it,' said Mum. 'Is it summer already?'

The bedroom looked strange in the daylight. Squeezed and washed out. We were used to lamps with thick shades and tiny low-watt bulbs.

'I don't know,' she said. 'Look at us. We could be sunbathing. We could be out in the back, dripping with Ambre Solaire.'

I tried a smile and went and sat with her. She moved an arm across, and her eyes swivelled softly in a pool of bloody red. She coughed and had to hold herself.

'Listen to me,' she said. 'I'd be better off with low tar, but they haven't any taste.'

I lit her another cigarette. It had felt strange at first. I'd never liked them much. I wasn't one of the gang who bought fags with their dinner money. But now I didn't mind. I could hand them to her, strike up a match. I was even willing to drag on it a bit if she was desperate.

'It's not your fault,' she'd been saying, over and over again. 'Don't blame yourself. It's him. He's changed somehow. I don't know. He's worse. He keeps seeing himself Up There.' And she'd moved her hand as if she was showing me the stage at the London Palladium. 'You know what he's like,' she said.

The sun felt strong as we huddled under blankets. They were creased now, and greying. You could see where we'd spilt tea, blood, fizzed-up soluble aspirin.

'We wouldn't do for visitors.' She was rubbing at the crusts that had built up round her eyes. 'Imagine. And I'd feel so ashamed,' she said. 'Just look at us.'

DAD? WELL, OF COURSE HE'D BEEN OPTIMISTIC. HE KNEW those clubs opened late. Didn't they have special licences? Tables with lamps on them. Wine. And then there were the parties afterwards. Small select gatherings in the dressing room. Drinks. Hangers-on. Celebrities. They went on for hours. He'd been looking forward to that side of things.

But really, even for an optimist, there was only so long you could wait.

It was after three o'clock when he'd slammed his fist into the armchair.

'Jesus fucking Christ!' The floor had rattled. There was blood everywhere. His hand had gone right through the springs.

For hours he'd been sniffing, pacing, staring at the telephone. Then every so often he'd looked long and hard through the window, as if that Jag might suddenly reappear, full of champagne, contracts and bikini-clad girls that just couldn't wait until morning.

We couldn't go to bed. We sat there, sharing his pain. We didn't talk. It didn't seem right when the only sound he'd really wanted to hear was the trilling of the phone.

I don't know if I remembered before he found out. Maybe I did. Maybe for a second I went cold and nearly said something. Wanting to. Relief. A jerking of the head, teeth apart, tongue back, almost saying, 'But it's not your fault, Dad. He's probably been trying to ring us up all night with the good news. It's the phone. That's all it is. The telephone. My fault. Would you believe it? I went and forgot to plug it back in again.' Then laughter all round. A bit of a slap on the back.

'Well, aren't you the idiot, son? Never mind! Phew, that one was close! I'll phone him in the morning. I'll tell him. It'll go down in showbiz history, will this. He'll have a good laugh. He'll be telling this story for years!'

But of course I said nothing. It was always best to say nothing. Even when he'd found it. Even when he was standing on the rug with the wire hanging out of his hand, his jaw dropping as we stared at the clump of limp coils. Of course he couldn't believe it. No one could believe it; except, of course, for me.

'You scheming fucking bitch,' he'd muttered, looking down at my mum, dripping his blood all over her knees. 'You little piece of shit. You've let me sit here all night like an idiot. Just what were you trying to do?'

'Nothing, I—'

'Nothing? Nothing? So?' he'd spat. 'Just how long were you planning to keep it like this? Weeks? Months? What? Go on, Evie. You Tell Me.'

'I didn't know, Joe. I really didn't know.'

'Well, they don't unplug themselves.' He was still looking at it, as if it might just ring. Hoping. Hoping. His hand full of blood where the springs had scraped it back. Raw knuckles. His suit ruined. 'What a bitch. What a bitch. I never took you for such a fucking bitch. Evelyn. Look at me. Look at me. Look!' He'd jerked her face around. I couldn't move. I'd hung on to those cushions as if they might just fly.

'It was me. I—'

'You've let me sit here all this time. What sort of a wife are you? Laughing behind my back. You're crap. Stupid. Useless. Look at you.'

'What?' her voice had trembled. She could hardly open her mouth.

'Well just take a look. You're all skin and bones. You're more like a kid, and they're right. Yes. I could have a hundred pretty girls. A thousand. What the hell am I doing coming back here every night?'

'But it wasn't—'

Mum drew back. She was trying to make herself small. Smaller. Huddled in the corner. Tight. Surely if she closed her eyes, then maybe she could disappear into the deep black warmth of her eyelids? And then suddenly, he flew at her, and all I could hear was the thudding.

I'd wanted to do something. I'd tried. I'd tried pulling, pushing, shouting. But my voice went to nothing, and then I was sick, and his arms, they'd kept getting in the way.

When she was down, more than down, he'd stamped his way upstairs. He'd smashed open the wardrobe and filled a couple of carrier bags. He'd ripped up a dress and used it as a bandage. Then he'd left. Revving the car like a maniac.

That first night, we hadn't moved. We couldn't. I'd brought a couple of blankets down and filled a hot-water bottle, and we'd snuggled up close, even with the pain. Mum couldn't stand the silence.

'It's killing me,' she'd said. 'Go on. Go and put a record on.'

So, stumbling over bottles, glasses, the puddle of my sick, I'd pulled off 'King Creole' and thrown it to the side.

'Which one?'

'Oh any,' she'd whispered. 'Just the first one in the pile.'

I'd picked it out. I could just about see the shiny white cover, as the arm slid across and the needle slipped down. It had crackled at first, and we'd huddled on the cushions, while Bobby Darin sang 'La Mer (Beyond the Sea)' to us, over and over again.

A LINE OF DUSTY DAYLIGHT HAD GOT BRIGHTER ON THE carpet. It was late in the morning when I'd bathed her head with Dettol and dabs of ice-cold water, and she'd struggled up and walked about a bit, checking for broken bones. Her arms. Wrists. Her tiny, birdlike ribcage.

'You need an X-ray.'

'I don't need anything.'

'You might be really hurt.'

'I am really hurt.'

'You know what I mean, Mum.'

But she'd managed to get up the stairs and she'd rolled herself into the bed.

'And this is where I'm staying till it's all sorted out. And you're not moving, either.'

'What? What about food?'

'We can always find something.'

'Milk?'

'We don't need milk. I'll drink black tea. Anyway...'

'What?'

'It's fattening.'

And we'd managed to laugh about that, shaking, crying, then laughing again.

I dragged the telly off its stand and heaved it up the stairs. It was heavy. My knees kept giving way, trembling. But she didn't want to move.

'Look what's on,' she said, as I stood by the door with the aerial. 'It's that Marilyn Monroe film, the one where they dress up as women.'

My arm ached, but whenever I put it down, the picture went. Eventually, I managed to jam it on top of the door, and we both sat watching the film, until we fell asleep again. Then later, I went downstairs, jumping barefoot round the kitchen, looking for something that was nice and easy to swallow. There was an egg left. Some chicken noodle Cup-A-Soup.

'Where do you think he is?' I asked. Whenever we mentioned Dad, our voices turned to whispers. 'Do you think that he'll be back?'

She plucked at the blankets. 'I suppose so.'

'Where do you think he is then?'

'I haven't even the foggiest.'

'Do you think he'll be all right?'

'All right? Of course he'll be all right. It's me who's not all right.'

'Yes.'

'So?'

'So, I was thinking, he might have gone to find him. Max. He might be in Rotherham by now, singing.'

'Rotherham? Ha. I bet there was no bloody Rotherham.'

'But Dad said—'

'You know what he's like, Jack. You've seen him. How he gets these fancy ideas.'

I closed my eyes and swallowed. I wasn't sure that I could say it.

'Do you want him to come back?'

Mum sank down. His things were still all over the place. His shaving foam was dribbling by the sink. The gonk sat and stared with its crooked plastic eyes. His slippers.

'I don't know. I just don't know anymore. Do you? When this happens. Well. Ask me again. Ask me again in a fortnight.'

It had already been nearly a week. Just us. We hadn't answered the door, but I'd peered through a crack in the curtains. Mrs Murphy. Sean. The milkman.

I'd called Mr Gentleman on the Monday, saying that Mum really was ill, and it wasn't an excuse, and I must have sounded worried because he'd believed me straight away. Then Vince rang, and the sudden noise of the phone had frightened us to death. What if it was him, all sad and sorry, on his way home with an armful of flowers and another cut-price annual?

'Where's your dad this morning?' Vince asked. 'He should have been in hours ago. There's a queue of clients and our girls aren't really trained for the toupee side of things.'

'He's gone,' I whispered.

'Gone?'

'Yes.'

'Gone? Oh, *gone.*' Then suddenly he'd softened. 'Are you okay? Both of you? I mean, is there anything you need? Anything at all? Would you like me to come round?'

'Oh no,' I said. 'I mean, can I phone you? I don't think Mum wants any visitors just yet.'

'Well, of course she doesn't. I understand. But if he turns up here, I'll tell you. I'll discreetly let you know.'

'Thanks.'

'Take care now, Jack,' he said. 'And don't worry yourself about here.'

Now the afternoons were full of films. Black tea and Dora Bryan. Big-eyed Ingrid Bergman. *Calamity Jane.* The tapping Ziegfeld Follies.

'We saw a show like that,' Mum said, as their legs crisscrossed out of view. 'Before you were born. I can't remember what it was called, but all the girls were beautiful, and it made me want to dance. That night it was raining, pouring down, but your dad took me straight to the Palais, and he whisked me round the dance floor. Funny, but I felt like a million dollars, just thinking about that show. My hair was wet. My dress. And all the lights were soft that night because they'd had a power cut and half of the bulbs had blown.'

After *Flying Down to Rio*, she managed to have a bath. She said she felt all right, but I sat tight against the door outside, listening, just in case.

'Go away, Jack,' she said through the steam. 'I know you're there but I'm fine. Really.' But I was comfy. I wasn't going to budge.

'I'm fine!' she kept shouting. 'Fine!' But I knew that she was crying, whenever she ran the taps.

We weren't going anywhere, but we waited for the postman as

if it was our birthday. Every morning at half-past seven I'd be wide awake when the letterbox clicked, and I ran downstairs to check it, shuffling through it, nervous, hiding all the red bills and any brown envelopes, just to soften the blow. There was a postcard from France. A sad-looking mule with parcels on its back.

Dear All, We've arrived safe and sound. The house isn't ready so we're staying with Michel. Tried to call on Friday but you were out again. Dad is helping with the plastering. It's sunny, but cold. All the best, with love from Mum and Dad. xxxx.

'Well, look,' she choked, holding it out as if she couldn't quite see. 'That's French that is. French.'

'It's a donkey.'

'I know what it is,' she said. 'God. And I knew it would happen like this.'

'Like what?'

She opened up her arms. 'Like they've all gone and left me all at once.'

There was a get-well card from Mr Gentleman. A long-faced woman in bed. 'Chin up,' he'd written, and he'd signed it, *with all best wishes, from Ted.* Mum looked pleased. She stood it next to the postcard.

'I told you I wouldn't lose my job,' she said. 'I'll soon be fine and out of here.'

'Of course you will,' I told her. 'And it won't be long before you're better. Don't worry, Mum. Don't worry about me. About anything. We can do without him. Easy. Can't we?'

And she nodded her head, concentrating on whatever film was on.

'Look at Richard Burton,' she said. 'You wouldn't think he was a miner's boy, would you?'

In the afternoon, a torn scrap of paper came fluttering through the letterbox. *Are you ok? From Sean.* So the neighbours had heard. I didn't tell Mum. I ripped it into shreds and put it in the bin underneath some soggy chicken noodles. Then I put my ear against their wall. I could hear their Hoover going. Moving furniture. Normal things.

'You think we would have heard,' said Mum. 'You think he'd have come back, just to see if I was still a bloody live.'

'Never mind,' I said, repeating, repeating, repeating. 'You're better off without him.'

It had been a week. On Saturday morning a letter came. Dad's handwriting. Addressed to me. So, finally. I sat on the doormat and stared at it. Smelled it. My heart was thudding, my hands felt like lumps of cotton wool. I peered at the stamp. It was stuck on upside down. Postmarked, Bolton East. He was still here then? I looked out of the window. What if he was watching?

Fumbling, I opened it. Plain white paper. No address.

Dear Jack, I'm sorry. I hope you are all right. Tell your mum I'm singing. She couldn't stop me. I'll see you around sometime! Love from your Dad.

I screwed it up hard. I wasn't going to cry. I went into the kitchen, to put the kettle on. The letter was balled in my hand. It felt heavy for paper. Cold. I gave it one last squeeze and put it in the bin, made some tea and took it out again. It was stained from the tea bag. Soggy. I wiped it off and put it in my zip-up anorak pocket.

'Black tea?' said Mum. 'I'm beginning to get used. I can do the Special K diet now. It was the black tea and coffee that always put me off.'

'You don't need a diet.'

'No.'

We sat and stared at the TV. There was never much on in the

mornings. Schools programmes. *Picture Box.* A man in a long fur coat was talking about Russia. His feet were covered in snow.

'I've never liked fur,' said Mum. 'I had a jacket once. Real it was. Coney. I hardly ever wore it. Was there any post?'

'Just a couple of adverts.'

'Adverts? What for?'

'You know. Film developing. Catalogues.'

'Oh, not more catalogues,' she groaned. 'Littlewood's. Christ. I owe everybody money.'

Food was already running out, because there wasn't much in to start with. We weren't that hungry, but then sometimes we got ravenous, especially late at night when we didn't want to sleep. We ate strange combinations. Whatever we had left. Soup. Pickled beetroot and pineapple crackers. Beef paste on digestive biscuits. Paxo and baked beans. We drank a bottle of flat lemonade with some syrupy half-cling peaches.

'It's like being in a war.'

'It is a bloody war,' she said. 'And I don't even know what side I'm on yet. Do you?'

I was fed up with Rasputin, so I decided to clear up downstairs. I opened all the curtains – if anyone came to the door, I'd just say that Mum was out, or I'd hide. The sky was a brilliant blue. It made the room look worse. The first thing that I did was to hide the hole in the armchair with the best and never-used tea towel. It didn't look bad. It was stiff red tartan. A Gift From Bonnie Scotland.

Everything was coated. There were bottles. Fag ends. Sick. The top of the record player was up and there was dust on Bobby Darin.

I moved things. I felt better doing something. I felt warm at last. Busy. I found a pound note screwed up by the rug. So now I could go for supplies.

'But that's not the point,' Mum said. 'I've got a bit of money. There's money in my purse and money in the teapot.'

'But we should get some fresh things. Fresh air.'

'Can't we just open a window?'

'I could get some bread.'

'Bread? We can do without a loaf.'

'Well I . . .'

'Oh, all right then,' she said. 'But you'd better have a wash and change your trousers. I don't want people saying you're being neglected.'

Just stepping outside made me shudder. It felt huge out there, and dangerous. The world kind of tipped and the pavements were warm. I could feel them through my gym shoes.

An ice-cream van was parked at the top of the street and three little girls were staring at the pictures of Orange Maids, whipped-up cornets and Raspberry Splits; their eyes bulging, their money jangling in their tiny screwed-up hands.

My mouth was watering. I could taste that Mr Whippy, but I walked with my head down. Quick long strides. I couldn't see anyone. I couldn't talk. How could I talk about this? Every so often I'd take a look over my shoulder. What if Dad was around? Sitting in his Minx? Watching me?

I went into a shop I didn't know. Bread, milk, potatoes. I bought Mum a magazine with How To Feel Happy on the cover, and a packet of ten Regal. I was nervous, but the woman didn't mind. The shop was closing down. Most of the shelves were empty.

'Weather nice,' said the woman, counting out my change.

'Yes.'

'The sun makes people smile. Don't you think so?'

I nodded. The beads on her sari sparkled and her arms were rattling with a hundred yellow bracelets.

'So? Tell me. Aren't you going to smile? Don't you like the sunshine?'

'Yes,' I said. 'It's nice.'

The woman giggled as her friend came into the shop. 'Asha.'

'Nisha.' They started chatting, and on my way out a perfumed hand brushed flat against my hair.

'Nice boy,' she said. 'Smile.'

I blushed. I could still hear their voices behind the closed glass door. Chatting. Laughing. Why didn't Mum have friends like that? She could be sitting with them now. Smoking. Drinking. Moaning about men. But the women Mum knew were all a part of Dad. The girls he'd worked with. Clients. The couples that he knew from the clubs. Mum hadn't bothered with her own. These were hers now. 'Why should I?' she'd said. 'We've plenty of friends. And there's always something going on for us, somewhere if we want it.'

I swung the plastic bag between my fingers. In and out, in and out. *Slap.* The sun made me squint, but I saw it straight away. Pink chalk. Big letters. I stopped. How could I have missed it? How long had it been there, down by the side of the door? Days? Hours? Minutes? Quickly I began to rub it off. My hands were turning pink. Sore. The shopping all over the pavement.

In fat, smudged writing, some joker had written: Elvis Has Just Left The Building.

'WAY BACK THEN, BEFORE WE EVEN THOUGHT OF HAVING you,' Mum said. 'It seemed like we were happy all the time.'

'So I spoilt it.'

'No.'

'What then?'

'We were young. We had no worries. Nothing very serious.' Mum was downstairs. She had a dress on under her dressing gown and brand-new tights. Her eyes looked better. They weren't quite as swollen and the red was fading into a blotchy kind of white. 'All we did was go out to work, dreaming of the night time. The dances. The pictures. Pubs. We loved going out. Nothing mattered. We'd have nothing, but when we did have a bit, we'd spend it all on records. Lipstick. Daft things. And everyone had a job back then. It's true what they say. You could walk out of your job in the morning and be doing something else before dinner.'

'So what did you do?'

'Well, nothing clever,' she sniffed. 'Not like our Claudine with her books and her waitressing job in the evenings. I sewed sheets. Pillowcases. Towels. It wasn't bad. It was easy enough, though my little arms ached day and night. God, did they ache,' she rubbed at them, remembering. 'The girls were nice though. You remember Sandra? And we did have a laugh.'

And I could imagine it. I'd seen what she'd looked like back then. Small, of course, and young. She'd worn high heels and she'd combed up her hair. 'Oh, anything to make me look taller.' And she'd worn those little tight dresses that were so puffed out from the waist, you'd think she'd topple over, or fly, if a sharp gust of wind came and hit her.

'Those were the days,' she said as she sat and shuffled the bills about. She'd found them in the knife and fork drawer. Manila. Red ink. Most of them final demands. But she'd laughed. 'What were you trying to do?' She'd said. 'Have us cut off? We'd be sitting in the dark and freezing cold. And have you seen what they charge, just for reconnection?'

After a very small brandy, for Dutch, she phoned up the gas and electric. Afterwards, she looked flushed, relieved, almost happy.

'We'll be okay,' she said. 'They've put us on a scheme. And if that doesn't work, Mike says we can always have a meter.'

'Mike?'

'The electric man.'

'Will we have to move?'

'No chance,' said Mum. 'Wherever your dad's buggered off to, he still has obligations.'

She limped to put a record on, but after the first few bars, she went and lifted the needle.

'He's everywhere,' she said. 'God. Even Alma knows.'

BUT IT WASN'T MY FAULT. WAS IT? WOULDN'T HE HAVE gone and done it anyway? Mum said yes, but I wasn't all that sure. I'd seen his excitement. 'He said I was a genuine new talent!' His eyes had lit up. Dad had never been happier. He wouldn't be hitting her, happy.

I SAT ON THE BACK STEP. THE SKY WAS FADING ORANGE. Violet. A line of small black birds were moving round in circles. It was warm. Next door had their gate pushed open and a Murphy boy was crying.

'But I wanted a Raleigh. Not just a bike. A gold one. A Raleigh. Four-speed. I thought I was getting a Raleigh.'

The sobs turned into shuffles, the sound of a bike being pushed, then, 'Look what you've done. Sean! Look what you've done to my bike!'

I still couldn't ride a bike. When I was seven my dad had come home with a bike he'd found in Willie's Canny Junk Shop. It was pink. How could I ride a bright pink bike? Even at seven, I just wouldn't get on it.

'It's only a colour. Get on,' he ordered.

'But it's pink.'

'It's a bike. It works. Get on.'

By then, the backstreet was full of kids hanging round. Having a look. Listening. 'Can't we just wait till it's painted?'

'Painted? I'm not painting it. Look. It's almost brand new. There's hardly a bloody scratch on it.'

I looked even closer. The seat had flowers on it, faded, but there. More pink. The logo was a doll, smiling up at me.

'I can't ride a bike anyway,' I swallowed. 'Not a two-wheeler.' Behind us, boys were sniggering, hitching up their jeans.

'Shit, Jack, I know you can't ride a bike. That's why I'm here, dummy. I'll hold you on for a bit. We'll soon have you whizzing round the block.'

'But I can't.'

His face was getting redder. He started jabbing me. 'I know you can't. Yet.'

'But there aren't any stabilisers.'

I could feel myself trembling. My face. Lips. I could feel the tears at the back of my eyes, burning to get out.

'Stabilisers? You don't need stabilisers. You've got me. I'm here to hold you up. Get on. What are you doing?' he hissed. 'You're fucking showing me up.'

So I had to get on. The bike had felt too big and stuck between the cobbles. Why couldn't we go on the pavement? It moved from side to side whenever I lifted my feet. I'd never be able to do it. Not without stabilisers. Not like this, with everybody watching.

'I like your little bell,' a boy called out.

Dad turned. 'Shut it, wise guy.'

He was holding on to my waist. Squeezing. Hard. I was trying not to cry. I could already feel those cobbles. Taste them. I knew I was going to fall.

'What are you doing, Jack?' he shouted, giving me a push. 'Head up. Head up. Look where you're going! Steering! Use your eyes! You have to bloody steer the thing!'

He let go. I fell.

'Get back on, soft lad. And don't start blubbing cos you've had a little fall.'

I got on. He let go. I fell.

'Now you're not even trying!'

My teeth were chattering. I didn't look down at my knees. I could feel the blood oozing. The grit was sticking in my pants.

'On.'

My hands were sore. Scraped. The kids were just a blur.

Laughing faces. The tears were streaming down and blocking up my nose. I just couldn't stop them.

'*On.*'

I got on. He let go. I fell.

'On. Try. On.'

'But I can't.' My chin felt smashed. I could taste blood at the back of my throat.

'Of course you can. Don't act wet. Everybody can ride a bike. Even a fucking three-year-old can do it.'

'But—' my teeth were chattering. I'd really had enough.

'On.'

I just looked at him.

'Get on, Jack, and stop being such a quitter.'

'No.' I was choking now, as quietly as I could, but he slapped me. I could see all the hard boys, staring at their boots.

'Get on. Do it. Do something useful. Learn to ride a fucking bike.'

'But I don't want to, Dad. Not today. Not really. Please?' I felt terrible. I felt so bad I didn't care what I said. Suddenly, he turned, pushing the bike with his foot, smashing it down and the bell rang, *tring*. Someone gave a nervous giggle.

'You are a fucking ungrateful bastard,' he spat. 'I get you a bike. Hell, I went and paid good money for that bike. Shit, Jack. Now who wants a bike?' he asked. 'If you want a free bike, just take it, because soft lad here can't cope.'

No one moved. The bike just lay there, pink on the cobbles, the doll smiling up with its red cupid lips. Dad strode off, kicking anything. He slammed and splintered the gate. My clothes were torn. I was wrecked. But what should I do with the bike? Should I leave it? Would he change his mind if someone else went and took it?

I looked up. No one seemed interested. I tried to lift it. My hands were ripped, shaking, the bike weighed a ton and it kept slipping out of my hands.

So I left it.

Inside, Mum patched me up and gave me strawberry Angel Delight. We watched cartoons. Dad had already gone out.

'It's only a bike,' she'd whispered. 'It's not the end of the world.'

When he came back from the pub I was crouched in my pyjamas, my legs and elbows full of plasters and soft yellow lint. He said, 'So, where is it then?'

'What?' But I knew straight away what he meant.

'The bike. Where did you put the bike?'

I looked at Mum. 'I left it.'

'Left it? Well, go and get it back again. You might not want it, but I can sell it to that Jim from down the pub. I might as well make a few bob back if I can.'

'But you said—'

'Just go and get it, Jack, and stop all this arsing about.'

It was getting dark. I felt small in my pyjamas. I could see Mum in the kitchen doorway, waiting in the light.

The street was empty. The cobbles brown, like little loaves of bread. They glistened. Someone had written Paki on Mrs Chattejee's gate. I liked saying that word. Chatterjee. Chatterjee. Chatterjee. I looked up and down, but of course the bike had gone. It was bound to go. Kids always wanted bikes, pink, black or rusting, a bike was a bike, especially if it was free, and you could ride it.

I went back in. Mum kissed the top of my head.

'Don't worry,' she whispered. 'I'll tell him. I'll see to it. You just go to bed. Go on now, quick. It's really getting late.'

Lying in the dark, I could hear them. The door slamming. Tears. Somebody said they were leaving. They might. It was all my fault again.

'How do I look?'

She gave a little twirl, trying not to grimace.

'You look fine,' I said. 'Normal. Nice. You look better with the make-up.'

'Honest?'

'Honest.'

'So, what was it you told him?'

'I can't remember.'

'Great.'

'I just said you were ill, that's all. I didn't go into the details.'

'Okay, okay. I'll make something up on the bus. Something gynaecological. That should shut him up.'

She was on her way into work. She said she felt up to facing the world. The catalogue man had been.

'Why did I buy that coat?' she said. 'I didn't even need another coat.'

I walked her to the bus stop. We kept stopping by shop windows. She looked nervous, but whenever someone passed, she gave them a little nod and a smile, whether we knew them or not.

'Well, you never know,' she said. 'Your dad might have his spies out.'

SEAN WAS ON THE STEP WHEN I GOT BACK, WAITING IN THE sun. He got up when he saw me, brushing down his jeans.

'You all right then?'

'Yes.'

'You got my note?'

'Yes. Thanks.'

'Your mam's gone back to work then?'

I nodded.

'My mam wants a job. She says she's bored of being a housewife. She says all that work for nothing.'

'Right.'

'My dad's not keen.'

'No?'

'He'll take some bloody persuading. Do you want to come in for a drink?'

His mum was at the market buying T-shirts. His brothers were at school.

'Orange? Tea?'

'All right.'

He put the kettle on. Their house was like ours, but the other way around. It seemed smaller, full of things. Dark wood furniture. Knick-knacks. Running trophies. There were pictures all over the walls and in cases. I stood awkwardly looking at the photographs. Sean and his brothers. Little baby Niamh, tiny and pale on a shawl.

'I've never seen so many photos.'

There were people that looked the same as Sean but they were wide, with older faces. A line of six children. A woman with red springy hair.

'That's my auntie Jo. Mam's sister, Josephine. She's a nun now. Sister Seraphina. She lives in New York.'

'Wow.' I didn't know they sent nuns to America.

'Mam says she's just minutes away from the Chrysler Building.'

'Right.' I didn't know what the Chrysler Building was exactly, but it sounded great. It sounded like the place where they made all the cars.

'You haven't been out much then?' He handed me a mug. It had Taurus on the front. A gold puffing bull in the lines of constellation.

'Not really. You see, Dad went and left and I couldn't leave Mum on her own.' I burnt, looking down at my hands. Well, I'd said it now.

'No way. When Roddy Simpson's dad went and left home for the third year in a row, Roddy did a bunk. He ended up in a dosshouse in Fleetwood. His mam had a breakdown. She was bad for ages. You can't leave your mam on her own.'

'No.'

'Right. I wouldn't.'

'No.'

We sat and looked into our teas. A fly was buzzing round the window. A bluebottle. It landed in the sugar bowl.

'So, do you want to do something now?' he asked, flicking it away. 'Now she's back at work and everything?'

'I don't know. Like what?'

'We could plan that trip.'

'What trip?'

'Winter Hill. Remember?'

'Oh yes,' I smiled. 'You and that Stacey-Ann Maguire. Have you got any further? You know.'

'Well, I sent her a postcard,' he said. 'But I haven't heard back. Not yet.'

We walked to the small branch library. The sun burnt our cheekbones. Sean wore his John Lennon sunglasses.

'We'll plan our route,' he said. 'The shortest way, of course. We're not bloody going for the walk.'

It felt strange being outside, just walking without Mum. I saw Mrs North from the butcher's. She smiled and gave me a nod, and I wondered if she knew, because she'd never nodded before, even when I was buying pork chops for my dad and asking for the kidney. We walked past the club. We had to. I tried not to look, but I went and turned round in the end. There were cars in the car park. An old fish and chip van with the paint peeling off. A smiling purple haddock.

'Greasy Bert's,' said Sean. 'He parks it all over. He lives in it. Well, he used to. Mam says his wife died in that van, from the oil fumes.'

But I wasn't bothered about Greasy Bert and his wife. I wanted to look behind it. I stood on a couple of bricks. The poster was still there, stuck inside a window. *Tonite at 8.30!* But it

was an old one. Next Saturday a woman was on. A singer called
Sammy-Lou Evans.

'Sammy-Lou Evans?' said Sean. 'Well, she looks like a bit of all
right. Are you sure she isn't a stripper?'

'WE'LL NEED TO CHECK ALL THE WEATHER REPORTS,' SAID
Sean, looking brainy over his sunglasses. They had pink mirror
lenses and I could see myself in them. My face looked squashed,
like a bubble. 'I'll ring Sky-Line. I won't tell Mam. I think it costs
a fortune. I'll do it when she's out.'

The library was nearly empty. In a chair across from us, a
woman was talking to herself, studying a knitting pattern,
shaking. 'Knit one, pearl one, knit one, slip.' She was doing all
the actions with her invisible needles. We were trying not to
laugh.

Sean spread the Ordnance Survey map across the table. It was
full of rips, coffee rings and dirty strips of Sellotape.

'Right. Does this make sense, to you?'

We stared at it. We found plenty of picnic spots. Belmont
Reservoir, and a disused pit (or quarry). We found Winter Hill,
eventually, but we couldn't see how to get up it.

'I can't tell which way would be the quickest,' said Sean. 'Can
you?' The hill looked tiny on the map, with its squiggly orange
lines. It didn't look high at all.

'We could ask Stuart,' I said. 'He came fifth in Geography.'

'We could ask him,' said Sean. 'But Fat Boy Stuart wouldn't
actually make it to the top. Knowing our luck, he'd be D.O.A.'

'What?'

'Dead On Arrival. I saw it on *Angels* last week. My dad fancies
one of the nurses.'

'DO YOU KNOW WHERE HE IS THEN?' SEAN ASKED. 'DID
that agent like him?'

'I don't know.'

'Our Michael said he saw him on Friday.'

'Where?'

'In town. Coming out of Marks & Spencer's.'

'No way.' Dad would never go shopping. And not in Marks & Spencer. He thought it was a rip-off. 'Cheap stuff made to look fancy.' Mum liked walking round, touching things. 'Feel that,' she'd say, handing me a kid's woolly cardigan. 'Go on. Feel how soft. Lamb's wool. And no irritation.' She never bought anything. She said she wouldn't dare.

Sean sniffed. 'That's what we said. We all said he was a liar.'

'Well I . . .'

'Oh, he's always making things up. He does it all the time. I told him that your dad would be miles away by now. Manchester. London. That's where all the big singers end up. They don't end up round here.'

I squeezed my library books into my chest. They were heavy. Hard covers.

'Did you hear him?' I asked. 'Did you hear him go?'

'Yes. We all heard him. Bleeding hell, Jack. You can't hide that with a wall.'

The sun was so bright that you couldn't see its shape. Flat white heat and haze. Sean bought a *Star Trek* comic, and we read it, sitting on our piles of library books in a dusty square of shade.

I was late getting back. Mum would be home from her first half-day at the office. So what had she told them? Had they all noticed that she couldn't quite lift her arm without screwing her eyes up first?

I stopped outside. You could still see the ghost of the chalk on the wall. Mr Gentleman's car was waiting. His shiny red Midget.

'I got a lift,' said Mum.

They were drinking tea from the remains of our best rosebud tea set. Mr Gentleman turned round. He was a blob of brown tweed with a cigar in his mouth.

'And that's not all,' he smiled. His face was red. The ripples on his forehead were moving up and down. 'Tell him, Evelyn. Tell the boy what I've done.'

I stood back. What had he done? Don't tell me that she'd already found Dad's new replacement? I could almost hear her. '*At least the money will be steady,*' she'd say. '*Forget what he looks like. Just think of our station in life!*'

'What's that?'

'I've got extra hours,' she beamed. 'I'll be nearly full-time.'

I couldn't help smiling. 'Great.'

'Well . . .' he flicked his chubby hand about. 'When you're in my position, it's always nice to be able to help out. And your mother's good. She makes people feel at their ease. She's a marvel. A wonder with the divorcees. The women can get a bit tearful. You know . . .' He coughed, embarrassed. He knew then? And now he'd put his foot in it. His brown shiny lace-up. His old man's shoe. But it was his line of business after all. Maybe we'd get a discount if it came to it? But I still couldn't imagine no Dad around, no Mystery Trains, and Mum on her own without her glittery wedding band.

As soon as he'd gone, she went to put a record on.

'You've cheered up a bit.'

'Well, there's no point in moping. And with all those extra hours I can start to feel useful again and pay off a few of my debts.' The record started. Alma. She moved her waist a bit, then stopped. 'Mind you,' she said. 'I still couldn't stomach "Delilah".'

I sat in the bath with my library books. The block of soap had stained my skin bright green. It made my eyes sting. You were supposed to wash clothes with it. Scrape it over collars and trails of sweaty grime. Mum always forgot there were two kinds of Fairy, and the darkest, which was the cheapest, wasn't for skin.

I was reading about Leo in *Astrology and the Universe.* My birthday was 21 August, so I only just made it. I felt nothing like a Leo. Confident. Impulsive. Influential. Apparently, William

Gillette was a Leo. Who? William Gillette. American actor. Portrayer of Sherlock Holmes. The book was getting damp. My birthstone was a peridot.

Downstairs, Mum was on the phone to France. She was sat with the egg timer and three minutes' worth of sand. I could hear her.

'We're fine. Great. No, no, nothing's wrong at all.'

I sank lower into the water. My chest was getting cold.

Throwing the book on to a dry bit of mat, I looked at all the clutter and the cracked white tiles. Damp spots. Mould. A collapsing box of razors.

'I still haven't heard from Claudine. No. Not since we left them at the airport. Well, they didn't want a lift.'

Claudine lived in luxury. She wouldn't dip her big toe in a bath like this. She'd have a walk-in shower. Fluffy white towels. Yucca plants.

'Jack says they've moved. But they can't have moved. Can they? Well, I haven't got their new number.'

Piled up by the bath, the books were running with steam. You could write your name in them, the letters running rivers.

'They'll let us know eventually,' said Mum. 'Oh, you know what they're like.'

I clambered out, freezing. I found Dad's dressing gown on the back of the door. It was cold, creased, silky. It didn't actually warm you. There was a fag end in the pocket and a dirty blue comb.

'Is there any gas at all?' Mum was saying.

Sitting hard against the bath, I could feel the lost heat as it poured from the top of the water. It gurgled. Downstairs, Mum was still talking. 'And I always thought they, oh, well, bye then, bye now. Goodbye Mum. Take care then. I will. Bye now, Mum, I will.'

She was sniffing. The sand had gone. I tried sniffing with her, but I was too busy thinking about supper, and how she'd promised us pizza and chips to celebrate her extra working hours.

'We'll get them from Rocco's,' she'd said. 'But we won't go mad.'

GRANDMA TRENCH WAS ILL. SISTER ELIZABETH HAD called. She said they'd had the doctor in. 'Twice. And he's talking about hospital.'

'Well, we'll have to go,' said Mum.

'But . . .'

'But nothing. She's old. She has no one else. And you just leave the talking up to me.'

We walked to save the bus fare.

'But it's miles.'

'Rubbish. We'll have a bit of a sit-down. You can take a can of Tizer or something. We'll get ourselves a suntan.'

Mum looked nice in the new summer dress that she'd bought from Mr Patel. 'I know we're stony broke,' she'd said. 'But you can't go around looking like you are.'

The dress was halter-neck. You could see red lines where her bra had dug into her shoulders. She jiggled a bit.

'Do I need a bra or not? I should have bought one of those combination thingies,' she said, 'with three kinds of straps, but they aren't cheap, and I haven't got much of a chest to start faffing with.'

It was hot again. Springtime Scorcher! Dad's still-delivered *Sun* was full of women on beaches in tiny micro bikinis. A film star had fainted in the lobby of the Hilton. She was snapped face down, showing long shapely legs and a glimpse of frilly knickers.

'The heat hit me, pow!' she'd told their ace reporter. 'And I just blacked out after that.'

We walked in silence, watching people. Girls pulled at their clothes and their mums made fans out of brown paper bags. On street corners, men sold water pistols, visors, and fans that buzzed like little plastic aeroplanes.

We were aching. Roasting. Baked.

'My God, I'm going to think about ice,' said Mum. 'I'm going to picture the bloody North Pole.'

Halfway there we sat on a bench, surrounded by dog shit and litter. Mum lit a cigarette to ward off the smell.

'I know he's gone,' she said, circling her fag end. 'But I don't exactly feel single.'

'You're better off without him.'

'Am I?'

'Yes.'

'I don't know,' she said, fiddling with her fringe. 'I'm useless on my own.'

SS PETER AND PAUL'S GLOWED WHITE AT THE BOTTOM OF the hill. There were chairs across the lawn, and in the shade care assistants sat holding crooked hands and white plastic beakers.

'Tea, love?' But the old women weren't looking. They had their heads down. They were wearing giant sun hats and woolly winter slippers.

'Come on, Lil,' said one. 'You don't want to go inside. You want to make the most of it.'

'It's waspy.'

'It's not.'

'I can hear them.'

'Well, I'll bat them away then. Look.'

'I want to go in,' she said. 'I hate sitting out, on show.'

We waited by the desk, with its red silk roses and the statuette of Our Lady. I picked Our Lady up. The face was smudged pink plastic and her eyes were different colours. When I put her down, the statuette swayed from side to side. I suddenly felt nervous.

'Maybe Dad knows all about it,' I said. 'He might have been already, on his own.'

Mum didn't say anything; she just arched her eyebrows, mouthing a silent *as if.*

'Well, you've missed him.' Sister Elizabeth sailed towards us. She was holding a bottle of sun cream as if it was something nasty.

We turned our heads.

'Who?'

'The doctor. Doctor Leonard. I think he wants a chat.'

'*Oh?*' Mum breathed. She looked relieved. Then she blushed even redder. 'I'm sorry we're on the late side. You see, we walked it, and we didn't think it would take us quite this long.' Her voice sounded posh. 'We did it for the exercise.'

Sister Elizabeth looked at us. We were sweating. Dripping. We looked like we might just collapse.

'Well, you can go on up,' she said, wiping her hands on a tissue. 'But don't expect miracles.'

The room looked different. She had the curtains closed and the telly wasn't on.

'Is that you?' Her face was turned to the side. The bed sounded crackly when she moved.

'It's us,' said Mum. 'It's Evie and Jack.'

'And here's me expecting Des O'Connor.'

We didn't go right in at first. There was a smell. We hovered by the bed end, wondering what to do.

'I'm on new tablets,' said Grandma. 'They make everything taste like metal.'

We sat and watched her lying there. Her eyes started watering and Mum wiped the tears with a hankie.

'I'm not crying,' she said. 'Don't think that I'm crying. It's water.'

'Are you feeling any better?'

'They all say that I am. But I'm not.'

The room looked eerie in the half light. The sun made strange pink shadows on the walls that moved up and down, rippling over faces in the photographs.

'I won't ask,' said Grandma.

'Ask what?'

'If my Joey's with you. Because I know very well that he won't be.'

'No. Well. You know what he's like, he's just busy.'

'He's a good boy. I know that he'd come if he could. He'd be here.'

'Yes.'

'What about you? Don't you have a job to go to then?'

Mum swallowed.

'She's just been given promotion.'

'Well, not exactly promotion . . .'

'Are you still behind that desk?'

'She's the receptionist,' I told her. 'She greets all the clients.'

'Greets? I thought so. That's a woman's job, greeting. You wouldn't get a man standing behind a desk, answering the telephone, saying nice hellos to strangers.' She closed her eyes, but the tears still ran out and dripped down the side of her cheeks. Mum tried to catch them, but she moved her face away.

'I'm all right,' she muttered. 'Just leave me.'

Across the drawers, where she kept all her nighties and the alpaca coat that she came in, there were new packets of tablets, prescriptions and some deathly-looking prayer cards.

'What have they told you?' she asked. 'Because they're all telling me that it's nothing.'

Mum moved closer. 'They say it's an infection and it's spread a bit, that's all. But that's what the tablets are for. Antibiotics will see it off. You'll soon be back to normal.'

'Will I?'

'Yes.'

'I don't want to go into no hospital.'

'Why not? It's the best place to be when you're ill. They know what they're doing. They have all the proper equipment.'

'They're all posh in hospital. And the doctors think that they're film stars.'

Mum looked at me. We didn't know what to say. The room was like a fish tank.

'Look at you. What are you wearing?' said Grandma. 'I can just about see. What is it? Are you showing off all your shoulders?'

'Yes. It's a halter-neck dress.'

'You want to be careful, at your age.'

Her voice was like a cackle. I sat on my hands.

'You're still skinny then?' she said. 'You always were a rake. Do you eat?'

'Yes. Of course I eat,' said Mum.

'We're on summer food. We had shrimp cream cheese last night.'

I stared down at the floor, with its thin grey carpet. There was a small dark stain and a red boiled sweet in its see-through Cellophane wrapper.

'Hospital. When I was young, hospitals were always the last resort. Myrtle died in hospital, when she should have been at home.'

'Well—'

'What would you know? It was terrible. And not because she was dying, though that was bad enough, but because they treated us like children. Like nothing. They told us where to stand. What to say. And they made us go home when the doctor did his rounds because they said we were in the way and we made the place look messy. Myrtle felt lost and she slipped away without us. But that's what it was all about back then.'

'Yes.'

'Is it still the same? Do you have to be tucked in a certain way before the doctor will give you a glance?'

'Oh,' said Mum. 'I doubt it.'

'Connie could have married a doctor.'

'Connie?'

'Arthur's Connie.'

'Oh?'

'She could have married a doctor, but she went and fell in love with that queer-looking waiter and she pined all through the fifties.'

'I didn't know Connie,' said Mum.

The room went dark for a second. The sun had gone in. Grandma closed her eyes.

'When my Joey gets home, tell him to send me a kiss. He doesn't have to come. He could send it through the air. He'll know,' she blew gently through her lips. 'He'll know what I mean,' she said.

'I WISH WE COULD TELL YOUR DAD. I WISH I KNEW WHERE he was. God.' She quickly lit a fag, sucking it in, as if it was doing her good. 'He could be anywhere now. He could be on that bloody cruise ship on his way to South America.'

'I doubt it.'

'Well, you never know with him,' she said. 'He can talk his way into these places. He has charm. He has the gift of the gab.'

We started walking back. It was all uphill. We went past The Victory, and Mum got a wolf whistle, craning her neck, to see if Dad was there.

'It's nothing,' she blushed. 'It's just this halter-neck.'

We walked slowly, shuffling our feet that were swelling in our shoes. My ankles rubbed and the soles were starting to flap. I could see people staring. I looked like a cripple.

'Can't we get the bus?' I said, as one sailed by full of bare-armed passengers, staring through the windows, cool. 'We're at least halfway there. It won't cost much. Not now.'

'No. Come on. We can do it.'

'Can we?'

'Well, we haven't any choice,' she said. 'And I left my purse at home, just so we wouldn't be tempted.'

We dragged ourselves past benches, because we knew that we'd never get up again. In the park, children were chasing butterflies and throwing up a ball.

'Look at them,' said Mum. 'In this heat. I don't know where they get all their energy.'

I didn't know. I was eleven but I felt about eighty.

'Do you think she'll be all right?' I asked. 'Grandma?'

'I don't know, love. I've really no idea.'

'She looks bad.'

'Yes. But have you heard her?'

'Do you think she's going to die?'

'Well,' said Mum. 'She might. She's old. But she's a tough one, Jack. And we've said all this before. A couple of years ago. There was a cold snap. She had that really bad flu.'

'Yes. I know. Dad gave us the money to light her a candle.'

'You remember that?' she said.

By the time we got home, we were dehydrated, collapsing. We had red and white stripes where our clothes touched our skin.

'Do you think he's somewhere hot?' Mum asked, rolling her lemonade glass on her forehead. 'Is Las Vegas in the desert?'

I looked behind the door. The letter bulged in my anorak pocket.

'It's hot everywhere,' I told her. 'It said so, on the news.'

She fell asleep, streaked in ancient After-Sun, her eyelids going mad, dreaming, muttering, 'I'll get it! I'll get it! My turn!' I didn't want to wake her. She was probably in a bar somewhere, having a brilliant time.

On the mantelpiece there was a new pile of bills – 'where did that lot spring from?' – and a note from the newsagent's in angry red Biro. No More Papers Until You've Paid Us For The Last Lot.

Dad had left in a hurry, but he'd taken his account number,

and the TSB bank book that we'd used for all the bills. The account was in his name, so we couldn't touch a penny. We were living off Mum's tiny wage, Family Allowance, and the bit that she'd stuffed in the teapot.

She'd tried to cancel Rhyl.

'It'd be great if we could get the money back,' she'd said. 'Or even half the bloody money back.'

'Oh, I'm sorry,' said the voice. 'But it's all there in the small print. No refunds. No selling the rooms on to anyone else. Personally, I wouldn't mind. It makes no difference to me who comes down for their toast in the mornings. As long as they're decent and leave the place tidy. But the association has its rules, and I don't want to get into any trouble.'

'Well, that's bloody that then,' said Mum, grinding out her fag. 'No money back. No holiday.'

'Why can't we just go away?'

'Because we can't afford the transport, not to mention all the extras.'

I thought about it. The journey. The first time we'd gone down in the heat of a blue-skied August. We'd chugged our way down there. We'd made slow progress. We'd had to keep stopping because the boot kept springing open, showing off our three tatty suitcases (two for clothes, one for food). 'I don't care what they say,' Dad had snorted. 'The grub's always cheaper in England.'

The sun had scorched through the glass. Mum had her window open. Both mine in the back had jammed.

'I know you're hot,' Dad said. 'Just take your bloody T-shirt off.'

But I didn't. I just sat there sweating, my knees sticking to the smooth, cracked vinyl as I slid from window to window.

'This is the life,' said Mum. 'Sun. Sea. And no getting up in the morning.'

Dad winked and grinned. He sang 'Summer Holiday'.

'Summertime Blues' (twice). He sang 'The Banana Boat Song', and Mum tried joining in, but she didn't know the words and her voice trailed off in a whine. Dad drummed on the steering wheel, posing through the mirror.

'Here's looking at you, kid!' He chewed through the side of his mouth. Fag flopping over. Ash dropping down on his beige summer pants.

We were the slowest in the slow lane.

'Oh, they might be whizzing past, in their flashy Ford Cortinas,' he said. 'But our little Minx here is a classic.'

'Yes, love.' Mum was rooting through her bag of bullet-hard mint imperials, while we were suddenly overtaken by an elderly couple in a patched white Zephyr. 'It's better to be careful.'

By the time we'd stopped, near Chester, the boot had opened nine times, the car had ground to a halt – 'it just needs a little cool down' – and a tiny flying stone had cracked the side of the windscreen.

'That's nothing,' Dad said. 'It's a scratch. I won't bother claiming for that.'

But we weren't the only ones that year. Cars with steaming bonnets were at every other junction. People got their deck chairs out and made the most of it before the repair man turned up. Children ran up and down the embankments, crying, screaming, laughing.

'They're going to kill themselves,' said Mum. 'They'll end up squashed under something.'

We had our picnic in a lay-by with the car doors wide open. Boiled eggs. Tomatoes. Warm luncheon-meat sandwiches. Whenever a car sidled past, looking for a parking spot, Dad would suddenly belt out 'Halfway To Paradise', making Mum splutter, losing half her tea on the tarmac.

'See him?' Dad pointed to a bald-headed man in a Mini. 'That could be England's Colonel Parker.'

'In a Mini?'

'Well, there's nothing wrong with a Mini. They're sporty. They do bloody rallies in them. Now shut it, titch, and let me concentrate on the directions.' He put his tea on to the dashboard and banged out the map. 'Yes. We're halfway to paradise.'

'We're that close then? Really?'

'That's what I'm telling you, Evie.'

'Well, thank goodness for that,' said Mum, blowing down her dress. 'I'm sticking to this vinyl. It's hard to feel comfortable in this kind of heat.'

We set off again, shooing the flies and the angry-sounding wasp that Dad had been annoying.

'It's going to sting you,' said Mum. 'And I've no TCP in my handbag.'

'That little thing? It's half a bloody sleep. It doesn't stand a chance.' And crunching it down he wiped its dead wings off the side of his hand, leaving a dirty black smear. 'Cheeky little bugger. Well, you're not so cocky now.'

Mum smiled, relieved. The gears stuck. I shivered. The boot flew open. Cars pipped.

'Out!' said Dad. 'Jump to it!'

It was my job to run and slam it down again.

'At least your legs get a bit of a stretch,' said Mum. 'I can hardly feel mine.'

Jumping back in, I looked up at the sky as it faded over buildings. Blue. Light blue. White. Birds looked like seagulls now, and behind Big Bargain Sam's Cut Price Carpet Warehouse, I was sure that I'd caught a glimpse of the sea. It was blinking at me. Surfers. Yachts. A beach the colour of biscuits.

'No, love,' said Mum. 'That was a billboard. It was an advert for Bacardi. We've miles to go yet.'

We passed a broken-down ambulance. The driver was lounging in a wheelchair with his cap tipped over his eyes. Then the boot fell open, a car pipped, and I got out again. There was a slight breeze now. It was warm. Dry. There was salt at the back of my throat. The sea was right at the back of those houses. It had to be. I could see a line of turquoise. I could hear it.

The sign said: Croeso i Rhyl a Phrestatyn!

'Look at that,' Dad grinned. 'I told them all at work I was taking you abroad.'

Mum giggled. 'Well, it does look kind of foreign. What do you think, Jack?'

I'd nodded enthusiastically. My backside was numb. I was burning. I just wanted to be there. To escape. Stuart had said it was easy to escape on your holidays. He'd been to Blackpool for a week. 'I palled up with a lad from Bury,' he'd told me. 'And the only time I saw Mum and Dad was when we were having our breakfast.'

'Now keep your eyes peeled for the Bron-y-Bryn.'

We drove up and down the promenade. White railings. Silver lamp posts. An edge of greeny brown sea.

'We'll take a chance up here,' said Dad. 'This looks a bit like the picture. That one. That one there. Pink curtains. Is that it?'

'No,' said Mum, fanning her face with a leaflet. 'That's the Windsor. And look, Joe, it has its own private cocktail lounge!'

The side streets were the same. Flaking. With painted plaster guesthouses and back-to-back hotels. We couldn't see Kerry Street. Dad had forgotten to ask for directions and he'd refused to call the woman back, saying it couldn't be that bloody hard for him to find.

'It's just off the prom. Turn right, it said in the brochure.'

'I remember that,' said Mum. 'Two minutes away from the sea.'

We circled the roundabout, with its parched red flowers and pebbles, and a man with a radio was lying on its dry yellow lawn.

'Look at him,' said Mum. 'All that beach and he goes and chooses a roundabout.'

'Never mind the scenery,' Dad sweated. 'I said keep your bloody eyes peeled.'

We drove down a dead-end street, full of cardboard boxes and red plastic milk crates. A man in a grubby chef's jacket was leaning against a wall, smoking and reading a paper.

'You could ask him for directions,' I said.

'No way, José. He'll think I'm bloody stupid. We might be next to Kerry Street. We might be bloody on it, and I don't want to be showing myself up.'

'Well, at least we're here,' said Mum.

When we were low on petrol, Dad circled the roundabout with his window rolled down and shouted to the radio man, who was lying with his eyes closed. It took another three circles before we got an answer and a grunt in the right direction.

'Up past the chip shop?' said Dad. 'Left at Jumbo's Ice Creams?'

The man gave the thumbs up and went back to his radio.

'What did I tell you?' said Dad. 'I knew it was past the bloody chip shop.'

'But which chip shop is it?' said Mum.

There was Captain Cod's. Barry's Golden Fish Bar. There was a stripy caravan with a Frying sign, and steam pouring out of its window.

'I think I'll go for the cod,' Dad said. 'It looks more like a shop. If he meant fish bar he'd have said a bloody fish bar.'

'Well, yes,' said Mum, tapping the side of her head. 'But he might not have been all there.'

Dad turned right and we'd given a loud spontaneous cheer at the sight of Jumbo's Ice Creams on the corner, with its pink fibreglass elephant.

'What did I tell you?' he said, spluttering up to the Bron-y-Bryn. 'I knew that we'd have to turn right.'

The sun gives out energy in the forms of light and heat. Without this energy there would be no life on earth.

THE SKY TURNED WHITE, AND ALL ACROSS TOWN PEOPLE WERE
shuffling in the heat, looking upwards, just waiting for the storm
that the weathergirl had promised on the early evening news.

'And she's always right,' Mum said. 'Oh, she never gets it
wrong.'

By late the next morning, the weather had broken, and kids
played outside, hollering in their swimsuits and shorts, running
up and down, dripping in the fast sheets of rain that made rivers
down the tarmac, as the thunder rumbled, and the lightning
cracked in perfect zigzag lines like a Hammer horror film. I
watched it from my window. I could see Mrs Murphy dancing in
the yard, the rain flattening her perm; she was doing the
Charleston, swaying her arms, laughing. Downstairs, Mum was
nervously huddled on the sofa, smoking extra-strength with the
plugs out of everything. As soon as it slackened, the doorbell
rang, and Dad just stood there, dripping.

Mum stepped back, letting the rain drift in. I could see her
head adjusting, as she quickly straightened her hair, kicking her
scruffy red slippers round to the back of the door.

'So, you've found your way back then?' her voice was gentle;
friendly.

'I only knocked out of politeness. I won't be knocking again.'
'No?'
'No.' He came inside and sniffed around a bit. Mum went up

to him for a hug, for something, but he just stood there, so she went and threw a towel at him.

'Where have you been, Joe?' she said, lighting a couple of fags. 'I've been that bloody worried. Honestly.'

'Oh, I've been around and about. Working. Singing. I've packed the wig job in.' He dried himself off. He looked like he'd just stepped out of the bath.

Mum turned the fire up, tidying bits and pieces, folding up the towel. It was as if she couldn't keep still, and Dad looked enormous, strange, just standing there.

'You've packed it in then? Well, that's great,' she said. 'It's what you've always wanted.'

'I just did a runner, so no bonus there.'

'That's a shame.'

They sat and looked at each other. Dad kept cracking his knuckles and messing about with his teeth.

'Aren't you going to welcome me home then, Jacky boy?'

'You've come back then?'

'Well, it's my bloody house, isn't it?'

'Of course it is,' said Mum.

'And I thought I'd be doing you a favour.'

'You did?'

'Yes. I know what it's like with the housing people. All those bloody waiting lists. I thought I'd let you stop here,' he said. 'You can be my lodger.'

'What?'

'You heard. You can move into the spare room. I've got it all planned. You can pay me reduced rent if you keep up with the housework.'

It was like I hadn't heard it at first, but as soon as I looked at Mum's face I could feel an invisible fist deep inside my belly. I swallowed and slipped behind the door. I sat on the floor, hugging my knees in a bit of wet draught. I could hear them going on.

'But I thought you'd come back. Properly. You know.' She was cracked with disappointment. She didn't care what Dad did, because they were only one-offs, and they did have a laugh. She was always wanting him back.

'What do I know?'

'I've been thinking, Joe. I've missed you. I've missed you such a lot. We could start again. Couldn't we? After all these years, it'd be a shame just to chuck it all away.'

'You sound like Mills and Boon.'

'I mean it.'

'So do I.'

'But I love you. I'm well, I'm here. I'm your wife.'

'Wife? Wife? Don't make me laugh. You don't know how to be a bloody wife, Evelyn. I've had more support from total bloody strangers than I have had from you.'

'I'm always here for you. I want to be.'

He laughed. 'It's too late. Way too late. I'd just about had it when that phone sitting there got the pull.'

'It was me,' I said, jumping up. 'I unplugged the phone. I didn't mean it. I didn't do it so you wouldn't get the job. It was when Mr Gentleman rang and he was going on and on, and he said he'd ring back. I just forgot to plug it in again.'

'Jack,' Mum breathed. 'It was you?'

I nodded, holding on to the door handle just so I wouldn't fall down.

'*Jesus.*'

'Sorry. I thought I'd told you.'

'No,' she said. 'You said something or other, but I didn't hear that.'

'Well, there's no need to be sorry, son. It doesn't matter who it was. You did me a favour. I've made my bloody mind up. I've done a lot of thinking myself and that spare room isn't bad. It'll do for you, won't it, Evie? It just needs a bit of a tidy.'

'But. Well, Joe. How's it all going to work?' Her voice was fluttery, but her face just looked defeated.

'Like I said, reduced rent for cleaning, cooking and that. But you'll help me pay the bills just the same, and, of course, I'm not going to bloody pay for the past few weeks because I haven't been here. I've been paying my way somewhere else.'

'Go out, Jack,' said Mum. 'I need to say a few things in private.'

'I'm sorry,' I mumbled. 'About the phone.'

'Don't worry, soft lad. It's the type of thing your mother would do. If you hadn't have done it, she would have done it in a flash. And why was that fancy bastard solicitor ringing you up anyway?'

'I don't really know.'

'Just go,' said Mum. 'Go on.'

I WALKED AROUND FOR AGES. THE RAIN HAD STOPPED AND the pavements were already losing their shine. I dreaded going back. I went down Manor Street and helped push-start a car. Five Asian men with their white gowns flowing, and me. At number twenty-four, there was a sign that said: Edith J. Marshall. Teacher of Elocution and Fine Dramatic Art. What did she mean? That she wouldn't teach you how to act out a part in *Bonanza*? *Coronation Street*? *Star Trek*? Dad said that's where all the money was made. That you could earn a year's wages in a day. An hour. Half a bloody hour. Through the open window I could hear a voice saying, 'Come on now, Veronica, *enunciate*.'

It was early evening when I headed back. The street was full of tangerine light and wet-haired girls with their skipping ropes singing songs about sisters they didn't even have.

I braced myself. Closed my eyes. Swimming breaths.

Normal.

Dad was sprawled with a can of Skol between his knees, conducting *Elvis Live*. His hair was dry and he'd changed into his never-used-for-running shorts. There was a wide pink plaster on his hand.

'Listen to this,' he said. He sounded excited, as if 'Don't Be Cruel' was a brand-new hit record that he'd never heard before. 'It's all in the timing and the interpretation. Oh yes, I've been learning all sorts from the pros.'

'But you're a pro now,' I said. 'Aren't you?'

'I surelybloodyam,' he drawled. 'I'm Joey Seville, on my '79 tour of the nation.'

'So, what happened?' I asked, dropping down beside him.

'I've been doing bits and pieces,' he said. 'Nothing too grand. Like I said, it's getting your foot in the door. Your name around town. People talking.'

'So where?'

'Rotherham.'

'I told her.'

'Halifax. Barnsley. That was a great night that was. I got a standing ovation. They even had a stage.'

'Did you ring that Max?'

'Of course I bloody rang him. I've signed up. I'm with him.'

'So what does he do then?'

'Everything. He sorts me out. He gets me gigs and promotion. He takes ten per cent.'

'But what about Pete?'

'Pete just does the backing. He comes with me now and then. But he's not on the books.'

'Why not?'

'Max only deals with the front men.'

'Oh.'

'So, how's your mother been?'

I looked behind me. 'Awful.'

'She's not had anybody round then? No funny gentlemen callers, if you get my bloody drift?'

I thought about Mr Gentleman, twirling his cigar, his shiny little Midget at the door.

'No,' I said. 'Nothing like that.'

'Not that I'm bothered, good luck to her, though I won't have it going on around here. If she was lodging somewhere else she wouldn't be allowed to have blokes up in her room. Oh, and by the way, son, you won't be paying me. You're rent-free.'

'Thanks.' The word slipped out. It sounded stupid saying thank you for your bedroom.

'Now, can you get us another one of these cans and turn the record over? Just don't bloody touch it with your hands.'

Mum was upstairs, moving dusty cardboard boxes and a suitcase full of clothes that she hadn't worn for years.

'All out of fashion,' she said, holding up a skirt. 'I thought they might have come back, but they didn't.'

She'd been crying but her face looked all right.

'Are you okay?'

'I don't know,' she shrugged. 'But at least I know where I stand. Well, I think I do. I wonder how long he's going to keep this up for? It's freezing in here. The window doesn't shut properly. It's warped. It hasn't been shut for years.'

'You don't have to stay.'

'I know.'

'So?'

'So, will you help me move these boxes? I've got the ladders down from the attic. The Christmas decorations can go up there, and this tree. And now you're here, I might as well put this lot up as well.'

The spare room was tiny. Single-bed size. The wallpaper hadn't been changed since Mum and Dad had moved in on their wedding night. Faded green. Flowers in a basket with occasional speckles of mould.

'I'll be all right in here,' she said. 'Don't you worry about me.

I'm already making plans. I've got big ideas. He's not the only one. He won't even know what's hit him.'

I stood on the ladders, feeding boxes into the hole. It was raining silver lametta.

'It's a long way off,' she said. 'Christmas.'

At teatime, Mum didn't quite know what to do.

'Should I make him something?' she whispered. 'Do you think I should go in and ask?'

'Lodgers don't do meals,' I said.

'But it's your dad.'

'Okay then, I'll ask him.'

We sat in our usual seats watching the local news. A plate of bacon butties each, tomato sauce, dripping.

'That Bob Greaves has changed,' said Dad. 'I've been watching him in black and white for a fortnight. He looks washed out in colour.'

Mum nodded. She still hadn't asked where he'd been, but Dad had come home with his clothes in different carrier bags, and one had said Zizi's Perfumery, in swishy pink writing.

'By the way,' said Mum. 'Your mother's ill.'

'I know my mother's ill.'

'You do?'

'Well, she's in a bloody nursing home, isn't she? Nursing? Nurses. It stands to reason.'

'But it's different, and the doctor's been a few times. She looks bad, Joe. That doctor whatsit said she could do with being in hospital.'

'Then why isn't she?'

'I don't know,' Mum sank back, playing with her crusts. 'She isn't all that keen.'

'She'll be all right. She'll have those flamin' nuns running after her, like headless bloody chickens.'

'I don't know ... '

'They'll see she's all right,' said Dad. 'Now stop bloody fussing and just let me listen to Greavsie.'

'MATTIE'S COMING.'

'Why?'

'He's got the binoculars.'

'And what about Stuart?'

'He's a liability.'

'But it's not that far. It's not an actual mountain.'

'All right, all right,' said Sean. 'Christ, all we need now is a dog and we'll be the bloody Famous Five.'

'So, when are we going?'

'Well, I can't go next week because my uncle Con's coming from London and he'll be taking us out nights and that, and I've not got to make any plans. Dad said he might take us all to the greyhounds. That should be a laugh. He's loaded, our Con. He's got his own dry-cleaners.'

'So when then?'

'A fortnight next Friday? Something like that?'

'A fortnight?' I sank. 'I suppose so.'

'I'll ring the Sky-Line people nearer the time, but I'm sure we'll be okay, now it's summer.'

'What did your mum say about you going up there?'

'She wasn't keen. I told her it was a science project, but she didn't really go for it, not with the school being cinders and all.'

'So?'

'So, I begged her. And I'm washing up all next week. Pans. Cooker. Everything.'

We flicked through the planet guide, *An Introduction to Astronomy*, but somehow it all looked dead in the book. I wasn't that bothered about right ascension, declination, the north celestial pole. I was fed up with reading. I was suffocating. I didn't care what they were, or how they got there. I just wanted to see them. Live.

'Your mam's all right with it? Is she happy now that your dad's turned up again? Has he changed his ways?'

I nodded. 'Something like that.' I could feel my face rush red. How could I tell him that she was just renting out the spare room, and doing all the cleaning?

'So?'

'So, she said I could go.'

'And your dad?'

'He won't even notice that I've gone.'

MUM WAS EATING WHEN I'D ASKED HER, LOOPING HEINZ spaghetti round her fork. Dad was in the bath. He was eating out, 'on the road'. He had a gig in the middle of Stockport.

'We're thinking of going up Winter Hill,' I told her. 'Star gazing.'

'Star gazing? What do you want to do that for?' Her mouth was an O, oozing sloppy orange.

'Because I like it. Well, I think that I do.'

'But you've never liked all that stuff. Have you?'

'Can I?'

'When?'

'I don't know yet.'

'That's handy. Well, who are you going with?'

'Sean and Stuart.' I hadn't mentioned Mattie. Mum still went on about the time he'd been caught sniffing Uhu in the bus-station café.

'What time will all this be going on till?'

'Late. Very late. I'll be out for most of the night.'

'Crikey.' She looked up at me, then sighed into her plate, her shoulders disappearing into the tiny loose sleeves of her dress. 'Oh, I suppose so. Though I don't know what your dad will say. I know you're sensible and at least you get to have a social life. Look at me. Your dad's only been back a couple of days and I'm thinking of being an Avon lady. Then at least I'll get to go out nights.'

'You could go out anyway.'

'Who with? Because it won't be with your dad just yet, that's a cert.'

'I don't know. What about Maureen? Or someone from work?'

'There's no one at work. Not like me. The secretaries keep to themselves. Karen and Christie eat *rolls*, and they're young enough to disco.'

'So are you, I mean, aren't you?' She didn't look great, but I'd seen other women queueing in their mini skirts. Stuart's dad went out. He had a great time.

'Me? You must be joking. Just think what your dad would say. Lodger or no lodger, he wouldn't let me go. Have you seen what they wear? And the music.' She let her fork clatter down by her soggy toast triangles. 'So, I'll be staying in, washing my hair again. Still, I'll get my own way eventually,' she gave a wobbly smile. 'You'll see.'

'So, I can go then?'

'Where?'

'Up Winter Hill?'

'Oh yes,' she'd sighed. 'I suppose so.'

IT WAS LATE AND THE MOON HAD A FACE IN IT OVER MRS Brady's chimney. You could see it. Calm. Peaceful. Smiling. It looked just like a drawing in a nursery-rhyme book.

'Looks dead innocent,' said Sean, 'but that moon could be causing a tidal wave on the other side of the world.'

We were lying side by side on the tarmac. We couldn't see much. It was cloudy. Too light. We were just trying to get in the mood. But I was watching the mauve getting darker and darker. The clouds had a bright silver edge to them. The whole of the sky was swaying.

'We went to the London Planetarium once,' said Sean. 'It was when Mam was expecting our Niamh. We had to stand for ages in the queue, and they were all pissed off with me, because they wanted to go to Madame Tussaud's next door, but I wouldn't let them, and I got to choose because it was the day before my birthday.'

'I'd rather see planets than wax,' I said. 'Any day.'

'I don't know. The planets were great, when we finally got in. But it wasn't the same. It was full of people. Packed. Most of them were there because they'd just seen *Star Wars*. The kids had their lightsabers with them.'

'Crap.'

'Yeah. Total crap. I had one though, but it broke the day after I got it. Our Matthew stuck it up the chimney, said he was making the route clear and safe for bloody Father Christmas.'

'The light-up ones are good,' I said.

'Well. They're okay.'

'Did you see it then?'

'What?'

'*Star Wars*?'

'Yeah. You?'

I shook my head. 'Dad was going to take me,' I said. 'But he didn't in the end.'

'Oh well. May the force be with you. Tussaud's is supposed to be good. They've got everybody in wax, just standing around. Kevin Keegan. Charlie's Angels. They've even got a chamber of horrors with blood and guts. And a fatal car crash.'

'So?'

'So, I wished we'd gone there instead.'

'It can't have been that bad, the London Planetarium. It sounds great.'

'Yes. And they showed it all. Space travel. The life and death of a star. But when our little Niamh died, I heard Mam talking. She said she'd felt like there was something wrong that day when we were queueing. And she hadn't looked well. Dad had to go and ask the ticket man for a drink of water, and they let us all in through the gate.'

'But you said it was her heart. The baby's.'

'Yes.'

'And don't you have to queue up at Tussaud's?'

'True. And that queue went on for ever. People had fishing stools. God. They were queueing before it even opened. At least we had a sit down for the show. At Tussaud's they just make you keep walking.'

We rubbed our eyes. The sky was dark now, but the lights from all the windows fell across the street. You could smell chips. Petrol. Dogs. In someone's back yard something clattered. A bucket. Mrs O'Connor was already pegging out her washing.

'Hand me the pegs, Colin. I don't care how bloody dark it is, I won't have time to do this in the morning. Pick it up. Look what you're doing. Careful. I'm not washing this lot out again.'

'We'll have to take torches,' said Sean, standing by the gate, swaying in his gym shoes. 'Food and supplies and that.'

'Yes.'

'I can borrow my dad's rucksack,' he said. 'It's old but it looks great. It's from the Army Surplus. He used to take it fishing, but he works on Sundays now.'

'What time will we have to set off?'

He looked at his watch, tapping his nail. Calculating.

'Nine-ish? That should give us time to get into position.'

'Do you know where we're going?' I hadn't a clue. Winter Hill always looked miles away, with its tall television masts and its line of winter snow that lasted until April. Whenever we came back from anywhere, we thought we were nearly home when the masts came into view, but then it seemed like ages again, more streets, more roads, more houses.

'Stuart does. He's drawn out the instructions. His uncle goes drinking in the pub out there.'

'There's a pub up Winter Hill?'

'Well, no,' he said. 'It's just near the sign with the arrow.'

THE FIRST NIGHT WITH DAD HADN'T BEEN ALL THAT different, because he'd just passed out in the armchair, and Mum had said she was glad she didn't have to put up with his beer breath and the death-rattle snores that kept stopping and starting, just to fool you; but now it was well past two o'clock, and he still wasn't back home from Stockport.

'He's got himself a woman,' said Mum. 'That's what it is. God, I hope he doesn't bring her back here. Imagine. I'd die, I would, I'd die. Jack?'

'What?'

'He wouldn't do that to me, would he?'

I was sat on her bed in the spare room, waiting for the sound of his car. Anything.

'It must be a woman,' she said. 'Has to be. What would he be doing buying things from Zizi's fancy perfume store?'

'Aftershave?'

'He has aftershave coming out of his ears.'

'He might not have bought anything. He might just have found it.'

'I don't know. He looked like he was flaunting it. Did you see the way he threw it down, so we could read what it said on the front?'

'It's just a carrier bag, Mum.'

'Yes. And I'm sleeping in the spare room.'

She lit another fag and I sat and held the ashtray. She'd refused to put the light on, because it would look like we'd been waiting.'

'This is worse than him being away,' she said. 'It's a thousand times worse. I don't know how I'll manage.'

I nodded in the dark. I knew what she meant. We'd be miles better off, knowing nothing.

'Listen to us,' she said, suddenly sitting straighter. 'Here we are, calling him blind. We don't know what might have happened. Anything could have happened. You know what he's like. He's probably lost. What if he's stuck somewhere, driving round all night in the middle of nowhere? What if the car's packed up on him? We didn't pay the AA. We haven't done for years. We just kept the badge. He might have had an accident. We should be phoning round the hospitals. What do you think?'

'He'll be all right.'

'Yes,' she said, as she hunched into the blankets. 'I think you're probably right.'

We lay there. I kept rolling near to the edge, putting my foot down on the carpet, just to stop myself from falling. I was lying sideways now, right at the end of the bed. I couldn't feel her feet, they reached nowhere near the bottom, but I was cramped and cold. I'd hardly any blankets.

Mum was snoring when the Minx clattered on to the pavement. It was light. 5 a.m. So how many doors would go bang? I tensed myself up and listened. *Slam.* So there was only Dad. Wasn't there? I closed my eyes, swallowed, then I crossed all my fingers, quickly breathing, *please.*

He didn't bother with Elvis. He came straight upstairs, to bed. One lot of footsteps. He stopped outside the door. Farted. Yawned. Then he slammed his way into his bedroom. He was snoring in ten seconds flat.

'MY DAD LEFT HOME ONCE,' MUM SAID. WE WERE SITTING on the bench waiting for the bus that would take her into town, to her extra new hours. 'He went for a whole week, then just kind of slipped back in again with a box of chicken pasties. He'd got them from a man on Bury market. He'd been gone for a week, but Mum just put the oven on and we sat in the kitchen and ate them. No one said a thing.'

'So, why did he go?'

'I don't know.'

'But you must have heard them talking?'

'Like us, do you mean?' She had her head inside her handbag, rifling through her change.

'I suppose so.'

'Well, I heard all right,' she said, 'but they always talked in French about things like that. Shouting. Hissing. Moving their bloody arms about. I just blanked it out. And I didn't want to learn it because I didn't want to know. Claudine used to run off with her hands clamped over her ears.'

I swallowed, picking bits of mud off my shoes. I turned my foot over. There was a chewing-gum stain, and a couple of drawing pins stuck inside the sole. I pulled them out, examining the dots that they'd made in the rubber.

'But wasn't it worse, not knowing?'

'I don't know. Maybe it was.' She clicked her handbag shut and looked across the busy main road. In front of us, a woman was dodging traffic, holding out her shopping bag as if it was a shield. 'So. Would you rather we just went?' she said. 'Would you rather we just got out and went somewhere else? Plenty of people do it. They do it all the time. We could do a midnight flit – only, knowing your dad, we'd have to do it later.'

'But where could we go?'

'I don't know. Maybe we should get that ferry you were on about?'

'You're joking?'

The bus appeared and stopped, and let a line of people off. A couple stepped out from the shelter, arms folded, waiting for the doors to hiss open at the front.

'I don't know. You'd like that, wouldn't you?'

I nodded. I didn't really know. All I could think about was the sea. Fresh air. Being miles away from here.

'I bet they'd have a shock.' She looked at me. 'But who knows? France? We might even like it.'

The bus driver gave her a nod.

'Hurry up, love, I've got workers in the back.'

'Well then, Jack,' she turned and gave me a wink. 'Now don't you start worrying about all of this.'

'No?'

'No. I've got a bit of something up my sleeve.'

DAD WAS STILL ASLEEP. I FELT ON A HIGH. LIKE I HAD THE best bloody secret in the world. I went into my bedroom and pulled the map from underneath my bed. You could see the little lines where all the ferries went. The wide Atlantic Ocean. I whispered the names of some of the places in Finistère, *Douarenenz, Hanvec, St Nic,* and I wondered if I was saying them right.

Dad got up for his dinner. He looked a mess. I'd forgotten what a mess he always looked when he hadn't made an effort. He just came and sat at the table in his vest and gaping dressing gown, pulling a squashed half a fag from the pocket.

'Brew us some tea,' he said, trying to straighten it out. He lit it, the end flaring up in bright orange splinters. He coughed. 'And where's the bloody paper? It wasn't here yesterday or the day before.'

'We had to cancel it.' I put the kettle on. How could he just sit there, as if nothing had happened? It was like he'd never even been away.

'Cancel it? Shit.'

'We hadn't paid the bill. I think we still owe them.'

'You mean your mother does.' He threw some money at me. 'Run and get us a paper,' he belched. 'I need to keep up with the showbiz column. See where everybody's up to. Go on. Don't look at me like that, it'll only take you five bloody minutes.'

I took the money and smiled. I didn't care anymore. Mum had a plan up her sleeve. She was right. He wouldn't even know what had hit him. We'd just bugger off, without even so much as a note.

MAX RANG. DAD WALKED AROUND, STILL HALF undressed, with the phone tucked under his arm.

'Well hey,' he said. 'Sure. No way? Excellent. I'll drive on up there and we can get it all sorted. Yup. That sounds great. Sounds like it was meant for me. *Meant to be.* I'll see you there then, about five.'

Dad danced around, his dressing gown swishing, singing, 'That's Amore'.

'So?' I was flicking through the paper that I'd had to walk a mile for. I couldn't go into our newsagent's, we owed them too much money. I was reading about a boy from Runcorn who'd been struck by lightning in the storm. His hair had caught fire. His bomber jacket had melted. He'd been playing on the railway line.

'So, Jacky boy, it looks like Max might have found me the big one!' He hummed, trailing the wire around with him, hugging the telephone as if it was a baby. 'I'm going to the office to get his best advice . . .' He danced and carried on with the song. *'That's amore!'*

'You love him then?' I smirked.

'Shut it, big mouth,' he said. 'You'll bloody love him if this deal comes off. You'll be kissing his toes by our swimming pool.'

MUM CAME HOME, LOOKING EXHAUSTED. SHE DROPPED IN the chair with her coat still on.

'Where's your dad?' she mouthed.

I pointed to the ceiling.

'He's got a big meeting with his agent,' I told her. 'This might be The One.'

Her eyes lit up. She smiled and got up, then sat back down again.

'I'm whacked. I'm not used to standing up all day. And that desk is too tall. I need higher heels.' She pulled off her work shoes and threw them by the side of the fire. 'I've been on my bloody tiptoes all afternoon.'

Dad appeared. 'Hello, hello, hello.' He was scrubbed and wearing his work suit. He smelt of something musky.

'New aftershave?' said Mum.

Swivelling his shoulders, he swaggered to the record player.

'It's that stuff your Claud gave me,' he said. 'Why? Am I giving you palpitations?'

Mum sniffed, easing out of her coat. The record started. Dad lit a fag and it hung from the side of his mouth, while he polished up his shoes.

'You look like you're in a good mood,' Mum said.

'Yup.'

'Anything happened?'

'Yup.'

'Like what?'

'Well, my sweet, like I'm going to meet up with my agent. Have a little drinkie from the cut-glass decanter that he keeps on a tray by his desk, and we're going to have a little chit chat about my fucking glorious future.'

Mum smiled. 'I'll make you something to eat,' she said.

'No need.'

'I don't mind.'

'Well, go on then. Some cheese on toast wouldn't go amiss. I need to put a bit of a lining on my stomach – though I won't go over the limit. Max won't let me. He doesn't want to see me in the fucking *News of the World* before I've even started.'

'That's good,' said Mum. 'Because neither do we.'

She looked happy waiting for the grill to warm up.

'What do you want to be looking after him for?' I whispered. 'You're not his slave. You've been at work all day. He's been lounging about, doing nothing.'

She tapped the side of her nose. 'Ah ah,' she said. 'You'll see.'

Dad munched happily. Tissues stuck all down his front and spread across his trousers. His chin was shiny with grease. His head was jerking, like he was lost inside the music. Then suddenly, he stopped.

'Do you fancy coming with me?'

'Coming with you? Well, I wouldn't mind,' said Mum.

'Not you, face ache. I mean soft lad here. Do you fancy coming to meet your father's theatrical agent?'

'Well . . .' My throat was a knot. Mum was trying to hide her disappointment, tapping her fingers, and smiling.

'Come on. I've seen sons in his office before. You know how to act, and when to keep your mouth shut.'

'But . . .'

'Come on,' he said. 'Put a shirt on. Have a wash. Hop to it.'

'So,' said Dad. 'What was the first Elvis song ever to be played on the radio?'

I looked at him. 'No idea.'

'Go on. Have a guess.'

'Well . . .'

'Well, come on,' he was tapping his fingers, smiling, as if he knew something wonderful. 'So?'

'"Blue Suede Shoes"?'

'Nope.'

'What then?'

'Keep guessing.'

'"Heartbreak Hotel"?'

'Nope.'

'"Hound Dog"?'

'Nope. Think early. Think of those great raw Sun sounds.'

'"Mystery Train"?'

Dad blew out his cheeks. 'No. Come on, Jack. Try.'

'"That's Alright Mama"?'

Dad whooped. 'You got it! "That's Alright Mama". And the response was so strong that the station played its B side over and over all night. So what was the B side?' he asked.

'I can't think.'

'"Blue Moon Of Kentucky",' he sighed. 'Christ, are you thick, or what?'

We moved slowly through the traffic. The car rattled whenever we stopped, as if it was a washing machine on rinse and final spin.

Dad lovingly patted the dashboard.

'Well, my little beauty, we might not be driving you for very much longer, but we won't forget you. We won't throw you out on the scrapheap.'

'We won't?' Whenever we slowed, I slunk down in embarrassment. People on the pavement would turn to look at the noise.

'No way. This car can be the start of my classic collection. Okay, so we'll be driving around in a Roller.'

'Great.'

'Though we might have to start off with something a bit smaller. I've heard it can eat a whole tank of petrol in an hour can a Roller. We might have something like an Escort. But we'll get the bugger customised. Fur trim. Alloy wheels. The number-plates.'

I wanted to believe him. I tried. But what about going to France? Talk about bad luck. We'd get our tickets for the ferry, just as he's moving into his own mini Graceland, with the swimming pool, jungle room and all the fancy trimmings.

'My classic collection will be housed inside the garage. And I don't just mean any old garage. It'll be the size of a couple of houses.'

'It'll have to be.'

'What?'

'I mean,' I spluttered. 'If you want to have a collection, you have to have the room.'

'They don't cost much.'

'What don't?'

'Garages. They're all breeze blocks and concrete,' he sniffed. 'Though I might have to have a bit of heating, if I want to be showing people round.'

'We could charge.' I was getting into this now. I'd already planned my bedroom. A kind of *Star Wars*/Natural History theme. I'd have fossils. A telescope. I might have to talk him into an observatory. I might not even want an observatory. If we were rich, I might have other interests. 'You could be like that bloke,' I said. 'That Lord Beaulieu.'

'I won't have the time,' sniffed Dad. 'I'll be touring.'

MAX'S OFFICE WAS IN A QUIET SIDE STREET. THERE WAS A brass plaque, and a couple of Jags outside.

'Well?' he said. 'What do you think?'

'It looks all right.'

'It looks all right? Come on,' he said. 'This is where it happens.'

It was small inside. Smoky. The walls were full of black and white photos, like the ones Dad had spent our Rhyl money on. There were bands. Women with bouffant hair-dos and sparkly low-cut dresses, with names like Roxie, Charlene and Lucki.

'Hiya,' Dad smiled to the woman on the desk. She looked slumped. Bored. She was wearing a cardigan with a hole in its sleeve. 'I'm here to see Max.'

She didn't say anything. She just moved a stack of envelopes and knocked on an adjoining window. She reached for a fag and Dad bounded to her with a light. She didn't say thanks.

'Joey!' Max appeared, holding out his arms. He was small. Grey. Chubby. 'Come on in. I've been waiting.'

'I've brought my son,' said Dad.

'Your son? Come on in!' he said. 'Phew, it's a good job I moved all the pictures of my new exotic dancers.' He jiggled his collar. 'Talk about hot stuff. The pictures were just melting in my hands.'

'Oh, Jack doesn't mind,' said Dad. 'He's wise to the ways of the showbiz world.'

Max's office was full of stuff. The walls were piled high with stacks of stapled papers. 'Scripts,' I thought. I wondered if he had anyone on his books that had a part in *Coronation Street*. There were more framed photos. Theatre posters. An autographed Hughie Green.

'Scotch?'

'Don't mind if I do. Just a small one. Thanks.'

The decanter clinked.

'So . . .' Max hummed. 'How are things?'

'Great.'

'I hear Barnsley was a good one.'

'Good? I haven't done better,' said Dad. 'They were lapping it up.'

'Yes,' said Max, 'so I heard. But let's get down to business. I've not much time. I've an act up in Rochdale tonight. I said I'd make an appearance. They're going to be the next Little and Large. So . . .'

'So?' said Dad. 'What have you got lined up for me?'

Max shuffled some papers. 'Like I said, Joey. This is a good one. A beauty. I've told them all about you.'

'Who?'

'The panel. They're looking for a male vocalist.'

'Me?'

'You.'

'They're thinking big time here. You know. London. Record contract.'

I could hear Dad breathing.

'Shit.'

'So, all you have to do is go and meet them in Manchester – it's just by the Granada Studios – and sing them a couple of songs. Give them what you've got. Have a chat with them, and so on.'

'That's just bloody great!' He turned around and looked at me. He was patting me hard on the knees. He couldn't keep it in.

'It isn't a dead cert,' said Max. 'Nothing's a dead cert, you know that. And you're a little bit over the age limit, but I'm pinning my hopes on you. I know you can do it.'

'Yes?'

'Of course he can. Can't he, Jack? You've seen him?'

I nodded.

'Well, you'll have heard it. Seen it. He's got charisma. He's got the voice of an angel and the devil all in one.'

Dad slapped him on the shoulder. 'Best bloody thing I did in my life was signing up with you.' He was close to tears. His bottom lip was twitching.

'Surely not? You musn't forget your family, Joey. You're going to need your family, because your life might change, like that.' He clicked his fingers. 'And there'll be plenty of rough sailing, there's bound to be. Well, you know all about it,' he said. 'You can pick up any paper and read the whole sorry story.' He handed over an envelope.

'It's all in there,' he said. 'Time. Date. Place. Two songs. One upbeat. One ballad. But that's a piece of cake for you, Mr Joey, Get 'em Going, Seville.'

'Shit! Shit! Shit! Shit! Shit!' Dad danced around outside. His nose was running. He kept leaping up and down on the pavement. I was shaking. Running close to him. I was pulling at his arms and pushing at his back. It hardly felt real, but I'd heard it. I could see it. Dad's name spinning round on a record.

We jumped into the Minx and rolled our windows down. Music on. Full blast. We sang along. Whooping. 'Lawdy Miss Clawdy'. My hands were sore from clapping. I didn't care about the looks we were getting. Who were they anyway? Girls who worked in Woolworth's? Shelf stackers? Typists? They were nothing. My dad had charisma. Look at us. Look over here. We don't care what you think, because he's something. He's Mr Joey, Get 'em Going, Seville.

We stopped at a motorway service station. We were walking on air. Whenever someone looked our way, it was as if my dad was already being recognised. He ducked his head a few times, practising. Like he wanted to avoid any limelight.

'Come on, son,' he said. 'Let's grab ourselves a drink and a bite. Get a tray. Get anything.'

We slid along, past the little glass compartments full of plates of cheese and gateaux. I looked at him before I picked anything, but he just kept giving me a nod and a smile. Roast beef salad. Coleslaw. Bread fingers. Chocolate cream pie. Coke.

'This is how it's going to be,' he said, as we stretched out at our table. Dad had fish and chips. The fish was so big it was falling off his plate. 'Welcome to the good life.'

Below us, the cars looked like Dinky toys as they whizzed past in the fast lane. Dad forgot his food for a while, staring out, imagining the car that he'd soon have to put in an order for. 'They have waiting lists,' he'd said. 'You can't just walk into any old garage and buy one.'

My salad tasted great. Like some exotic foreign food. But then I saw a woman with a boy about my age. They were smiling about something. The woman picked cotton from the boy's fluffy jumper and he blushed, batting her hand away.

'What about Mum?' I asked.

'What about your mum? She knows the score.'

I looked at my plate. The beef had a curly line of fat around it. It was gristly. Dry.

'You're really going to leave her?'

'She left me.'

'She didn't.'

'Well, she left me no choice.'

'But it was me who left the phone out.'

'You think that was it? It wasn't that. I would have gone anyway,' he puffed on the end of his fag. 'I needed a break. I had to get my head together. I knew something big was on its way. Something gigantic.'

'Where did you go?'

'Bolton Royal Infirmary,' he said, holding up his hand. 'I needed a couple of stitches.'

I swallowed. I could feel the food inside, just sitting there. The slimy onion coleslaw and the thick white bread.

'She thinks you've got a girlfriend.'

'Oh, she does, does she?' he was grinning through the window. He ruffled out his hair. 'Well, well, well.'

'So, have you?'

He sniffed. 'There's plenty of women who like me,' he said. 'It's the way it is. I can't help it. What do you think I'm going to say when a girl plops herself down on my lap? It's natural. It goes with the job.'

'But Mum . . .'

'What about her?' He looked at me, then sighed, scraping back his chair. 'Oh, don't you fret. I'll see she's all right,' he said. 'If it makes you feel any better. I mean, I don't want her badmouthing her way to all the papers.' He suddenly looked stricken. 'She wouldn't do that to me? Would she?'

'No. I don't know. But you could try being nice to her.'

'Fuck.' He pushed his plate away. 'I hadn't thought of that.'

'What?' I wasn't sure what he was getting at.

'The papers. The fucking papers, the telly and all those smarmy big-gob reporters. It can kill you off. I've seen it happen. Miffed wives telling porkies just to make a few bob on the side.'

'Don't,' I said.

'Don't what?'

'Well, Mum wouldn't do that. She's not like that.'

'You just wait.'

'What do you mean?'

'Well, no one's like that till their ex-husband's got a million in the bank and fucking fame and fortune. Then, suddenly, they change.'

'Ex-husband? Are you getting divorced?'

'I don't know,' he said. 'I'll have to think about it. Maybe it'd be better to get it over with while I'm still poor.'

Dad rubbed his eyes. He looked exhausted. Old.

'Oh, your mother's all right, I suppose.' We were in the gift shop. He was buying her a box of Meltis Fruit Jellies. 'Just to keep her sweet.' He bought me a *Beano* summer special and a giant packet of Revels. When we were nearly home, he said, 'I don't want to give them to your mum. The jelly things. Just keep them for yourself. Or tell her they're from you.'

Dad parked up. 'What a night,' he said. 'High. Low. Look at me. I'm supposed to be celebrating.'

He left me at the door. I watched him walking down the street with the envelope tucked inside his arm. He was going to The Victory. He'd buy a couple of rounds. He was feeling flush. He might even start up a sing-song.

'It went all right then?' Mum was in her dressing gown. She had lipstick on. She'd done something curly to her hair.

'Yes, I met that Max. Dad might have this really great job coming up. He bought you these. I mean, I bought you these.'

She took the box and smiled.

'Lovely. I haven't seen these for donkey's years. Has your dad gone down the pub?'

'Yes.'

'Right, well I'm off to bed, before he brings the bar back with him.'

But Dad was in by eleven, with his 'Mystery Train' on low. It was a comfy sort of sound, without all the clattering; without the things that could easily break. Then later, the phone woke me up, and he was singing 'Love Me Tender'. It sounded beautiful, all hushed and unaccompanied, like a lullaby. He sang the whole song through, then he laughed, and for five long minutes he whispered a hundred goodnights.

In the cold spare room, the light was out, and Mum was crying, muffled inside her blankets. It was quiet downstairs as I stood against the door. I could see her now. Her face was wet. She was twisted in net. She was pressing herself to the wall.

In Le Faou, Finistère, the house with the shutters had a view of the sea. I studied it. How many windows? How many bedrooms? It looked tiny. How many rooms would the four of us need?

I'd taken Gran's leaflet upstairs, the photograph and a tourist's guide to Brittany. I was going to learn French. A bit of Bretonese. I sat in my bedroom with the book spread out, saying, braz, *large*, bihan, *small*, mor, *sea*, mor-bihan, *small sea*. That foamy wild sea. I could hear it, crashing. Booming. It was full of rocks and unlucky sailors, still in their broken-up boats. I had the number of four different ferry lines. SNCF railways. Brittany is one hour ahead of Greenwich Mean Time. Electricity is generally cheaper than in the UK. The current is 220 volts.

'Ding, dong! Avon calling!' My mum put her head round the door. My grandma was in hospital, in a single private side ward.

'You again,' she said.

'I'm practising.' Mum pulled out a bulging make-up bag. 'Would you like to try out a few of my great new samples?'

Grandma was hooked to a monitor. I didn't know exactly what it was for, but every so often it bleeped and the numbers flashed in red. None of the nurses seemed worried. They just walked past, with charts and covered bedpans.

'Look at me,' said Grandma. 'I'm covered in electrics.'

Mum found some hand cream and a tube of greasy lipstick.

'You want cheering up,' she said. 'I'm thinking of going into Avon. They've sent me a trial pack.'

'You want to be careful,' said Grandma. 'You don't know whose bell you're going to ding dong on.'

'They give you strict guidelines,' said Mum. 'Would you like to try my Misty?'

Grandma lay still while Mum rubbed her hands with sticky pink cream; it came out of the bottle farting.

'You'll feel better after this,' said Mum. 'They're very drying, hospitals.'

We sat and listened to the bleeps. They were going off all over the place. A nurse came in and pressed something.

'Is everything all right?' Mum asked.

'Fine. They're temperamental. They just need a bit of adjusting.'

Grandma looked tired. The light was bright in the room, but there weren't any windows, just a sign that said Fire Hazard. There was a clear plastic water jug. A bedpan made of paper. Something called Sani-Spray.

'He's coming then? Really?'

'Yes. Joey's definitely coming. He promised.'

Grandma looked at the door. The whites of her eyes were yellow. Her mouth had dropped into itself.

'He's really coming?'

'Like I said, definitely.'

'Well, put a bit of lipstick on me then. Nothing too bright.'

Mum bent over; she was trying to find the line where the lipstick ought to go. The lipstick was called Shelly. It was pale pink, it was hardly there at all, but on my grandma's face it looked shocking.

'That's better,' said Mum. 'You're ready for him now.'

Dad was definitely coming, but he was walking the long way round, through the front entrance, avoiding certain wards. He said he didn't really mind the walk, 'at least it's all indoors', and he didn't want to bump into any of his old clients, or worse still, come face to face with the man who'd got his job. 'He's only temporary,' he'd said. 'And he hasn't had much training.'

'My doctor here's a foreigner,' said Grandma. 'Doctor Beau something. Do you know him? I can't tell half of what he's saying, but he does have lovely teeth.'

'Hello, hello, hello, and who do we have here?' Dad was in the doorway. We could smell him. He was covered in musk again. 'Is it that film star? That Divine Mrs Gloria Trench?'

'Get away with you.'

She was smiling now, and holding out her hands.

'What do you think?' said Mum. 'She's been trying out my Misty.'

'Soft as a baby's botty,' said Dad. 'And look at those lips. Where are you off dancing to tonight?'

Grandma swallowed. She was smiling, swallowing cries, now that Dad was here.

'Move up, Evie,' she said. 'Let the lad sit down. Have you been working hard, Joe? You must be worn out.'

'I'm always working hard. And has our Jack told you? I've jumped right in at the deep end. I've gone pro.'

'No,' she sounded cross. 'You never told me that, Jack. Why didn't you tell me that? It would have kept me going.'

I shrugged and kept out of the way. I was trying not to listen, concentrating on a doctor outside who was talking to a porter. I looked at his hands. I imagined them, deep inside a body, fiddling with the guts.

'And I'm doing fine. More than fine. I'm doing great. They're talking records, Mother. They're talking London.'

'Palladium?'

'Well, probably not quite the Palladium. They can get Bruce Forsyth for that.'

She smiled. 'Oh, he is doing me proud,' she clapped. 'Isn't he doing me proud?'

We nodded. I'd started feeling sick.

Mum looked at me.

'Jack,' she said, 'shall we go for a little walk? Shall we leave them in peace for ten minutes?'

'That's the best thing I've heard in ages,' said Grandma. 'You go. And if there's a shop, will you get me something to suck. Not too sweet, mind. Something nice and lemony.'

We left them.

'Oh, isn't he doing her proud?' said Mum. 'Christ. If only she knew the half of it.'

WE SAT AROUND THE TELLY. A HORROR FILM WAS ON. DAD kept looking at the phone.

'It's plugged in then?'

Mum just stared at him.

The doctor, with his busy hands and straight white teeth, who wasn't foreign after all, had prepared us for the worst.

'You could wait here,' he'd said. 'She might not make the night.'

'Might not make the night?' said Dad. 'Look at her. She's sat up laughing. She's got some bloody lipstick on.'

'She's old, Mr Trench. We tried. We've done everything. Really. She's had the greatest possible care, but it's only a matter of time.'

When he'd gone, Mum said, 'Are you waiting then? Are you going to be with her, just in case? She might want to hold your hand, or say a few last words.'

Dad looked worried.

'Well . . . I'll stay another half hour,' he'd said. 'That's all I can just about manage of this place. And now he's told me she might, well . . . I can't stand the bloody suspense. She'll be better off without me. Anyway, they can always ring us up.'

'I could stay,' said Mum.

'She says she doesn't want you going to any more trouble. She says she's seen you more than plenty, lately.'

'She has? Well, I'll just go in for a minute. I'd like to tell her goodnight.'

The horror film was old-fashioned. You could tell the blood was make-up.

'We shouldn't be watching this,' Mum said. 'This is a horrible thing to be watching with all that you-know-what going on. Joey?'

'What?'

'Can't we turn it over? Can't we watch something that's a bit more pleasant than this?'

'Like what?'

'Like anything.'

'There isn't anything else on the box that's worth watching.'

Mum opened the paper. 'There's a quiz on,' she said. 'A pop quiz. You'd like it.'

But then the phone rang, and Mum wasn't quick enough with the switch, so the doctor had to tell my dad that his mother had died with all the blood curdling screams in the background, and some crazy mad axe man shouting, 'Murder!'

'DID YOU SEE IT IN THE PAPER THEN?'

'What?'

'Mattie.'

'What about him?'

'He's been done for shoplifting.'

'No way?'

'And you'll never guess what it was that he was nicking?'

'Fags? Booze? *Playboys*?'

'No,' said Stuart. 'It was a load of stuff from Mothercare. Jeeze. Can you imagine it?'

I shrugged. I didn't want to think about it. Mattie with some of those Babygro things tucked inside his sweater.

'Do you think he'll get off?'

'Probably. He's only a kid.'

'They could shut him in some borstal.'

'I suppose so. Christ.'

We were sat at the back of the Wimpy. Because my grandma had just died, a couple of the neighbours had been round with sympathy cards, and they'd thrown all their bits of loose change at me. Of course, Mum hadn't let on that she was just a paying guest. They probably wouldn't have believed her anyway, the way she'd kept running into the kitchen to make fresh pots of tea for them all.

Stuart had an old school exercise book with him. It was covered in drawings that were supposed to be naked women, but they looked more like chickens laying eggs. Inside, he'd drawn Winter Hill. The road where the path started, and little purple arrows that would lead us to the top.

'It's going to be great,' he said.

'I didn't think you'd be into it.'

'Stars? Well, I'm not. I'm just going for the laugh.'

'Have you seen the size of Winter Hill? You won't have the breath to start laughing.'

'My brother's been up it. He says it's a piece of bloody cake.'

'Your brother? What was he doing up there then? Sheep rustling?'

'It was an April Fool's Day thing. Ages ago. Someone told him and his mate that aliens were going to land up there. They knew it was a joke like, but they were going up with some lamps from Rigby's Garage – his mate Ian works there; they were going to flash them around a bit, make it look like they'd just stepped out of a spaceship.'

'And?'

He blew into his milkshake until the glass was just pink bubbles and a waitress rolled her eyes.

'He said they were scared shitless. It was pitch black, freezing, and the TV masts kept making funny singing sounds.'

'Pitch black? So what about the lamps?'

'Oh,' he said. 'They didn't know how to work them. They said it was too dark and they weighed at least a ton.'

'Fantastic organisation.' My cheeseburger had arrived. The waitress wiped the table with a sopping grey dishcloth. Stuart lifted his book up and grinned. 'You know where we're going then?' I asked.

'Jeeze,' Stuart pointed to the drawing. 'What's this then? A crossword? I've got it all planned. It took me bloody ages.'

'Well . . .' People were looking, listening, smirking. The café was quiet. It was early. Market day. 'We don't want to be going on a tour of the local countryside,' I said. 'We don't want to have to call out Search and Rescue.'

'Search and bloody rescue? Christ, Jack, it's not Snowdonia. There's bloody arrows and signposts to the top. There's little picnic spots with benches.'

'Okay. Okay.' But I wasn't all that convinced.

'So,' said Stuart, drooling at my burger. 'What are we going to see?'

I looked at him. 'Stars?' I said.

'Come on Patrick Moore. You can do better than that.'

'Well . . .' So, I'd read the books. I was always going on about it. Asteroids. Meteors. I knew that if we were using Mattie's old binoculars we wouldn't be able to detect the rings of Saturn. But what exactly would we see up there? I didn't know. I just knew it would be sparkly. Immense. 'It all depends on the night,' I said. 'Sean's calling Sky-Line. We'll tell you when we get there.'

'Do you think Mattie will be coming?'

I shrugged.

'He might have done a runner.'

'No way.'

'We're all going to Kelby, you know. The letter came through this morning. I nearly shit myself.'

'It won't be that bad,' I said. 'At least we'll all be there.'

'True.'

But I'd already been to the library, looking up schools in the Finistère region. Most of them were church schools. Small. And I couldn't really tell if they were for infants or for seniors. I might have to go to a special school anyway, seeing as I'd only be able to understand about three of the words they were saying.

We walked back through town. It was still full of kids, but they'd all had too much summer. New handwritten signs said: No Unaccompanied Children, By Order of the Management.

'I'm sorry about your grandma,' Stuart said. 'My mum reckons she's going to the funeral. Apparently, they used to work in the same factory, years ago.'

'Right. You coming?'

'No fucking way.'

I left him at the bus station. He was going to get a haircut at a place where it only took the barber three minutes. He'd been in the paper, holding up a stopwatch. He was famous for it. He didn't even look at your head half the time.

'Jack?'

My heart sank. I recognised the voice. I didn't know what to say. I couldn't escape. Vince.

'I'm sorry about Dad,' I blushed. We walked to the railings and stopped. 'He's singing full time now.'

'I heard. I couldn't believe it.'

'He's good,' I blurted.

'I know. But after all these years. I felt terribly let down.'

'I'm sorry.'

'Don't be. It's not your fault. And I always knew he was a dangerous boy.'

I laughed.

'I didn't advertise for ages,' he said. 'I thought he might

change his mind. Come back. Do you think that he might still change his mind?'

'I doubt it. He's got a really great job coming up.'

'Can't he do both?'

'I don't think so.'

'Oh. I was sorry to hear of your grandma. I saw it in the paper.'

'Thanks.'

I shuffled a bit. Vince looked too smart for the bus station. He was wearing a dark blue suit and a cravat that looked like water was stuffed inside his shirt. A hat. People kept looking.

'You know, I owe your dad a bit of money. I haven't forgotten. I'll send it.'

'Could you send it to my mum?' I asked. 'She's nearly full time at the solicitor's, but she needs all the help she can get.'

'I wish I could,' he coughed. 'I'll think about it. But what if your dad finds out?'

I nodded. I knew exactly what he meant.

'Look, if you ever need me for anything, just pop into the shop. Or give me a ring. And if Joey's working on a weekend, you and your mum could come up to the house and have a bit of tea. Like we used to. Remember?'

'Yes.'

It had been something of a ritual. Every Sunday afternoon we'd driven to his house with its long winding drive and the pockmarked, wingless cherub. Dad would have the paperwork, new catalogues, strands of nylon hair. The house was huge. It had felt like a museum with the paintings and the bronze statuettes on the fireplace. I'd sit with my mum drinking tea and eating crustless sandwiches. Dad would be with Vince in the kitchen, checking through their orders, but then he'd get the brandy out, sweet Italian brandy, and lemon squash for me, and he'd play records that he'd thought we'd all like. The Beatles. Lulu. Early Elvis Presley tucked in between his opera and *Ella*

Sings The Blues. If we were staying, Dad would loosen his collar and sing a couple of ballads. 'It's Now Or Never'. 'Blue Moon'. He thought they sounded better, with Vince's high ceiling.

'You've got great acoustics.'

'I should invite people round,' Vince would blush. 'We could charge them for admission.'

But he'd end with something lively, bumping my mum around the furniture. Me and Vince clapping, shouting, More! More! More!

'What happened?' I asked. 'Why did it stop?'

'It was awkward,' he said, shading his eyes from the sun.

'Awkward? Why?'

'Well, I had a permanent visitor,' he said. 'And your dad said it wouldn't be right.'

OUTSIDE THE MURPHY HOUSE, THERE WAS A VAN THAT said: C.J.M. Dry-Cleaning. There was a picture of a coat. Trousers. The address said Brixton. Was their shop next to the prison? *Seven Sisters.* Next to it there was a Rover. A P5B sedan. It was black, with pale leather seats. A 3.5 automatic. I was looking through the windows when the Murphys' door opened and they all came out in a sheepish broken line, and all of them dressed to kill.

The uncle was fat, but he looked how Sean's dad would have looked with a beard. Tottering. Red hands. His wife wasn't pretty. She had snappy blonde hair and a face like a whippet's. They were organising. Shooing. Clucking. The boys were wearing ties and sharply pressed trousers. Of course, Sean pretended like I wasn't even there, but Michael gave me a wave. Mrs Murphy was doing something to her shoe. She was wearing a long white dress that was dirty where she'd tripped on it. She looked like a drunken bride.

'Come on you lot,' said the auntie. 'They'll be dishing out the entrees and there'll be no one there to eat them.'

Sean couldn't resist. He had to give me a look. He stuck his finger in his mouth and went cross-eyed. He got a crack on the head from his dad.

THE ROVER BELONGED TO MR ERNEST JEREMY FARTHING, undertaker. He was in the front room with a coffin brochure. Mum had been told to keep out of the way. She was listening from the kitchen. She was making more tea and arranging chocolate wafers.

'The pine is popular,' the undertaker was saying. 'We have a variety of linings. We have steel or brass ornaments, and the plaque will come as standard.'

'It's a cremation,' said Dad. 'So we don't want to be spending the earth on something that's going to go whoosh.'

Mum closed her eyes, but she came out smiling.

'Mrs Trench left us plenty of provision,' she said, wobbling the saucers. 'It's not that we want to seem mean.'

Dad hissed through his teeth. 'You just leave the choosing up to me.'

'It's a hard time,' said the undertaker, as he sniffed into his teacup. 'It's a time of great sorrow, and strain.'

'Tell me about it,' said Dad. 'She's been nothing but a strain since I met her.'

'YOU DIDN'T HAVE TO CHOOSE THE CHEAPEST,' MUM SAID. 'Talk about showing us up.'

'What do you mean? Showing us up? What's it to you anyway? Why should you care what we burn my mother in?'

Mum let out a choke. 'How can you be so heartless? How can you talk about your mother like that?'

'Like what?'

'You know. Saying things.'

'Saying what things?'

'Burn. You don't have to say things like burn.'

'Well, that's what she wanted, isn't it? Cremation, like my dad. We can bury the urns together.'

'But you don't have to be so cold about it.'

'Cold? I thought I was being red hot!' He laughed and slapped his belly. He abandoned the tea and found a can of lager he'd been saving for the funeral.

'Joey . . .'

'Well. She was old, wasn't she? I loved her. I'll miss her, but it's better to talk plain instead of skirting the issue. What's the point of wasting all that money when it's going on a bonfire?'

'I thought you were going to be rolling in it?'

'Too right.'

'And so what about your mother? How do you think she'll feel lying on show in the undertaker's parlour, in something that's shaped like a coffin but feels like an orange box?'

'Feels? You see, there you go again, Evelyn, putting feeling into it. When you're dead, you have no feelings. Even if I were a millionaire today I wouldn't go over the top. Just what is the point? They don't make coffins like that for nothing. Why do you think they put them in the brochures?'

'Oh, I don't know,' Mum sighed, exhausted. She lit herself a fag, looked at it, then handed it to Dad. She lit herself another. 'They have to have a range.'

'Exactly. And who's going to know? People are hardly likely to turn up to a funeral and say, "Oh, nice coffin, how much did that set you back then?" It's not a bloody motor.'

'All right, all right, I'm fed up of arguing.'

'Me too.'

'Good.'

'So, what about your rent?'

'Rent? Now?'

'I see you've got yourself a few bob working overtime for Genty.'

'But I need that for the catalogues. Not to mention the paper bill.'

'You should have stopped them quicker.'

'How could I? After that. Well, I couldn't get out of my bed for a week.'

'So?' Dad swirled his can around. 'You should have sent soft lad here. He could have done all your errands.'

'Are you going to let me off then?'

'Hmm. Well, I won't let you off. I'll just put it on tick. I'll get myself one of those little spiral notebooks and I'll jot down what you owe me. How's that?'

Mum said nothing.

'Oh, well go on then. I'll let you off half of it this week. I thought we'd have a party after the funeral. A little wake, like. If you get the beers in for that, I'll let you off half your rent. How about it?'

'Well, have I got any choice?' she said.

When Dad went round to his mate Terry's, Mum said, 'Please don't think that I'm awful, but I'm going to have a little root through his things. Just to put my mind at rest.'

'I'll come with you,' I said.

Mum hadn't been in the big bedroom since she'd taken her things out. She gently pushed the door. She made us take our shoes off.

'We don't want to leave any marks on the carpet,' she said. 'You know he's like Columbo when he wants to be.'

The room was a mess. Clothes. Beer cans. Papers.

'He'll never be able to tell. It looks like we've been broken into.'

'Don't bank on it,' she said. 'And don't you touch anything.'

The only tidy corner was his 'dressing room'. The suit was still hanging there in its plastic. Tom Jones had had a wipe down. Even the gonk's purple hair looked combed.

Mum was being gentle, searching through his pockets. She didn't find much, just a few snotty tissues and some matches.

'I don't know,' she said. 'Maybe he was drunk that night. Being daft, on a high, singing down the phone.'

'It was probably a joke. You know what he's like.'

She struggled through his jeans. She found a bus ticket and examined it. 'It's smudged,' she said. 'I can't tell where it was he went to.'

'And he didn't ring her,' I said. 'She rang here. Why would a woman ring here when she knows you might answer the phone?'

'It was definitely a woman then?' said Mum.

I didn't know what to say. 'It could have been a bloke,' I managed, trying to sound convincing. 'He might have been doing the song as a wind-up.'

'A wind-up? Yes. I don't think he's turned into a Vince.'

'I saw Vince.'

'Was he mad?'

'A bit. He says he owes Dad money. I asked him if he'd send it all to you, but he said he wasn't sure.'

'Well, it is your dad's. He did work for it.'

'But I thought we could use it. Your little plan? You know?'

She looked at me. She'd found some screwed-up paper that she didn't want to open.

'My little plan? Oh, yes. Well, I do need money for that. Still, it wouldn't be right. It'd feel like I was stealing.'

She screwed the paper tighter, then quickly smoothed it flat. It was Dad's handwriting. It said, 56365, Caz.

'Do you think that's it?' she said.

'Nah,' I swallowed. 'That could be anything. And if it is his girlfriend's number, why would he have screwed it all up?'

'Yes. You're right. And if it's her,' she said, 'it might mean that they've finished.' She put it back, smiling. 'Caz? What's that supposed to stand for?'

'I don't know. Carol? Karen?'

'*Caz,*' she said. 'Well, just how bloody common can you get?

Sean said the ferries were great. They had shops on them. Cafés. He said the last one he'd been on had an arcade full of Space Invaders, and you wouldn't even notice you were in the middle of the sea if it wasn't for the floor that kept tipping every few minutes. 'It was just like being in the Fun House,' he said. 'And Matthew was sick in his sports bag.'

I practised in my room, whispering the words. It was too much to hear them out loud, and I thought I might sound daft.

'Quel est le prix du billet?'

'Un billet pour Brest s'il vous plait.'

Brest. It would have to be Brest, wouldn't it? And I thought of my dad eating breakfast. His page-three smasher winking over his bacon.

'Have you seen this here?' he'd say. '*It's Tit For Tat Says Sam!*'

MUM HAD BOUGHT A BOTTLE OF SHERRY, TWELVE CANS OF lager and half a bottle of vodka with the last of the teapot money. She'd spent the morning doing a buffet, listening to the Mario Lanza story on the radio. 'I think it's fitting,' she'd said. 'Your grandma always loved "Because You're Mine".'

She'd made pinwheel sandwiches, sausage rolls, boiled eggs with the middles scooped out and then mashed with salad cream. Dad emptied a few bags of crisps into Tupperware jelly bowls.

'Look at me,' he said, his black tie hanging over his shoulder. 'You can't say I'm not doing my bit to see that my mother's sent off right.'

'What's he like?' Mum whispered. 'He can't even do that right. Look at him. He's mixing all the flavours.'

'I heard that,' he shouted, blowing into a crisp bag and bursting it. 'I'm doing it on purpose. It'll make them more exciting.'

Mum was wearing navy blue. It was the darkest thing she had. Dad had his suit on. I was in my old school uniform again.

'Well, we might as well make the most of it,' said Mum, brushing down my collar. 'What a terrible waste.'

I smiled. I knew exactly what she meant.

At eleven o'clock, people started appearing. Grandma's old neighbours. A great uncle something. Stuart's mum was all in black. She even had a hat.

'Have you seen the state?' whispered Mum. 'And by the looks of it, she's already had a skinful.'

Dad's friend, Terry, appeared with a couple of bottles of Guinness. Terry was the kung fu fanatic. He hadn't brought his wife.

'These are for the wake,' he said. 'You still here then, Evie?' Mum walked off.

'Easy now,' said Dad. 'Remember what I was saying.'

My uncle Frank couldn't make it from Canada, so he'd sent a wreath the size of a tractor tyre. It had a sash that said, *Mother R.I.P.* It was purple. It looked like the kind of thing that Miss World might have worn round her swimsuit.

'It must have cost a packet,' said Dad. 'Have you seen the fucking size of it?'

When the hearse appeared, there was a little bit of sniffing. There was only one black car for the eight of us. The driver, with his drooping face and black bowler hat, said he was really only licensed for six, but if we were discreet, he'd let it go this once.

'You're a bloody gent,' said Dad. 'I'll see you right at the end.'

We were squashed, but it felt like we were sailing. The car was huge. Three lots of seats. Our own little light in the back. I found a glove in the side of the door. It had mud on it. We felt important. We held up traffic, and across the pavements people stopped with their shopping and crossed themselves.

'She'd be loving this,' said Mum.

There were more people at the crematorium. Sister Elizabeth.

Ronnie. A huddle of women that Dad knew from the club. Mum balled up her Kleenex.

'What are *they* doing here?' she said. 'They never even met her. Not once.'

'Just leave it, Evie. They've just come to pay their respects.'

The crematorium was supposed to look like a church. It had a stained-glass window with birds on it. Crosses. Pews. But you couldn't really disguise the chimney at the back. It was wide and square, and it was trickling with smoke when we got there.

'I see she isn't the first,' said Terry.

We went inside. Dad and Terry stayed outside with the funeral directors. They were having one last smoke before they'd have to bring the coffin in.

Mum looked upset.

'I never thought of your dad as a pallbearer,' she said. 'It's a terrible thing to see.'

A tape made music and the coffin appeared. It looked okay. It didn't look cheap, as they lowered it on to the conveyor belt. 'Please Dad,' I thought. 'Don't make any Brucie jokes.' He looked at me and winked. Then he brushed his shoulders as if something had been left on them. He didn't sit with us. He went on the front row with Terry, where they bowed and looked at their knees.

The priest was all right. He didn't go on. He didn't really know her. For most of her life, she'd forgotten to be a Catholic. Sean could not believe it.

'I've never known that to happen,' he'd said. 'One of my dad's uncles even married a Muslim and went to live in Birmingham. He was supposed to be converted, but when he thought nobody was looking he'd sneak in a confession. I thought all Catholics were like that?'

'Not my lot.'

'Well, you're bloody freaks,' he'd said.

We sang a few hymns, and as the tape played 'O Perfect Love', the conveyor belt started up and she went behind the curtain. It was hard to believe it was my grandma in there. No more talking. No more visits to her room on the second floor. And soon, she would be burning.

On the way out, people came and patted Dad on the back. The women hugged and kissed him. Mum went and sat in the car.

'"O Perfect Love"?' said Stuart's mum. 'I thought they only did that one at weddings.'

'She'd have preferred Des O'Connor's "Dick-A-Dum-Dum",' said Dad. 'But the priest put his foot down.'

'Oh, don't take any notice,' said Mum.

'You should have sang a song for her,' one of the neighbours piped up. 'She was always going on. My Joey this. My Joey that. My Joey, the next big thing on the box. You could have sung her something.'

Dad coughed. 'I thought it might upset me,' he said. 'But don't worry. I'll sing her off tonight.'

The house was full. Most people just turned up. They didn't even bother with the funeral. Mum made tea until the windows steamed up, but they soon went on to the sherry, the men slowly loosening their ties. Laughter.

The music was soft at first. Elvis ballads. Perry. We had no Des O'Connor.

'Your mum still here then?' Some of Dad's friends came and whispered in my ear. Their breath felt cold. Like they'd been chewing on their ice cubes.

But Mum kept busy, and the kitchen turned into a bomb site. She buttered cream crackers. Poured out vodka tonics. Her pinwheel sandwiches were something of a hit.

'I've never seen anything like it,' said Terry. He held one up. 'Did you go to that cordon bleu cookery school, or something?'

'Terry,' she said. 'It's just a bloody sandwich.'

When most people had left, it turned into a party. The records got livelier. Terry did a bit of kung fu.

At five o'clock, Dad hit the side of his beer glass and proposed a wobbly toast. 'To my mother, may she always rest in peace.'

Everyone said 'aye', though the people that were left wouldn't have known his mother from Adam, especially now they'd had a few.

'And now,' said Dad, pink-faced and sweating, 'may I sing a little song to drift her up to heaven?'

Mum looked away. The record Dad chose was apparently one of her favourites.

'She used to sing it all the time,' he said. 'Mind you, it didn't sound like this.'

It was Frank Sinatra. 'I've Got You Under My Skin'.

'So, this one's just for her.'

He put down his glass. Closed his eyes, and the record started behind him. All serious at first, he just stood there, but soon he was moving around, pointing his finger, and picking out people to sing to. It was how I imagined being in a cabaret lounge. Everyone was smiling.

Mum was washing up again. The room was too small. People were on the stairs, sat in twos. I heard a voice say, 'Carolyn'.

I went out into the yard. I'd hardly noticed the sunshine. I walked around a bit, kicking a dirty tennis ball. I could hear them all singing. Tom Jones now. Someone had brought a guitar.

Through the kitchen window, soaked with condensation, I could see Mum at the sink. She was nodding her head to the music. From down the backstreet a voice said, 'Listen to them, you'd think they were Irish or something.'

There was dancing now. Mum came out with her fag.

'I'll miss her.'

'Yes.'

'She was a funny old thing.'

'She didn't look like she was going to die. Did she? What was it she died of?'

'Old age,' said Mum. 'And septi bloody caemia.'

'What's that?'

'Blood poisoning.'

'Oh.'

'I thought you liked science,' said Mum. 'I thought you knew everything.'

'I do. Well, nearly everything.'

'I miss my mum,' she said. 'All the way over there.'

'In France they have the metric system.'

She looked at me.

'What?'

'Grammes, centimetres, litres.'

'We have them here.'

'Not really. Not all the time. Not every day. In shops.'

'No.'

'Do you think it'll be hard to get used to?'

She shrugged.

'And the office workers start early.'

'How early?' She flicked her fag into her hand.

'Seven thirty.'

'God.'

'But they have a very long lunch hour.'

'Well, thank goodness for that,' said Mum. 'They'll need it.'

I went inside again and left her to her breather. A few more people left. Terry was still at it. He'd broken something. A glass.

Dad wasn't there. Someone else was changing the record. Someone who wasn't being careful. I could already see the grease marks.

'Come on, Dave,' said a woman. 'Put something modern on.'

'Like what?'

'Blondie.'

'They haven't any Blondie.'

I went up to the toilet. I had to step up past my dad. He was on the stairs with a girl who looked a bit like my mum, only younger and longer. They were all over each other. His hand was in her T-shirt, going round in circles.

I had the quickest piss. I had to get out. I jumped back downstairs with my eyes half shut. I had to get back to my mum.

She was still outside.

'I wish I could plant some flowers,' she was saying. 'Something bright. We could dig up the flags. We could buy some pots, if we ever have the money.'

'Pots would look great. Sean's mum has some red things in her pots.'

'You can get them cheap on the market. Is Brian still here? I could ask him. He's got that I-Sell-Everything stall. They must do pots there.'

'It's awful inside,' I said. 'It's better out here.'

'My head's full of it.'

'You need some fresh air.'

'It'll soon be getting nippy.'

'I don't mind nippy,' I said. 'Nippy's all right. Nippy's great.'

She lit another fag. Her blouse had come undone. You could see the edge of her bra and a bright red scoop where her sundress had been.

'The sun's going in. Look at it.'

'I don't care. I could stay out all night. Shall I go and fetch you a drink?'

My mum had other boyfriends. Years ago. Before she met my dad. Before her night out at The Beehive when his packet of crisps had hit her in the face. It should have been a warning, but she hadn't even noticed.

'Oh, there were plenty before your dad,' she'd say. 'Well, one or two. But they were only bits of boyfriends, if you know what I mean. They were nothing very serious. Unless you count that Eddie.'

Eddie was different. He didn't like Elvis. He played tennis and he went to the grammar school.

'My girlfriends would have picked on me, only he was that good-looking. He looked like Tommy Steele, only nicer, and without all the teeth.'

'Who?'

'Tommy Steele. You know. He sang that "Little White Bull". Eddie was always suntanned, because he was outside all the time. They're all like that at the grammar school. Sports. Walking. Outside things.'

'So? What happened to this Eddie?'

'He went off to college somewhere. He wrote to me a few times. But you know what it's like. It soon fizzled out, and I never really minded.'

'Does he live in Bolton?'

I could picture this Eddie. He'd be tall. Strong. He'd rush up our street in his running shoes, and he'd come and rescue my mum.

'Eddie? I don't know. But he did get married, to a girl called Emily, and they have three very beautiful daughters.'

'How do you know?'

'Claudine told me. Well. She had her eye on him. He was more her type, anyway.'

LATER AND COLDER WE WATCHED PEOPLE LEAVING, WEAVing their way between cars. The woman had gone, and Dad was jumping in and out of the doorway shouting, 'I'll get some more booze from the offy! Come back you lot, it's early. It's a bloody wake, isn't it? They're supposed to go on for days!'

The men looked behind them, as if they'd run back if they could, but the women held tight to their sides, pushing their way back home.

'They've had enough,' said Mum. 'Come on.'

Dad sat on the front step.

'It's the end,' he said. 'The end.'

We left him. We threw everything into bin bags. Mum looked pleased. She'd found three packets of Players with fags still in them, and half a bottle of rum that someone else had brought.

The room was soon tidy, but the back yard was full.

'Still,' said Mum. 'It's better out than in.'

Dad looked small on the step. His shoulders caved in. There was a rip in the side of his trousers.

'She's had a good send off,' said Mum. 'And that coffin looked a treat.'

He nodded. It looked like he'd been crying.

'Put something on, Jack. And can you give the vinyl a good wipe down? You know what it's like when people have had a few. They don't take care when they should do.'

Dean Martin. 'Everybody Loves Somebody Sometime'.

Dad came in, and sat there, hugging one of the cushions. He was strange. Quiet.

'Stop giving me the eye,' he said. 'I'm thinking.'

We sat in a row saying nothing. I tried to think about Grandma, but all I could see was Dad's hand up that blonde girl's T-shirt. I felt terrible. Like some kind of sicko. And I must be, because it had made me feel like I'd wanted to have a go at it. I tried following the music, but Dad's hand was still there. Up and down. Squeezing. Going round in bloody circles.

'I can't fucking stand this,' he said.

'It'll get better,' Mum said. 'It's always bad when somebody dies. Your own mother, especially. But now the funeral's over with, you can think back on your memories.'

'Just what are you on about?' he asked.

'Your mother,' Mum swallowed. 'You know.'

'Well, I'm not fucking on about my mother. Shit. I'm thinking about next week and my fucking big audition.'

'Max says you'll walk it,' I said, staring at my shoes.

'I know I'll bloody walk it. But it's what I'm walking back to, that's doing my head in.'

'What do you mean?' Mum asked. *No. Please no.* I closed my eyes. I didn't want to hear.

'It's you. Look at you. You're supposed to be the lodger and you're everywhere.'

'So what do you want me to do?'

'I don't know. But take today for instance. I saw you. Handing round the drinks. Shuffling in and out. Taking over. Shit, Evie, you were putting people off.'

'I'm sorry. I thought I was helping.'

'You weren't helping. Like I said, you were putting people off.'

'Off what?'

'Me.'

'Well, I can't see that,' she said, looking at me. 'Can you?'

I said nothing.

'Lodgers don't hang around like a bad smell. They're supposed to hate their landlords. But you—'

'What?'

'Well, you're everywhere. Look at you.'

Mum got up. She went over to the magazine rack and found her old *Woman's Own*. She kissed me.

'I might see you later,' she said.

We sat there for a bit. Dean Martin was on to 'Volare'.

'I don't know,' said Dad. 'Just when you think you're all sorted. Look at me. I thought I'd got it made. And this time next week, I'll be somewhere else. I'll be bloody miles away.'

'Where? Where is it you're going?'

I could see him with the blonde girl. He'd be dragging her round show houses. They'd be staring at diamond rings on those little velvet love hearts. Kissing.

'Oh, I don't know exactly, but they'll be putting me up somewhere,' he said. 'Some fancy hotel on the Strand.' He stood up. His shoulders were going.

'Come on, lad, let's do it.'

'Do what?'

'Get up. Get up on the rug for "Volare". I'll start it again. Come on, Jacky boy. We'll have it on from the very beginning.'

I got up slowly. I could already taste the words that were crammed inside my mouth.

'Who was that woman?' I asked. 'You know. That girl?'

He looked round at me and smiled.

'That's Caz,' he said, wriggling his bum. 'She's a bit of all right is Caz, but once I'm on the up, well, she's the sort you leave behind.'

The music started up again, as Dad got into position.

'Look up. Look up. Jack. Are they there? Can you see them?'

'See who?'

I was swaying with him now. Floating my arms out, hula-style. We were in and out of the mirror.

'There. Front row – it's full of big stars tonight. And they've all come to see us. Imagine. There's Sinatra and his missus. The bloody cast of *Dallas*. There's even Brucie Forsyth. Look, he's tapping his feet, Jack.'

We carried on. 'Volare' finished. Dean Martin finished. But there were plenty more tracks.

The sun is surrounded by nine planets, which orbit, or travel round the sun all the time. They are pulled towards the sun, and held in their orbits, by an invisible force called gravity.

THE VAN WAS FREEZING COLD AS WE RATTLED ROUND THE BACK of it. There were bits of soggy carpet. Dog things. Mattie's brother was giving us a lift to the bottom of the hill. He was dressed like Ziggy Stardust. He was on his way to a Bowie night, somewhere near Wigan.

'You lot all right back there?' John looked at us through the mirror. It was dark. You couldn't see much, but the silvery zigzag stripe on his face was glowing.

'Fine.' Stuart was rolling around, trying to get up, crashing into the back of the doors. He'd lost his torch: we could hear it bouncing.

'Is it near you?' he kept on. 'It sounds like it's up this way.'

Suddenly it lit up. Mattie had found it. He waved the end about.

'Look at it,' he said. 'Some fucking use this is going to be.'

It was tiny, and shaped like the Batman sign.

'It's all I had,' said Stuart. 'I thought it was better than nothing.'

It flashed on the rusty white walls. Sean looked well pissed off. He had his arms crossed, his army rucksack on. He looked like a professional.

The van went into a pothole. We bounced again.

John put a cassette on.

'Space Oddity'.

'It's especially for you lot,' he said. 'You never know what you might see up there.'

'Shit,' said Sean, banging his head on the side. 'What a fucking shambles, and we haven't even got there yet.'

Suddenly, the van stopped and we slammed against the door. 'Everybody out!' said John. 'We've landed.'

It was twenty past nine, and dark at last. It wasn't pitch black, but it was getting there. John came round and opened the padlocked doors. He was wearing a white silk jump suit. Gold lipstick. We didn't dare laugh. He was huge. A fighter. He frightened us all to death.

'Do you know where you're going?' he asked as his legs started flapping in the breeze. 'What about you, Mattie? Don't go nicking any wildlife.'

'Fuck off.'

'I know where it is,' said Stuart, rooting through his bag. 'I've got the maps planned out and everything.'

'Great,' said Sean. 'I mean, what would we do without you?' He shook his head and started walking off without us, his long legs striding over the rocks sticking out of the mud. The van revved away and we followed on behind Sean. We didn't have rucksacks. We had carrier bags blowing. And Stuart had a lilo.

'What the hell's that for?'

'My arse. I'm going to blow it up when we get to the top. It's bound to be hard, just sitting there. I'll be nice and comfy on this. I've even brought the pump.'

'Jesus.'

We looked up.

'I can't see any stars,' said Mattie. 'Oh look,' he jumped. 'There's one.'

'Where?'

'There. Now which one's that?' He grabbed hold of his binoculars. They were old and heavy with thick leather straps. His dad had bought them for watching the football with. 'He had terrible bloody eyesight,' Mattie told us. 'They called him Mr Magoo.'

Sean grunted.

I looked up. I could hardly see a thing. Mattie passed me his binoculars. Now I still couldn't see a thing, but at least the clouds were in close up.

'It'll be better at the top,' said Sean. 'When the sky pans out.'

'Will you fucking listen to him?'

We didn't need a map. There were signs. Stuart flashed his torch, but it was light enough to read them.

I tried walking backwards for a bit, looking down behind us. It wasn't all that steep. The mud felt soft but the grass was parched. You could smell it.

'How will we know when we get to the top?' Stuart asked. He kept stopping. He'd already started gulping down his Coke.

'When we run out of grass.' Mattie grabbed his can. 'Give us a swig.'

'No.'

'Go on.'

'No. It's all I've bloody got.'

'Will you listen to them?' said Sean. 'They're never going to make it.'

It was cold. I had my hands in my pockets. I could feel the wind as it hit at the back of my throat. Whenever we stopped I could hear it through my anorak, going bang, bang, bang, bang, bang.

'You didn't say it would get this bloody cold,' said Stuart. 'It's supposed to be July. It was July down there a minute ago.'

'I'm not Michael bloody Fish,' said Sean. 'I thought you might have realised that the higher you get, the colder you get. Do you know nothing, or what?'

Stuart just wheezed. He didn't have the breath to answer back.

I didn't mind all that much. My eyes were watering. Our

carrier bags were flapping all over the place. Sean looked down at us.

'You could have made an effort,' he said. 'Have you see what you all bloody look like?'

'It's the fucking SAS,' said Mattie. 'He thinks he's Steve McQueen.'

It didn't seem that far. It wasn't like it was a mountain. It didn't even feel like a hill, though I suppose it did to Stuart. We were 1,498 feet up. Or supposed to be. I kept looking. Where had all the stars gone?

'A meteor,' said Mattie, waving at the sky.

But it was just the tail end of a plane, flashing on and off. I kept looking at the moon. Wondering where the footsteps were. And they'd still be there, because there's no wind on the moon, and nothing to erode them. They'll be there for years. For millions of years. Trillions.

When Neil Armstrong landed on the moon, he unveiled a plaque that read: HERE MEN FROM THE PLANET EARTH FIRST SET FOOT UPON THE MOON, JULY 1969 AD. WE COME IN PEACE FOR ALL MANKIND.

Then, while he was collecting forty pounds of rocks to bring to Earth, Aldrin pushed the flag into the ground. The Stars and Stripes, held up straight, by a thin piece of wire. After the flag-planting and rock-collecting, they left behind some medals and badges and things, then they climbed back into the *Eagle* and took their helmets off, before tucking into a snack of cocktail sausages and fruit punch, and then settling down for a well-earned sleep.

So, where was it all? The moon looked blotchy. Was the flag in one of those grey bits?

When we reached the top of the hill there was silence. We just stood and listened to it. The TV masts hummed, but you didn't hear that at first. At first you heard nothing. Then of course there was Stuart's wheezing, and the sound of him pumping up his lilo with a foot pump.

'So, where are all these fantastic-looking stars then?' said Mattie.

The sky was wide. It had a kind of street-lamp glow. White. Orange. You could see small buildings down below, a road, and an articulated lorry that was winding its way too fast around the corner.

'We're not that fucking high up,' said Mattie. 'Did you see that lorry driver? I could even see what colour shirt he had on.'

'Will you just shut up?' said Sean. 'Jesus.'

We sat there.

'Did you ring Sky-Line?'

'Yes.'

'So, what did they say?'

'It was a recorded message. It said the sky was clear. They gave it eight out of ten.'

'You should ask them for your money back.'

'At least there's a moon.' I said.

Mattie sat and stared through his binoculars. He rubbed his snotty nose.

'It looks just the same,' he said. 'Only bigger.'

'What did you expect?'

'I don't know. I thought it would look, well, different.'

'With those crappy things?'

'Well, at least I've bloody got some.'

'You'd need a telescope for things to look any different,' I told him. 'Something fork mounted.'

'Fork what?'

'It's one of the world's most popular amateur telescopes,' said Sean.

'It's still not much bloody use if there's nothing there to look at.'

'Well, we're here now,' said Sean, 'so shut it.'

We rummaged through our carrier bags. I'd brought lemonade. A Mars Bar. Mattie had a sandwich but then his bag blew away.

'Bet you wish you'd thought of this,' said Stuart, sitting on his lilo. He lovingly patted the ridges.

'You know a plane crashed here,' said Sean. 'Years ago. It was coming from the Isle of Man in thick fog. Loads of people were killed.'

The grass was cold. My jeans felt wet. My gym shoes were soaking.

'I suppose they walk about at midnight with all their bits and pieces missing,' said Mattie. 'Just like my mum and dad on the M62.'

We looked at him. We couldn't believe what he was saying.

'You don't mean that,' said Sean.

'Of course I don't mean it.'

'So why did you say it?'

'It was meant to be a joke.'

We looked at him. His mouth was full of jam. Eyebrows joined. He was sniffing.

'So, what's going to happen to you?' Sean asked. 'Have you actually been arrested?'

'No.' Mattie stood up; he shoved his hands in his pockets and looked up at the moon.

'I'm off,' he said. 'I'm going for a piss.'

We watched him as he disappeared behind us. Then we started staring at the sky as if it was full of something interesting.

'The moon's craters were formed when meteors hit the surface,' said Sean.

Stuart looked at him. 'God,' he said. 'You know fucking everything, you do.'

Mattie reappeared. His flies were undone and he'd splashed himself, but nobody said anything.

'I got a warning,' he told us, stepping on the lilo. 'They wrote it all down. Then they let me off. But I'll always have a record.'

'Well. It's better than being in Strangeways,' said Stuart.

'I'm too fucking young for Strangeways. Dickhead.'

'Anything's better than being banged up or cleaning graffiti off walls,' said Stuart. 'That's what my cousin had to do when he was caught with his car boot full of knocked-off cassettes.'

'What kind of cassettes?'

'Showaddywaddy,' said Stuart. '*You Got What It Takes.*'

'I've got that,' said Sean.

We were hugging ourselves now. I had my hands up my sleeves, rubbing all the warmth from up and down my arms.

'We should walk around a bit,' I said. 'At least we'll get warmed up.'

'I'm not walking,' said Stuart. 'I'm stopping here.'

I got up with Mattie. Sean had his serious-looking torch out and he was flicking through a book. He had his eyes down, squinting at 'Extending Our View Of The Universe'.

We walked down the hill a bit. It was harder walking down. You had to dig your feet in, or you'd gather too much speed. Finally, we sat on a clump of rocks. We were frozen. We could hardly feel our hands.

'It's big,' said Mattie. 'Well, it looks big.'

'What does?'

'Out there.'

'Yes.'

'Wouldn't it be great,' he said, 'if we could run down here, and fly like fucking birds? Up, up and away! Shit. We could go anywhere.'

'Yes. So where would you go then?'

'I don't know,' he sniffed. 'I've got an uncle in Morecambe.'

'You'd want to go further than that.'

'Why?'

'You just would. Well, I would.'

'Yes,' he said. 'I can just see it. You'd land in fucking Hollywood on top of Olivia Neutron-Bomb.'

'Well, I wouldn't mind.'

'Me neither.'

We laughed. When we stopped, it was quieter than anything.

'I really am going away,' I said. 'I'm really going to France.'

'No kidding?'

'It's for my mum. My dad's gone and left her in the shit.'

'But he's back.'

'Exactly. He should have just pissed off and stayed pissed off. And you were right.'

'What about?'

'Him. You know. The women.'

'I don't know. I was only having you on.'

'No,' I said. 'It was true.'

We looked straight ahead. It was lighter than you'd think. Fields got chopped off. Buildings appeared. A roundabout.

'I didn't mean it,' he said. 'About the love child thing.'

'No?'

'No.'

'Well, I wouldn't be fucking surprised.'

'Nah. There's only you. Why did they only have you?'

'Because I'm enough bloody trouble,' I said. 'They can't cope with any more.'

'Trouble? No. You're okay. You never get into any real bother. But you're not a goody two shoes. Well, you are a bit, but you're not all wet like those two fucking idiots up there. Fat Arse and Swatty.'

I pulled at some grass. I let it trickle slowly out of my hand.

'I can't imagine having a brother.'

'You can borrow mine. He's supposed to act like my dad. That's what the social services came and said. And it wasn't clothes,' he went on. 'It was a musical cot mobile.'

'A musical what?'

'You hang it over the cot and you wind it up and it plays a

tune to send the baby off to sleep. They're great. They're fucking amazing. This one had four sheep on it with ribbons round their necks.'

'You just walked out with it?'

'Well, I didn't make it obvious. But the box was massive. And then I went and dropped it and the bloody tune went off and that was fucking that, really.'

We laughed, and then we just sat there, breathing. We fell back and looked straight up at the sky. A choppy ocean. I could even see a boat. Islands. Clouds had always been islands.

'You won't say anything will you? About France?'

'No.'

'It's Mum's big plan. It's her secret.'

'Right.'

'I'm not supposed to say anything,' I said. 'He'll have the bloody shock of his life.'

'Well, it sounds like he fucking deserves it.'

'Yes.'

'And shit, it's just like me.'

'What is?'

'Well, they don't want me there, you know. Our John and Candice. They might do a runner, like you and your mum. No, they wouldn't run off. They just want the whole fucking place to themselves. Shit. If I were them I'd want the whole fucking place to myself. Wouldn't you?'

'They want you.'

He turned over, cocking his head to the side. 'This grass tastes funny.'

'A sheep might have pissed on it.'

'I might have pissed on it.'

We laughed, coughing, spitting out the bits that we'd chewed.

'I thought they'd like the cot mobile. It would have made a great present. You should have seen it. Honest. I hope they have a girl,' he said. 'I could be her minder.'

'My dad might need a minder. He's got this big job coming up. He's says he's going to be a star. Big car. House. The lot.'

'Shit,' said Mattie. 'He's good, but he's not that good. He isn't actually Elvis.'

The others were already walking back.

'I knew it would be a disaster,' said Sean. 'I just knew it.'

'You could have fucking waited for us before you set off home,' said Mattie as we hurried down to meet them. 'We could have been sat up here for hours.'

'Well, we couldn't see you. You were smooching under a rock.'

Stuart was on his lilo. He was trying to use it like a sledge, but it kept stopping, and he kept on rolling off.

'It's your weight,' said Mattie. 'Or are you eating for two?'

'Just think how much money you'd make,' said Sean. 'If you were a man and you got pregnant, you'd make fucking millions. They'd have to pay you for experiments. They'd make films. Write books. You'd be made.'

'You'd be a freak show.'

'You'd be a rich freak show,' said Stuart. 'I wouldn't mind.'

'You'd have to find someone to have sex with first. Someone going blind.'

'I knew you'd say that. You're so fucking original.'

It was early. It wasn't even midnight. When we got down to the road, people were still hanging round outside the shut-up pub. They looked at us. Lilo. Grass stains. Mud all over our clothes. We just walked out of the darkness and smiled at them.

'Good evening ladies and gentlemen,' said Mattie. 'What a fucking long walk it is from Blackpool.'

We sang down the pavement. We had to. We had to do something to keep from just collapsing. We passed houses with nice gardens. Caravans in the drive. Houses with lights still on in them. You could see people through the windows. Warm. Doing nothing. Just watching TV. Eating biscuits.

'I wished I lived there,' said Stuart. 'I wished I lived in that car, because at least I would be home already.'

'Just keep going,' said Sean. 'Come on.'

'I've worn three inches off my legs,' said Mattie. 'I'll be a fucking midget by the morning.'

IT WAS PAST TWO O'CLOCK.

The light was still on. It was blazing through the curtains. I could hear something, before I put the key in. Dad talking. Music. 'And Little Things Mean A Lot'.

I stepped back. Waited. Knocked. I didn't want to walk in on my dad and the blonde, just doing it, there on the carpet.

Mum opened the door. She was wearing a fantastic-looking dress. It was silver. Strappy. Shiny. She looked like she wasn't my mum.

'What are you doing back here? All night, you said. Remember?'

'There weren't any stars,' I told her. 'There was nothing.'

'Who the fuck is it?' shouted Dad.

I went inside. He was sitting with his shirt half off. Belt undone. Flies. I just stood there. I was freezing to death in the warmth.

'Oh, it's you,' he said. 'I thought it was my fan club. I thought they'd tracked me down. Shit. Get us a drink then, Evie. You might as well, now that you're up.' His voice slurred as he started doing something to his toenails. Picking. Scratching. 'Ouch.' His best socks and shoes were melting by the fireplace. 'Go on then, girl. Chop, chop.'

We went into the kitchen. The dress made a swishing sound.

'What do you think?' she whispered. 'You know. Like I told you. My little plan.'

'Your what?'

'This. The dress. It's a one-off,' she said. 'Well, nearly.'

'But what about France?'

'What about it?'

'That was the plan. It was your idea. Wasn't it?'

'Your dad has been talking about holidays. Barbados.
Lanzerote. Somewhere hot. Somewhere Caribbean.'

The kitchen was a mess. I didn't look at Mum. I looked at
empty packets. Kenny's Fried Chicken. Cans. Across the draining
board, the best Sunday plates were smeared with dirty gravy. I
could feel my face getting hotter and hotter.

'Go on,' she twirled. 'It won't bite. Look. Feel it.' Slowly, I
pointed out a finger. The dress felt cold. Hard. It felt like she'd
been polished, and when she bent down, you could almost hear
it breaking.

'It's a bit on the tight side,' she said, 'but that's the whole idea.
And it's working.'

'Why?'

'Because your dad thinks it's gorgeous.'

'He said that?'

'Yes. He's seen a dress like this on that Sally James from
Tiswas. You know.'

I knew.

'But she always dresses like a tomboy.'

'Not when she's out,' Mum smiled, rolling Dad's can gently in
her hands. 'When she goes out, she goes for something
glamorous. Really. Your dad's seen her picture in the paper.'

'Come on. What are you doing?' he shouted from the living
room. 'I'm dying of thirst out here.'

Mum looked happy. She closed her eyes and breathed into a
smile.

'It's the little things men like,' she said. 'It's when you make
the effort. That's when they notice.'

'Are you on strike then, or what?' Dad called.

Mum glided in there, looking back at me. I didn't move.
Suddenly, Alma had stopped, and the music was sliding into Elvis.